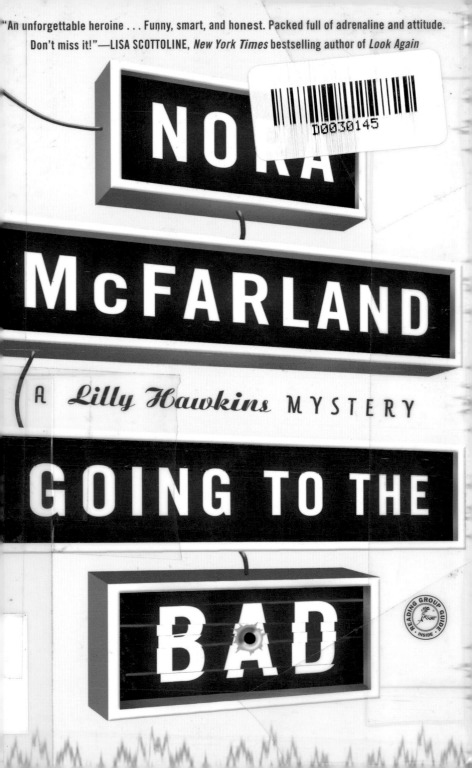

NORA

McFARLAND

A *Lilly Hawkins* MYSTERY

GOING TO THE

BAD

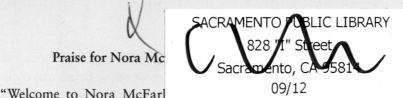
Praise for Nora Mc

"Welcome to Nora McFar[land]... Lilly, who's as lovably dysfunctional as any character you'll ever read! She's funny, smart, and honest, albeit occasionally tactless—in short, fully human. Packed full of adrenaline and attitude, *A Bad Day's Work* is a roller-coaster ride of a mystery. Don't miss it!" —Lisa Scottoline

"A wonderful debut novel! Action packed, with a heroine who's sure to win your heart." —Marcia Muller

"McFarland, herself a former 'shooter' for a Bakersfield TV station, nails the newsroom as well as her feisty, funny accidental sleuth." —*Publishers Weekly*

"McFarland's debut, the first in a planned series, is often both amusing and touching as Lilly discovers both the truth about the murder and enough about herself to change her life." —*Kirkus Reviews*

"Former Bakersfield camerawoman McFarland clearly knows her technical stuff. . . . McFarland has an appealingly flawed protagonist here, and fans of Julie Kramer's Minneapolis TV reporter, Riley Spatz, will likely take to Lilly, too." —*Booklist*

"A breath of fresh air to the world of lighthearted mysteries, Nora McFarland offers readers a charming new series. . . . Off the wall in the best way, McFarland never lets you see what is coming as one crazy antic swiftly follows another. The sequel to this excellent debut will be worth the wait." —*Suspense Magazine*

"More than a compelling mystery—it's a unique glimpse into the life of a small-town television news photographer. The story of Lilly Hawkins of Bakersfield, California, may be fiction, but the author's fresh voice and careful attention to detail make the intrigue real. . . . The next installment of this excellent new series can't come soon enough." —*BookPage*

"Readers don't know what McFarland's characters are going to do next, and that gives us a reason to keep turning the pages."
—*Southern Literary Review*

"What makes this book a winner is the honest-to-goodness funniness offered by first-time author Nora McFarland. Hers is a refreshing kind of humor and it's the key element that drives this fast-paced story about a feisty young TV photographer who solves the crime." —*Bakersfield Californian*

Praise for *Hot, Shot, and Bothered*

"Fun, funny, tautly suspenseful, and very smart. Lilly Hawkins, the heroine, is irresistible. I couldn't put it down." —Spencer Quinn

"Lilly Hawkins is a terrific protagonist—a straight shooter with her heart in the right place. You'll root for her from the very beginning of this feisty new mystery." —April Smith

"Nora McFarland tells a great story with an important moral lesson—rare in mysteries these days. The vivid descriptions of the rapidly approaching fire are so real they left me breathless. Literally." —*Suspense Magazine*

"Lilly, with her humanizing flaws, is both smart and strong-willed, and this adrenaline-fueled sequel ought to win her more fans."
—*Booklist*

Also by Nora McFarland

A Bad Day's Work

Hot, Shot, and Bothered

GOING TO THE BAD

A Lilly Hawkins Mystery

Nora McFarland

A TOUCHSTONE BOOK
Published by Simon & Schuster
New York London Toronto Sydney New Delhi

Touchstone
A Division of Simon & Schuster, Inc.
1230 Avenue of the Americas
New York, NY 10020

First Touchstone trade paperback edition August 2012

TOUCHSTONE and colophon are registered trademarks of Simon & Schuster, Inc.

For information about special discounts for bulk purchases, please contact Simon & Schuster Special Sales at 1-866-506-1949 or business@simonandschuster.com.

The Simon & Schuster Speakers Bureau can bring authors to your live event. For more information or to book an event contact the Simon & Schuster Speakers Bureau at 1-866-248-3049 or visit our website at www.simonspeakers.com.

Designed by Renata Di Biase

Manufactured in the United States of America

10 9 8 7 6 5 4 3 2 1

Library of Congress Cataloging-in-Publication Data

McFarland, Nora.
    Going to the bad : a Lilly Hawkins mystery / Nora McFarland.—1st Touchstone trade paperback ed.
        p. cm.
    "A Touchstone book."
1. Hawkins, Lilly—Fictitious character—Fiction. 2. Photojournalists—United States—Fiction. 3. Women photographers—Fiction. 4. Murder—Investigation—Fiction. 5. Family secrets—Fiction. I. Title.
    PS3613.C4395G65 2012
    813'.6—dc23
        2012006695

ISBN 978-1-4391-5557-8
ISBN 978-1-4391-7235-3 (ebook)

For
Trish Lande Grader
Sulay Hernandez
Lauren Spiegel

GOING TO THE BAD

ONE

I glanced out at the KJAY newsroom. My elevated position on the assignment desk gave me an excellent view as my co-workers prepared for our noon show. As is typical in most newsrooms this time of year, the food and frills of the holiday season existed side by side with the uglier realities of our business. Bloody crime-scene video played next to a platter of holiday cookies. A script detailing a tragic car wreck sat on the printer next to a pot of candy canes.

My name's Lilly Hawkins. I was born and raised here in Bakersfield at the southern end of California's Central Valley. I'm a TV news photographer, nicknamed a *shooter* in the industry, at KJAY.

I would have preferred to be sitting out in the newsroom with the newshounds and food—or even better, in the field shooting video—but Callum, our station's assignment manager, had taken a rare week off for Christmas. It was my temporary job to supervise newsgathering and ensure stories made it on air. I hated it.

I love KJAY and I love TV news, but spending my day on the assignment desk went against all my instincts—working inside instead of out, planning instead of acting, having to watch my tone as I gave orders to other people instead of brazenly ignoring orders given to me.

My mood both brightened and dimmed when I saw Freddy's mop of bleached-blond curls pass through the rear door of the newsroom.

He fired off finger pistols at a few old friends, but mostly made a beeline straight for me. "Dude, is it true what they're saying about the giant python?"

"I haven't heard about a python, but I'm going to go out on a limb and say, no, it's not true."

Despite the cold weather this time of year, Freddy wore his usual cargo shorts and flip-flops. His only concession to the season was a sweatshirt with a surfing snowman.

"And is it just me," I said, "or do you spend more time at the station now that you don't work here?"

He ignored me. Maybe he knew that I missed him. "Dude, seriously, tell me you have a reporter on this python-sludge thing."

"I've got the morning anchor and the dayside reporter both at the site of a multivehicle pileup." I glanced up at the dry-erase board where we laid out the day's stories. "A tanker truck carrying sludge was involved, but there was no snake."

"Dude, there totally was. Everyone's saying a twenty-foot python escaped during the crash."

"Who's everyone?"

Freddy's eyes shifted away. "This dude I do business with."

"Does the dude sell you weed?"

"I can neither confirm nor deny that."

"There is no missing python." I returned to sorting through press releases. "Sludge is all over the place, though. I don't think they'll have the roads open again until this afternoon."

Sludge is a waste by-product that other cities and counties pay Bakersfield to take off their hands. It's our biggest import.

"The city is in total cover-up mode because they don't want to start a panic." Freddy spread his arms wide. "Think about it. Twenty feet. That snake could totally gobble a baby."

"Did you drop in today to pass on fake news tips or are you thinking about coming back to work here?"

His arms dropped, as well as his enthusiasm. "There's totally no job for me. MMJs killed the video star."

MMJs, or multimedia journalists, were essentially one-man-band reporters who shot and edited their own video for television, the web, and mobile devices. When the station higher-ups announced we were joining the ranks of many other small-market TV stations and transitioning to MMJs, I'd predicted catastrophic failure. KJAY had always saved money by occasionally assigning shooters to stories without a reporter, but I believed the reverse was impossible.

I'd been wrong. Our staff of young reporters had proven remarkably adept at mastering the new digital cameras and editing software. To my horror, as a group they were both comfortable and competent shooting their own video.

Freddy and the rest of the videography department had all lost their jobs. At least I'd kept my title of *chief photographer*. The only hitch was that now instead of managing a department of shooters, I trained the reporters on how to use the cameras, handled equipment issues, and shot video for the older anchors and reporters who would never adapt to the new system.

"I'm not looking to come back." Freddy glanced across the rows of battered metal desks to the rear of the room. "College is awesome. I'm here today for the Tedster. He needs good vibes and moral support."

The Wonder Twins, as Teddy and Freddy had sarcastically been nicknamed when they were the laziest and least responsible shooters on staff, no longer looked anything alike. Teddy, the shyer and nicer of the two, had cut off his bleached-blond curls and become KJAY's junior sports reporter. As part of his TV makeover, his name had also been shortened to Ted—another of the many things I was having trouble adjusting to.

Freddy watched his best friend on the other side of the room trying to tie a Windsor knot. "This is a big day for my main dude. First time anchoring instead of just doing sports."

I shrugged. "They canceled the eleven o'clock show for the holiday so Ted only has to do the noon and five. And I've got the animal shelter coming to do an adopt-a-pet segment. That'll kill a lot of time and be all heartwarming. Should be cake."

The hallway door opened. Leanore Drucker, my best friend and the KJAY historical reporter, entered carrying a gingerbread house. "Hi, everybody. I'm dropping off a little holiday cheer."

Several mumbles from random places in the newsroom were her only thanks. Leanore didn't let the lack of enthusiasm dim her smile. She was an optimist; a strange and exotic species I'd never understand. Of course that optimism didn't prevent an occasional tart observation. Her news stories, although usually soft-boiled re-hashes of local history, always contained a healthy amount of wit.

"Good to know the spirit of love and goodwill flourishes in the heart of the newsroom." She tossed back her auburn hair. Since Leanore is in her sixties, the veracity of that shade was in question, but real or fake it had become her calling card on TV. "FYI, something major is tying up all the traffic."

I nodded. "Auto versus tanker. It turned into a real pileup."

"The tanker spilled its cargo." Freddy raised an eyebrow. "Sludge all over the road."

Leanore, always a lady, didn't react.

Freddy continued, "You know, sludge is like . . . waste."

Leanore removed a speck of lint from her jacket. "I understand what it is."

"You know, medical waste and sewage waste."

"Yes, I get it."

"It's poop."

"I understand, Frederick." For Leanore, using the long form of someone's name was akin to the nuclear option.

Even Freddy understood that and dropped the subject. "There's also a thirty-foot cobra missing from the wreck."

Leanore's eyes widened and shot to me.

"Don't worry, there's no snake." I turned to Freddy. "A minute ago you said it was a twenty-foot python. Next you'll say it's a fifteen-foot anteater or a forty-foot rat."

We were interrupted by a ten-thousand-year-old demon. (Full disclosure: I have no actual proof that the individual in question is anything other than a blond, twenty-one-year-old reporter.) "I'm coanchoring the noon and the five today with Ted. What's the latest on the lead story?"

I gestured behind me to the wall of monitors and video decks. "We're planning to open the noon with a live shot from the scene of the accident. Preliminary video should feed back any minute."

"I haven't been at KJAY very long, so I don't know how smart you are about these things." She spoke with the condescension of someone who'd planned for her first job out of college to be in a much bigger television market. "But I'm assuming you haven't had much real training in what makes good video. I need the sludge. That's the important shot."

Freddy and Leanore, alerted either by her condescending tone of voice or my body language as I reacted to it, each took an instinctive step back.

I leaned forward. "I know more today about what makes good video than you'll know at the end of your entire career, which will probably come in about ten years when you're passed over for fill-in weekend anchor in Fresno."

Her mouth compressed at the same time as her eyes widened. "There's no need to attack me. All I want is for my show to be as good as possible."

What she wanted was to get good video of her anchoring a newscast for an audition reel. Since I wanted her gone almost as much as she wanted to be in a larger TV market, we had a common goal.

I swallowed hard. "You're right. I'm sorry. I'm out of line. I promise we'll get video of the sludge."

She tore the candy chimney off Leanore's gingerbread house and exited toward the control room.

Freddy stepped back to the assignment desk. "You got some sand in your butt crack today?"

"Freddy," Leanore and I both said loudly and in unison.

"Dudes, I don't punch a clock here anymore. I can totally say all kinds of inappropriate stuff now." Freddy saw the look on my face and dropped his smirk. "Don't get me wrong, she was a total tool, but your reaction was a little extreme."

I didn't say anything.

"Freddy, I think Teddy may need some assistance with that tie." Leanore pointed across the newsroom. "He looks in danger of strangling himself."

"Call him Ted," I said. "He's talent now."

"I better go give a hand to"—Freddy paused to raise his fingers like quotes—" 'Ted.' "

Leanore waited for him to cross the room, then said, "Is Rod spending Christmas in LA with his family?"

Rod was my boyfriend and KJAY's senior producer. He'd negotiated the new title—*senior producer*, not *boyfriend*—after some high-profile reporting the previous summer. His coverage of a deadly wildfire had earned him job offers from all the major networks. He'd chosen to stay in Bakersfield.

"Rod changed his mind about visiting his family," I said. "He came back this morning unexpectedly. It's the first Christmas since his grandfather died and I think being at home was a reminder."

Leanore didn't say anything. She kept the same friendly half smile on her face and waited for me to elaborate.

"Rod and his grandpa were close. I think their relationship was sort of like me and my uncle Bud."

She continued her silence.

"We're having Christmas dinner with Bud tomorrow. He's still living with the little sick girl's mother. . . . Remember we used to do those tearjerker stories about the little girl who was going blind?"

Leanore treated this as a rhetorical question.

I tried to hold out. I didn't want to talk about what was really on my mind, but Leanore's silence was like a tractor-trailer hauling the truth out of me.

Finally, she raised one eyebrow.

It did me in. "I found an engagement ring in Rod's pocket."

The spell broke. Leanore actually jumped as her hands came together in a clapping motion. "A Christmas proposal! It's so romantic."

"It's only romantic if I say yes."

Her hands dropped. "But, Lilly . . ."

I refused to look at her. "Don't 'but, Lilly' me. I love Rod, but this is a huge step."

She tensed. "Does he know you found the ring?"

"No. I put it back and then ran out of the house for work."

"Good, then it's not ruined. You have to act surprised tomorrow when he asks you."

I leaned forward. "Leanore, did you hear me? I'm not ready for this. Everything is changing and I hate it."

"But you and Rod have been living together for over a year. He's handsome, smart, funny, and kind. What more could you possibly want in a man?"

"That's just it. He's perfect. When we met, he had flaws. He was terrified of going on camera and he let everybody walk all over him."

"Maybe he was a little too timid," she said. "But you're the one who helped him get over that."

"I know I did, but that was pretty much the only thing wrong with him, and it's gone now."

"Why is that a bad thing?"

I pointed at myself. "Because I've still got all my flaws. He's perfect, and I'm still me."

She shook her head. "Okay, now you're just making stuff up."

There was more to it than that, of course. I also worried that the still recent death of Rod's grandfather—whose loss had been sudden and painful—had driven Rod to take this big step.

In a few months when his grief receded and emotional equilibrium had been restored, would Rod regret proposing? That kind of rejection was excruciating to even contemplate. I had no intention of actually experiencing it.

"He's too perfect?" Leanore continued. "Lilly, I've heard of people sabotaging themselves, but this takes the cake. You're thirty-two years old. It's time to . . ."

Leanore continued, but I'd already stopped listening. The sounds of a voice under pressure had consumed all my attention. I tilted my head toward the scanner, but couldn't understand what was being said.

"Everybody quiet," I yelled while cranking the volume to high. "There's something on the police frequency."

Conversation in the newsroom abruptly stopped. Several people turned down the audio on their computers. All heads turned toward the small boxes behind me.

"Send ambulance and backup to my location ASAP. I've got a possible one eight seven with multiple gunshot wounds."

A small ripple of excitement passed through the newsroom. Ted and Freddy both got up and hurried toward the assignment desk.

The dispatch officer answered, "What's your ten-twenty?"

I recognized the location request and quickly searched for a pen. At the same time I looked over my shoulder at the dry-erase board of stories.

"Oildale."

I found a pen and scribbled *Oildale* while mentally doing the calculations of whom to pull off which story in favor of breaking news. It would be difficult because we were staffed so low for the holiday and already had the sludge crash.

"One seventy-three Jefferson Street."

I froze.

"One seventy-three Jefferson Street," the dispatch officer repeated back. "Ambulance was dispatched from original nine-one-one call, but it's been delayed."

Everything slowed down. I took a breath, but the simple act of filling my lungs seemed to take forever. I finally managed to speak, but it came out in a mumble.

"What's that, Lilly?" Leanore frowned. "Are you all right?"

Freddy was the first to realize the truth. "Dude, don't you and Rod live on Jefferson Street?"

"It's my address," I repeated, this time not in a mumble.

Leanore's voice rose. "You mean the shooting is at your house?"

I nodded.

"But Rod's in LA," Ted said. "He's not home."

Freddy nodded. "Isn't he visiting his folks for the holidays?"

"He came back this morning." I finally released my grip on the pen. "He was home when I left for work."

I started running and didn't look back.

TWO

I don't own a car. As chief photog I'm required to take a news van and gear home with me every night in case there's breaking news. I treat news van #4 as my own company vehicle. I've driven it from the station to where I live in Oildale more times than I can remember, but never faster or more recklessly than on that morning.

I slammed through downtown Bakersfield without pausing. The Christmas-themed store windows went by in a blur. I almost hit a car when I entered the Garces Circle without the right of way. I passed the Kern County Museum and the Bakersfield Drillers' ballpark going seventy-five. I slowed to fifty-five as I crossed the bridge into Oildale.

This side of the dry riverbed—the water long ago diverted for the irrigation of crops—is Bakersfield's rougher, less affluent sibling to the north. Originally constructed as company housing for the nearby oil fields, Oildale was where I grew up and where Rod and I had been living for the last year. We shared my uncle Bud's three-bedroom house, which Bud had inherited from my grandfather half a century earlier.

Two police cars were parked in the street. My last hope that Rod might be safe died when I saw his Prius in its usual spot out front. I abandoned the news van in park with the motor running and the driver's-side door open.

I ran toward the house. A uniformed officer walked out my front door and intercepted me at the bottom of the porch steps. "Hold on. This is a crime scene. It's not open to the press."

"I'm not the press."

"Do you think I'm blind?" He gestured to the van out on the street, then to me.

To be fair, I was dressed like a shooter in my sturdy hiking boots, jeans, and red KJAY polo.

He stepped forward trying to force me back. "Now do me a favor and wait out at the sidewalk."

"This is my house. I live here."

"You do?" His demeanor changed. "Do you have some kind of ID?"

I didn't. I'd left my wallet and everything else back at the station. Instead of explaining, I tried again to get around him. "My boyfriend lives here with me. Is he okay?"

I felt the inadequacy of the word *boyfriend* as I said it. Boyfriends were casual. There was no permanency or sense of commitment there. I wanted to add a qualifier. I wanted to tell him that Rod had a ring in his coat pocket.

"I'm sorry." The officer had taken a step back, but still blocked the porch. "We'll try and get this sorted out. But in the meantime, I'm going to have to ask you to wait out on the sidewalk."

Instead of arguing with him, I pushed. He was knocked off-balance and fell back on the steps. I used the opportunity to trample the rosebush and jump up onto the porch. I swung my legs over the railing and stumbled toward the front door. It opened and a second patrol officer emerged with his Taser out.

The one I'd shoved came up behind me with handcuffs. He sounded apologetic as he secured my hands behind my back. "You'll only be in the way in there. You could even make things worse."

I managed to look through the dime-store lace curtains covering the front window. Through the web of white polyester, I saw the outline of two figures clustered around someone on the floor. "Rod," I yelled as the two officers forced me down the porch. I continued to struggle as we crossed the lawn.

"You need to stop resisting," one of the officers said as we continued to the sidewalk. "I swear, they're doing everything possible in there to keep him stabilized until the ambulance arrives."

Stabilize him! Everything possible! My knees buckled and I sank down to the concrete. A noise in the street brought my attention to a second KJAY news van parking behind mine.

Ted got out and ran right for me. "What happened? Where's Rod?" The tie still hung loose in a deformed knot around his collar. "Why are you handcuffed?"

One of the patrol officers stayed next to me with his hand on my shoulder while the other one moved to block Ted's way into the house. "We need everyone to stay back. This is a crime scene. You'll have to move your news van. We're going to cordon off the street."

Under stress, Ted reverted to the speech patterns he'd tried so hard to abandon since becoming on-air talent. "Dude, is Rod, like, okay?"

The officers looked at each other. Finally one said, "Everything possible is being done."

Sadness, panic—those are words we can all relate to, but they don't begin to describe what I felt. It was as if my heart had been tied to a weight and then the weight dropped off a cliff.

"Where's the ambulance?" Tears were streaming down my face. "Why isn't it here yet?"

A Ford Taurus came to a screeching halt in the street. Out jumped our station's assignment manager, whose job I'd been covering all week. Callum is a big man with a big gut, and I wasn't used to seeing him move fast. I also wasn't used to seeing him with a week's worth of beard.

I looked at Ted. "You called Callum at home?"

"It wasn't me, dude. I followed you right out the door."

Callum passed my news van, paused to turn the engine off, then rushed to join us. "The ambulance is close. Thirty seconds maybe."

I recognized a small white cord running from the pocket of his

LA Dodgers jacket and up to his left ear. "You were listening to the scanners at home?"

He shrugged, but withdrew the portable radio from his pocket and adjusted something. "Traffic around the sludge spill delayed the ambulance. That's why they're not here yet."

In the distance I heard a siren. I focused all my attention down the street, praying the ambulance would come into view.

Ted's voice barely registered as he said, "Dude, you're on vacation and you were, like, home listening to the scanners?"

While we waited, Callum convinced the officer to unlock my cuffs. As soon as they were off, I started toward the house again.

Ted and the officer were slow to react, but not Callum. His hand shot out and gripped my wrist tighter than the cuffs had. "Don't be an idiot."

The siren reached a crescendo as the ambulance arrived. It parked and the noise abruptly stopped. Two more patrol cars followed the ambulance and blocked opposite ends of the street from traffic.

Callum still held me. "Right now you need to let the police and paramedics do their jobs. Your job is to wait with us. It's lousy, but that's what you have to do."

I glanced at the officer. He still held the cuffs, waiting to see if he'd need them.

I crumpled in defeat and let Callum pull me into a rare hug. Fear and adrenaline, not to mention the cold winter weather, caught up with me and I began shaking. Ted went to my van and retrieved my blue coat.

The new officers quickly created a perimeter. Police tape was unspooled just in time to stop a rival station's live truck at the other end of the block.

That's when I saw the detective nicknamed Handsome Homicide. He was getting a rundown from a patrol officer. They both stopped at the porch steps to put blue bootees over their shoes.

"Please," I begged him. "Tell me what's going on."

Handsome had once asked me out on a date, which I'd turned down because, despite his good looks, he was basically a jerk. I'd only seen him a few times in the last year, and always at crime scenes.

"I've heard that he's alive, but it's bad." Handsome continued up the steps. "I'll send someone out to brief you as soon as I can."

Ted took out a cell phone and hit speed dial.

We all heard Freddy answer, "KJAY, we're on your side."

Callum's eyes widened. "Freddy's covering the assignment desk? He doesn't even work at the station anymore."

"We're short-staffed for Christmas Eve." The usually easygoing Ted looked annoyed. He covered the cell phone's microphone. "And don't hurt on Freddy. He's better at stuff than you give him credit for."

Ted uncovered the phone. "Dude, it looks like Rod's been shot. The ambulance is here now. I'll call again when I know more."

The front door opened. We all jerked to attention. I expected to see either Handsome or the EMTs bringing out the stretcher.

A figure stumbled out onto the porch. Callum and Ted both gasped when they recognized him.

I tried to say his name, but I think it came out as a scream.

Rod reached the bottom of the steps. He looked around in a daze and then saw me running. "Lilly."

I threw my arms around him. "What happened? Are you hurt?"

"I'm fine. I promise, I'm okay."

Several officers had followed me, but stayed a step or two back from our reunion.

I didn't want to let go, but after a few moments Rod pulled back.

He wore the black shirt, shorts, and running shoes he routinely took to the gym. Something was wrong, though. My clothes were stained with blood where I'd hugged him.

I touched the wet, black fabric of his shirt. "If you're fine, then whose blood is this?"

"I'm sorry, Lilly."

My voice rose. "Why are you sorry? What happened?"

"I went to the gym. When I got home, I found him in the living room. I tried to stop the bleeding, but he'd been shot."

"Who? Who's been shot?"

From inside the house a voice yelled, "He's lost too much blood. We gotta go now." Moments later the EMTs appeared in the doorway. Rod and I jumped to the side as the stretcher was brought out.

I couldn't see the face underneath the oxygen mask, but I recognized the leathery, tattooed skin on the forearm.

Uncle Bud.

I watched in disbelief as they wheeled the stretcher to the curb and loaded it into the ambulance. I knew someone was talking to me, but I was too off-balance to pay attention.

"Lilly?" Handsome said sharply. "I asked why your grandfather was at the house this morning."

I finally looked away from the ambulance. "He's my uncle, not my grandfather."

It was an easy mistake to make and I shouldn't have been so irritated. Bud was my father's much older half brother. When Bud's father and stepmother both died back in the 1950s, Bud had raised my father, the infant they'd left behind.

"Fine," Handsome said, his annoyance growing. "But why was your uncle here?"

"I don't know." I glanced at Rod, who shook his head. "We were supposed to see him tomorrow for Christmas dinner at his girlfriend Annette's house. That's where he's been living for the past year."

A strand of my curly black hair had come loose from its ponytail. I pushed it away from my face and saw that my hand was shaking. "Was it a robbery? Is anything missing?"

"Nothing obvious." Rod put his arm around me. "I'm so sorry. I called nine one one as soon as I found him, but the ambulance took forever."

Handsome looked at Rod. "I understand he was unconscious and wasn't able to communicate anything to you about who might have shot him?"

Rod's body, pressed to mine as he embraced me, went rigid. "That's right."

"Did you see anyone when you got home? Anyone suspicious you might have passed on the street?"

Rod shook his head. "I wish I had."

A short burst of the ambulance's siren got my attention. "I'm sorry. We need to go to the hospital. Can you send someone to take Rod's statement there?"

Handsome gestured to a man in a suit getting out of an unmarked police car. "Let me consult with the detective sergeant."

We followed him down to the sidewalk where Ted waited. "I'm really sorry about your uncle, Lilly. He was a cool old dude."

"He's strong. He's going to make it." A moment after I said the words, I realized that I didn't believe them.

The ambulance siren cranked up to full. As it pulled away, Callum was revealed shooting video on the other side of the street. For a moment I stared directly into the lens. The camera was mine. Callum must have got it out of my own van.

He lowered the camera, then gestured down the street to our competitor's live truck parked behind the police tape. "I figured you wouldn't want us to get scooped on a shooting at your own house."

I was still trying to process that I was now a part of today's lead story when Handsome returned.

"Miss Hawkins, I'm sending you to the hospital in a patrol car." He looked at Rod. "But, Mr. Strong, we'd prefer to take your full statement while the details are still fresh in your mind. Maybe you can even come to headquarters."

Rod shook his head. "I'm sorry, but I need to be with Lilly right now."

"You're our only witness. We need—"

Rod cut him off with uncharacteristic aggression. "I told you already, I didn't witness anything. I can't help you."

Handsome took a breath and looked around. The gesture looked fake and I realized he was trying not to lose his temper. "It's possible you were the intended target. You got a lot of attention covering the wildfires last summer. You could have a stalker."

"That's ridiculous." Rod's voice was loud enough that other officers turned to look. "I don't even work in front of the camera anymore. You're deliberately trying to frighten me."

I was surprised by Rod's tone. Usually, I'm the one getting angry at police officers while Rod counsels courtesy. "Rod, maybe you—"

But Rod ignored me. "There's nothing more I can say in my statement that you don't already know. Bud was unconscious when I found him and I didn't see anything."

Handsome nodded. "Regardless, I suggest you cooperate. It would be very unpleasant for everyone if we were forced to detain you." He turned to me as if the matter were settled. "I'll get an officer to drive you now."

He left before Rod could argue further.

"Don't worry about me," I said. "Make a quick statement and get it over with."

I leaned in and kissed him. I hadn't intended for it to be more than a peck on the lips, but the drama of the moment tumbled into something more passionate.

"At least you weren't hurt," I finally said. "If only the same were true for Bud."

THREE

Christmas Eve, 9:19 a.m.

The uniformed patrol officer driving me to the hospital had to take side streets to avoid the accident with the sludge spill. It took fifteen minutes to reach Bakersfield Medical Center. I filled the time by criticizing the officer's route.

In my defense, nobody knows city streets better than a shooter. Identifying the most direct way to reach a destination can be the difference between getting amazing video of breaking news or getting nothing at all.

The officer escorted me into the ER and then suggested I sit in the crowded waiting room while he tried to get information. At least the news wasn't playing on the television mounted to the wall. I dreaded seeing the scene outside my own house replayed on KJAY—or even worse, on our competitor's broadcasts.

I couldn't help but think about the time I'd spent with my mother and sister in a similar ER waiting room. All I'd known was that my father had been in an accident on the job. He worked, and lived most of the week, seventy miles from town at an oil field out by Lost Hills. When I was little, he'd come home every weekend. By the time I was sixteen, and waiting in that ER for news of him, his visits had become unpredictable and rare.

When had I realized that my father was going to die? A memory of Bud surfaced. He'd come through the ER door and my spirits had briefly lifted. Bud was fun. He loved to use colorful southern slang and delighted in teasing my starch-perfect mother. Crazy uncle Bud always had a crooked grin on his face, unlike my father, who was quiet and withdrawn.

But the grin hadn't been there that day. That was when real fear had penetrated my teenage brain. I watched my mother embrace her seedy brother-in-law. I could hear her crying into his chest.

"Oh, hell" was all Bud said as tears began rolling down his face. That's when I'd felt it. The same feeling I'd experienced as I collapsed onto the sidewalk thinking Rod was dead. A feeling as if you'd do anything to change what was happening—make any deal, climb any mountain, make any sacrifice—but there was nothing to do because you were helpless.

The patrol officer returned and jerked me from the memory.

"They're prepping him for surgery. Someone will be out soon to talk to you." He sounded official, but polite. "Are there any other family members you can call to come wait with you?"

"No. My mother and sister live in Fresno now." I suddenly realized no one had told Annette, Bud's girlfriend. I explained and used a pay phone to make a collect call.

I hated telling her over the phone, but she took the news as well as could be expected. She promised to come as soon as she could find someone to stay with her daughter.

I returned to the waiting room just as Leanore arrived from the station. She hugged me and said, "I'm so sorry, Lilly."

We sat down together near a trio dressed as the three wise men. They all wore sneakers under their robes, and one had a bloody towel around his hand, but otherwise they were straight out of a Nativity scene.

"You're not going through this alone," Leanore continued. "Whether you like it or not."

Leanore had brought the messenger bag I used as a purse when I wasn't working as a shooter. After thanking her, I checked my phone for messages. There were two.

The first was from Rod and was sent a little after seven that morning. "Hi. I didn't hear you leave. Did you go in to work early? Call me, okay? I'm going to the gym, but I thought maybe we could go buy a Christmas tree on your lunch break." The message ended.

"You were right to yell at me earlier," I said to Leanore. "About Rod being too perfect to marry. I'm an idiot."

"You're not an idiot. You're just afraid of getting hurt. Welcome to the human race."

The door opened from the interior of the ER and a woman called my name. I was surprised to see the officer join us as Leanore and I went to speak with her. I shouldn't have been. This was a violent crime. Handsome had probably ordered the officer to keep an eye on us.

The woman directed us all to another floor where Bud would be taken for surgery. After a long walk and a brief elevator ride, we reached the surgical waiting room. I gave as much information as I could about Bud's medical background, age—which I guessed to be late seventies, but didn't know exactly—and of course insurance. When I'd finished those forms, I resumed checking my phone's messages and got a shock.

"Little Sister, it's Bud." Even through the phone's crummy speaker I could tell his voice was hoarse and tired. "If you're not answerin', then I figure you're at work. Rod's down visitin' his folks, right? I'm usin' the Oildale house for a meetin'. Just wanted to make sure I'd have some privacy."

I glanced at the patrol officer. I started to wave him over so he could listen to the message. Bud's own words stopped me.

"I got a situation needs tendin' and I need to be discreet like. The Law might not take kindly to this one, and it's best to keep you and Rod out of it."

"The Law" could only mean the police. Bud had a long history of shady schemes that skirted legality, but he'd vowed off those kinds of deals when he'd moved in with Annette and her daughter. Had he relapsed?

Bud continued, "Don't come home till you hear from me. I'm real serious, Little Sister." The recording ended.

I knew that I should forward the message to Handsome. He'd be trying to build a timeline of events, and the call might help. On the other hand, it sounded as though Bud had been doing something he didn't want the police to find out about.

Bud's girlfriend, Annette, arrived and interrupted my internal debate. As we hugged, I got a noseful of Chanel No. 5. It, and the nice dress she wore, reminded me of what Annette had been like when we'd first met.

Reeling from her daughter's terrible diagnosis, her husband's abandonment, and mounting financial troubles, Annette had exploited a flurry of attention from the media about her daughter's illness. I much preferred the jeans-wearing, down-to-earth woman I'd got to know as my uncle's girlfriend. I suspected her dressing up now, before coming to the hospital, was a way of coping with extreme stress.

Leanore kindly offered to go get coffee from the commissary while I filled Annette in on Bud's condition. Once I'd told her the little we knew, I gently maneuvered Annette to the opposite side of the room from the officer. He couldn't follow us without making his eavesdropping obvious.

"Do you know what Bud was doing at my place this morning? Was he involved in anything illegal?"

"Illegal?" The way she said the word was both a denial and a rebuke for even thinking it was possible.

"Bud has a history. Between you and me, was he doing anything he didn't want the police to know about?"

"Bud wasn't doing anything illegal, I'm sure." She straightened the green wool fabric of her dress. "But he was upset yesterday. I've never seen him in such a panic."

"That doesn't sound like Bud. I've seen him cracking jokes while narrowly escaping death." This wasn't an exaggeration. I literally had. "What happened to set him off?"

"He went out shopping for Christmas presents yesterday morning. Something he saw at one of the pawnshops upset him, but that's all he'd tell me. I don't know what the item was or why it was so disturbing."

"Pawnshops?"

She gave me a sheepish smile. "That's where Bud likes to shop. I realize how it sounds, but he knows all the owners. He's bought and sold for decades."

I didn't want to know the origin of the things he'd pawned over the years. Bud was never himself a crook, but he'd have no problem acting as middleman for shady merchandise. "What exactly happened when he came home from the pawnshops?"

"Like I said, he wouldn't tell me much. Bud ran right into the bedroom and started making phone calls. Then he went out again and never came back."

"Where did he sleep last night?"

Her eyes looked away as she admitted, "I have no idea."

"Any guesses?"

"I had hoped he was staying with you and Rod in Oildale. Most of his furniture and things are still in that house." When I shook my head, she continued, "And he's got that mobile home up at Lake Elizabeth. It's a drive, but he could have gone there."

I nodded. The obvious truth, that Bud might have spent the night with another woman, remained unsaid.

Annette addressed it, without addressing it. "Bud was wonderful to me when he was around, but he always made it clear marriage wasn't in his future."

"I understand." Actually, I didn't care. At the moment, the intricacies of their relationship mattered little to me compared with the intricacies of what got Bud shot. "Those calls he made just before leaving yesterday, did you hear any of them?"

She nodded. "He closed the door, but at one point Bud was shouting and I heard a name that I recognized." She paused for effect. "Leland Warner."

You could have given me a million years and gazillion tries and I would never have guessed Annette was about to say that name.

Warner was one of the richest men in California. I'd tangled with him a year ago when a young man named Val Boyle had been shot in one of Warner's many orchards.

At the time, I learned that Bud and Warner had a history, but each had refused to reveal the details to me.

"Did Bud ever talk about Warner?" I said. "I think they might have known each other a long time ago."

"Bud never talked about the past. He's all about having fun right now with no baggage."

Leanore returned from the commissary with a tray of Styrofoam cups just as a nurse was coming to speak with us.

The news sounded grim. Surgeons were currently working on Bud, but he had two gunshot wounds to the abdomen and had lost a substantial amount of blood. Assuming he survived, the surgery could run all day and into the evening. When I refused to sign a Do Not Resuscitate order, Annette began to cry.

The years fell away, and Annette, with her showy emotion, transformed into my mother. Bud, unreachable in the depths of the hospital, became my father. I knew what this day spent waiting would be like. I knew how it would end. I'd already lived through it once.

Except this time I didn't have to wait passively while my heart broke. I was no longer a confused, helpless teenager. I could take action instead of wallowing in the things I couldn't change.

As Leanore tried to console Annette, I made a phone call. When I'd finished, I took Leanore aside.

"I have to go," I whispered. "It's an emergency or I wouldn't leave." I glanced at the officer. I didn't think he could hear me. "Can you stay here and call me if there's news?"

"Of course, but what's the emergency?"

One glance at Leanore's sharp eyes and I knew I had to tell her the truth. "I need to talk with Leland Warner. I think he may know something about what happened to Bud. Can you distract the officer while I slip out?"

"Lilly, I'm saying this as someone who cares about you." Leanore put a hand on my arm. "Sitting here is probably going to be the worst day of your life, but if you don't face this, you'll regret it."

I fought the urge to tear my arm away and instead gently lowered it. "I'm not running away from bad news. Warner may know something about Bud's shooting that he can't share with the police because it's illegal."

Leanore looked torn, but then marched up to the officer and handed him one of the coffees. "This one's for you."

He took the cup and offered her a smile in return. "You didn't have to do that."

While they chatted, I made a show of asking the receptionist where the bathroom was. I followed her instructions, but kept going to the elevators.

Downstairs, I waited just outside the main entrance. The KJAY news van arrived a few minutes later. Ted must have left right after my call.

I opened the driver's-side door. Ted had already slid across to the passenger seat. "Thanks for bringing my van. You want me to drop you back at the station?"

"That would be righteous." He caught himself reverting to old speech patterns and frowned. "I mean, that would be nice. I still have to anchor the noon and five."

I put my seat belt on and drove out of the hospital parking lot. "Where's Callum? Is he covering the assignment desk? I doubt I'm going to be able to work this week."

"Freddy's still on the desk. Callum's going door-to-door in your neighborhood asking if anybody saw something. He wanted a reporter to do it, but there's no one available."

"What about Rod? I'm sure he'll pitch in."

"They took him to the Sheriff's Department headquarters."

My head jerked from the road to Ted. "Why? Is everything okay?"

"They threatened to arrest him if he didn't go." Ted looked uncomfortable with the topic, but continued anyway. "I'm sure it's just shock and stress, but Rod was acting sort of . . . I mean . . . he wasn't being very cooperative."

After I dropped Teddy, I mean Ted, at the station, I stopped for gas and phoned Rod's cell. He didn't answer so I left a message asking him to call me. I didn't really think Rod was in trouble with the police, but if Handsome was taking advantage of the situation to be a jerk, I wanted to know about it.

I filled up the gas tank, but didn't use my company gas card. I had a feeling this tank was going to be used exclusively for personal business.

Leland Warner has several properties around the county, and probably the world, but I only knew about two of them. The first was a vast ranch out past Shafter. I'd visited it in less than ideal circumstances a year earlier. The other was a mansion designed by a protégé of Frank Lloyd Wright's. When it was built in the 1970s, it was the most expensive structure in Bakersfield.

Not many people had seen it since then. The land around the house was well guarded and walled off from prying eyes. Leanore had been trying for years to gain access for one of her local-history stories. *Architectural Digest* had actually sent someone to Bakersfield when they'd devoted an entire issue to the now-dead architect.

I could have told them not to bother. Warner may be a disagreeable control freak, but he wasn't a snob. If he said no to Leanore, he'd say no to *Architectural Digest* too.

I drove to the northeast end of Bakersfield, where the wide, flat streets characteristic of the rest of town narrowed and sloped upward. This gentle climb came to an abrupt stop at an area called the Bluffs, where the land fell dramatically down a cliff face.

The real estate here is highly sought after. Houses actually on the Bluffs, the only ones in Bakersfield with views, were some of the most expensive in town. When Rod had moved from LA to work at KJAY, he'd bought a house in this neighborhood near the country club. He still owned it, but I liked the grit of Oildale and preferred to stay there.

For the first time I thought about what going home would be like. Could I stand to spend even one night in the house where Bud had been shot? What if he died? The house had been in my family for generations and I felt sick at the thought of moving. Then I thought about scrubbing Bud's blood off the living room floor and felt sick at the thought of staying.

The line of houses abruptly stopped at a massive concrete wall that marked the edge of Warner's property. It still took another five minutes of driving before I reached a gate made of two enormous copper doors. No markings or street numbers identified the property. The metal doors looked dull in the gray winter morning, their natural orange blunted down to brown, but I guessed that in summer they'd reflect the sun and the heat. I stopped and rolled down my window. I pushed the call button on a pad and looked up at a camera mounted to the wall.

"Yes?" a man's voice said over the speaker.

"My name is Lilly Hawkins. I'm here to see Mr. Warner."

The voice came back through the speaker before I'd even finished. "You may contact the media relations department at Warner Industries if you'd like to request an interview."

"I'm not here on business. Tell Warner that Lilly Hawkins needs to see him and it's an emergency."

"This is a private residence. If you insist on loitering, we'll call the police."

I was getting nowhere fast, which at least is better than getting there slowly. I was considering asking for Warner's head of security, whom I'd met last year, when a vehicle pulled in behind me.

After glancing in the rearview mirror, I turned full around. A little old lady sat behind the wheel of a large black pickup. She frowned at me, or rather at the KJAY logo on my van. She was a stranger, but the contemptuous twist of her mouth was not. I'd seen it many times on Leland Warner's face.

FOUR

Christmas Eve, 10:37 a.m.

I got out and walked to the pickup. Instead of rolling down her window, the woman glared at me.

"I need to see Leland Warner," I said.

"You're wasting your time." Her voice was muffled by the glass, but I could tell she spoke in short, clipped tones. "No interviews."

"I'm here for personal reasons, not as a journalist. My name's Lilly Hawkins and it's an emergency."

Something crossed her face at the mention of my name.

I guessed she knew what had happened last year when I'd first met Warner. "I'm the one who was involved in the murder at Happy Valley Farms last December."

She lowered the window just as the copper gates began to swing open. "What did you say your name was?"

Two uniformed Valsec Security guards rushed out.

"Lilly Hawkins." I put my hands on the truck door and leaned in. "Please, I need to see Warner. It's an emergency."

"Leland's sick," she said. "Even if you're here for legitimate reasons, you can't see him."

The guards hurried around my van. This was probably my last chance. "If you don't help me, I'll go on TV and tell everything I know about Warner and his family."

The guards stopped a few feet from us. They had their Tasers out.

"We're sorry about this, Miss Warner," one said to her. "Go ahead and drive up to the house while we take care of this situation."

"I know a lot," I said to her through the open window. "Stuff Warner wouldn't want on television."

She didn't react to my threat. Instead she calmly said, "And you say your name is Hawkins?"

"That's right."

One of the guards moved behind me. "This driveway is private property. If you don't leave, we'll forcibly detain you until the police arrive."

"Perfect," I said. "There's all kinds of things I can tell the police too."

The old lady leaned her head out the window and spoke to the guards. "Stand down. Miss Hawkins is coming to the house. She has business with the family." Miss Warner turned to me. "Get in. You can leave your van here."

The guards watched in surprise as I retrieved my blue jacket from the news van and got in the passenger seat of the pickup.

Miss Warner, as the guards had called her, had short, thin gray hair cut in a practical style. That and her plain jeans and sneakers contrasted with the exotic red tunic she wore. She looked to be in her seventies and made no effort to hide that behind makeup. I realized with a slight shock that her clothing was similar to my work outfit—jeans, red shirt, and practical shoes for traction and the unexpected.

"Why do you need to see my brother?" She hit the gas and expertly maneuvered around the news van.

"I know I just made a lot of threats, but I'm not the enemy."

"That's not what I asked." She drove the truck with a confidence that appeared to be second nature. She easily cleared the gate and then accelerated past a small guard post. "Why do you need to see my brother?"

I pretended to be distracted by the terrain on this side of the wall while I considered how much to tell her. "Is this a dirt road? I'm surprised the land is so wild and undeveloped. I thought Leland Warner would have spent money on landscaping."

She didn't take her eyes off the road. "Are you related to Allan Hawkins?"

My mouth fell open, but I quickly caught myself. "If you're talking about my uncle Bud, then yes. How does your family know him?"

"Your uncle Bud? You don't really call him by that stupid nickname?" The question must have been rhetorical because she didn't wait for an answer. "If Allan is really your uncle, then you must be William's daughter. Your father was a little boy last time I saw him."

The words were friendly on the surface, but her expressing knowledge of my family felt like a show of power, especially when I was so in the dark.

"My father, William, is dead. And you haven't answered my question. How does your family know Bud?"

"You're the one who hasn't answered my question. Why do you need to see my brother?"

I debated trading information with her. My instinct was to keep Bud's business as private as possible, especially since he might have been doing something illegal. "I need to speak with your brother before anyone else. I don't know the full situation yet myself. There may be things that, for Bud's sake, I simply can't talk about."

"I'd like to give you the benefit of the doubt, even if you won't give me the same." She glanced at me from the road. "Allan worked on our father's orchard when he was a teenager. He and Leland were best friends."

I took a moment to digest that nugget, then asked, "What's their relationship now?"

"There isn't one. They haven't seen each other in decades."

"Are you sure?"

"No." A smile filled out her thin lips. "Why do you think I brought you up from the gate?"

"I thought it was because I threatened to go on TV and embarrass your family."

"I could care less about that. I don't even live in this country anymore." She said it as though the United States and her family were both distasteful memories. "But I am curious to find out what Leland may be doing with Allan after all these years."

For some reason her calling him Allan bugged me the same way her knowledge of my father had. "Why do you keep calling him that?"

"Allan? That's his name."

I managed not to say that Bud must prefer the "stupid nickname" since he'd been using it my entire life. "When was the last time you saw Bud?"

"Over fifty years ago."

"If you don't mind my asking, what was your relationship?"

"I already told you," she snapped. "Allan was Leland's best friend."

"That's what he was to Leland. What was Bud to you?"

"I don't like your tone."

"If you don't like my tone, then what I'm actually thinking would really offend you."

She laughed. "I have a pretty good idea what you're thinking. You're not exactly a difficult person to read."

I knew this was true, but that didn't keep me from feeling annoyed. "I'm thinking that every time you call him Allan, you're raising your leg like a dog marking its territory. Most people aren't that possessive about friends of their brother's who they haven't seen in fifty years."

She gave the truck some gas and we climbed the short hill.

I continued, "And why haven't you asked me how he is? An old acquaintance who hadn't seen him in that long would be curious. He could be dead for all you know."

We cleared the hill and sailed over the crest. For the first time, we had an unobstructed view.

My breath caught and I momentarily forgot my questions.

"It's something, huh?" She glanced at me. "The architect actually had dirt trucked in to construct that hill we just came over. He wanted a dramatic introduction to his work."

"The house is the least of the drama."

The dirt road continued its path through the wild brush and ended at a long, two-story building made of glass and concrete. It barely registered as a house. Instead, the large structure, built near the edge of the bluffs, served as a complement to what lay below. Warner had built his mansion overlooking a working oil field.

Pollution was low today, so the view stretched for miles. Power poles and cables formed a black web over the land. A second network of shiny pipes connected everything on the ground. In several places, flames shot straight into the sky burning off gas. The derricks themselves bobbed up and down as they sucked raw crude out of the earth.

"This was where Leland dropped his first well." Her abrupt tone had been replaced with something gentler. "Before that, this land used to belong to our father. When I was a girl, I would cross the river just below the bluffs and climb up here. I could see the men picking fruit and sometimes even my father riding his horse out to check on them."

Her nostalgia turned wry. "I hadn't thought Leland sentimental, but after I ran away from home, he chose this spot to build his mansion. Maybe the fact that I was forty before I got the courage to leave made my desertion all the more unexpected."

The two-story building had been constructed of large blocks of concrete stacked in vertical lines, interspersed with columns of windows. A greenhouse capped each end of the building, with large trees inside reaching as tall as the house. They were either trapped or showcased, depending on your perspective.

As we approached the copper double doors set in the exact middle of the house, I spotted a man in a Valsec Security uniform. He stared at us with his arms crossed. I recognized him as Warner's head of security.

Miss Warner saw him too. She slowed and then stopped in front of the house. She put the pickup in park, but left the engine running.

"I brought a visitor up, Frank." She carefully stepped down into the dirt. She was even shorter than me. "This lady's the niece of an old family friend."

"It's okay, Miss Erabelle. You did the right thing." He gave me a curt nod. "Good to see you again, Miss Hawkins."

I came around the front of the truck and stopped. Frank was in his fifties with a spare tire and graying hair. He looked like someone who might be a friend of your dad's, but his blandness hid some nasty skills.

"Why are you happy to see me?" I said. "Looking for someone to assault and kidnap?"

Erabelle, as he'd called her, looked surprised. I guessed she really didn't know about the business last year.

Frank told a young guard to take the truck to the garage, then held open one of the copper doors for us. "Mr. Warner saw you on the security cameras and is eager for a private chat."

"I doubt Warner's as eager to see me as I am to see him."

I entered, followed by Erabelle. Another glass greenhouse containing a single willow tree sat in the exact center of the house. The branches had been decorated with white Christmas lights.

Frank shut the door behind us. "If you'll come with me, Miss Hawkins." He started around the tree.

Erabelle followed. "I'm coming too."

Frank continued to a wide staircase placed before a wall of windows. The view was of the oil field.

He spoke with politeness, but no respect. "Sorry, Miss Erabelle, Mr. Warner already gave his orders."

I followed as Frank climbed to a landing where the staircase split in opposite directions. It appeared each side led to a different wing of the house.

"I don't care what his orders were." Erabelle rushed to keep up on her older and shorter legs. "Tell him I insist."

Frank didn't pause before taking the stairs to the right. "Has that ever worked before?"

The answer was written all over Erabelle's defeated face. After watching Frank's retreating figure as it disappeared down a hallway, she turned to me. "Don't leave without seeing me first. I want to know what's going on."

I agreed and then hurried to catch up with Frank. "How sick is Warner?"

"He's got two nurses with him, round the clock." We reached a doorway at the end of the hall and Frank raised his hand to knock.

I stopped him. "Can we send the nurses out? I need to see him alone."

"Not going to happen, but the nurses are paid for their discretion."

The door opened and we each stepped back as an unusually attractive man exited. I think the best description was tall, dark, and handsome. He wore perfectly creased khakis and one of those polo shirts with a logo. "There you are. I don't think I've ever seen Dad this excited about a visitor, and that includes me."

I got a whiff of the same expensive cologne Rod wore. The smell provoked an emotional reaction. It was as though my heart lurched toward this stranger.

"It's really quite a compliment." He smiled and the spell was broken. This man might smell and dress like Rod, but his smile left me cold.

"I'm not flattered by empty compliments, especially from manipulative bullies like Warner." I entered and shut the door behind me.

The windows in this room offered views of the oil field on one wall and treetops on another. The master bedroom, sitting at the end of the wing, butted up against one of the greenhouses.

The furniture was in a hodgepodge of styles collected over a lifetime. The bed belonged in a New England beach house, while the brown tile floor was covered in a Native American rug. It felt as though Warner had given his architect full creative control to express a vision, then sabotaged that vision with his choice of furniture.

The man himself sat in bed, hooked up to monitors and IV bags. His drooping eyelids made it look as though he were dozing, but I knew better. He'd probably even heard my comment in the hallway.

I quickly crossed the room. "I need to talk to you."

"That's your opening move?" He stirred in the bed. "As a manipulative bully, I was hoping for something much more challenging."

FIVE

'm not here to entertain you," I said. "This is serious."

"And I'm seriously disappointed. I'd hoped someone with your damaged personality would make better conversation." Warner turned to one of the nurses. "The poor girl has almost no friends and more one-night stands than relationships. I suspect she's on the autism spectrum."

I should have stayed focused on Bud, but it's hard not to hit back when someone is kicking you in the gut. "So I hear you're dying."

A ripple went through the silent nurses.

Warner smiled. "That's more like it." He waved the nurses away with a flick of the wrist.

After they'd retreated to the other side of the room—where they could still hear us, but at least weren't hovering—I continued, "Who's going to take care of your daughter, Mary, once you're dead? Isn't she parked in a high-class mental hospital right now? It's a shame you won't be around to protect her."

He took a quick breath and let it out slowly. Instead of firing back, he said, "What did you need to see me about?"

Had I just won? Warner had to be in really bad shape. I actually felt a little guilty.

I sat down in a wingback chair set near the bed. "When was the last time you saw my uncle Bud?"

"That's why you're here?"

"I know he used to work for your father back when you both were teenagers. I heard you were friends."

"He was my best and only friend." Warner looked in my

direction, but his eyes lost their focus. "We were inseparable, right up until he turned eighteen and volunteered to go fight in Korea."

"Why didn't you go too?"

"No sensible person wants to go to war. And I had responsibilities. My father was sick and my mother was dead. Unlike Bud, I knew what I owed my family."

I straightened. "What's that supposed to mean?"

He let his head fall farther into the pillows. "Bud wanted adventure. When he came back from the war, he only stayed a year before going to Alaska to fight wildfires. He was addicted to risk."

I knew Bud had been a smoke jumper—his knowledge had saved my life last summer when I'd been covering a wildfire in the mountains—but I'd never thought of that or his military service as selfish.

Warner suddenly turned to me. "Why don't you ask Bud these questions?"

"He's been shot."

Warner's eyes opened as far as I'd ever seen, which is to say, a little. Still, he looked more sad than frightened. "I don't know why Bud insisted on living the way he did. Petty get-rich-quick schemes, associating with disreputable thugs. He could have been better than that. He wasted his life."

"You might try to hold back on all that sanctimonious judgment. Whatever got him shot involves you too."

He didn't move. Unlike before when he'd at least registered something, now he was a blank slate. "Why do you say that?"

"He saw something at a pawnshop yesterday that set him off in a panic. The first thing he did was call someone and shout your name into the phone."

One of the nurses made a small sound of recognition.

I turned fully to her. "What do you know about it?"

"Well, I think—"

Warner raised his hand. The skin was a yellow-and-blue patchwork of faded bruises from previous attempts to connect an IV with a working vein. But even in Warner's weakened state, that one gesture was enough to silence the nurse.

I got up and crossed the room. "What doesn't he want you to tell me?"

The nurses stared back at me. Clearly, supernurses of the rich and famous knew to keep their mouths shut.

"Where is Bud?" Warner said. "And what is his condition?"

I turned back to the bed. "He's in surgery at Bakersfield Medical Center."

Warner thought for a moment. His body remained still.

"I want answers," I said. "And I'm not leaving without them."

"Bud lived in a terrible neighborhood and had low friends. I'm sure whatever bad end he came to had nothing to do with me." Warner took a deep breath, but the air caught in his chest. "Why aren't you at the hospital? If Bud is fighting for his life, you should be with him."

I shook my head. "I have no intention of sitting all day in a waiting room like a useless piece of furniture. This time I'm asking questions and getting answers."

Breathing was becoming increasingly difficult for Warner, but his eyes shot to me. "This time? If unanswered questions about your father's death are motivating you now, then I'm truly sorry. That's my fault."

Last year Warner had tried to bribe me. Through corporate espionage, he'd supposedly obtained internal documents from my father's employers—a rival to one of his own companies, Warner Petroleum. These documents supposedly laid out a case that the accident that killed my father was a suicide. Since I'd refused to make a deal with the devil, in this case Warner, I'd never seen the contents of the file.

I'd thought about it a lot over the past year, not that I would have admitted it, even to Rod. I'd decided Warner had hit on a truth I'd been denying—that my father had been a withdrawn depressive—and then lied about the rest to manipulate and control me.

"Your father's death was an accident." His eyes looked directly into mine, despite his labored breathing. "I made up the business about suicide because I was desperate. I needed to silence you for my daughter's sake."

Even though his statement confirmed what I'd already decided, hearing the words loosened something inside me that had been tightly coiled.

But that didn't mean I was ready to abandon my questions about Bud. "I appreciate your telling me, but my father's death is old business. Right now I'm more interested in why Bud was shouting your name into a phone yesterday."

"I don't know, but it couldn't be related to his shooting." Warner was now having serious trouble breathing. "Go to the hospital and be with Bud. I won't keep you any longer."

He gestured to the nurses. One hurried over to the bed and adjusted his oxygen. The other opened the door and called to Frank.

"I'm not leaving," I said.

Frank approached from behind and took my arm. "That's not your decision to make." When I refused to yield to his gentle tug, he let go. "This is private property. If you don't voluntarily come with me, this can and will get physical."

Frank didn't make idle threats, so I relented.

After he'd shut the bedroom door behind us, his demeanor changed. "Thanks for coming. I've got an army of guys working security here, but it still would have been a pain in the butt to force you out."

"You could thank me by being honest. Has my uncle been in contact with any of the Warner family lately?"

Frank started down the hall. "Mr. Warner's not in the habit of taking the hired help into his confidence."

"You must know where enough of the bodies are buried to be considered more than hired help."

"I'm not complaining. Mr. Warner's been very nice to me over the years." He probably had—financially—but I doubted Warner's generosity had extended to actual kindness.

We exited that wing of the house and walked down the steps to the landing in front of the glass wall. Despite everything on my mind, I couldn't help stopping to look at the oil field. I wondered what the view would be like at night when all those beacons and flashing lights burned in the darkness. Would it actually be pretty?

I glanced straight down and saw the river Erabelle had mentioned crossing as a girl. A picturesque wooden bridge straddled it just below the house. Maybe Warner was sentimental if he'd left it standing all these years.

Frank chuckled. "I wouldn't have taken you for the stop-and-look-at-the-scenery type."

"It's not scenery. It's a freak show." I turned from the window and discovered that Frank had continued up the opposite stairs to the other wing.

"Come on," he said.

I hurried to catch up with him. "Thanks for letting me see Erabelle. I figured you'd throw me out."

He continued toward the end of the hallway. "I'm not taking you to Miss Erabelle. It's Mr. Warner who wants to see you."

"I'm pretty sure he was the one saying good-bye back there."

Frank stopped at the door at the end of the hall and knocked. "We have a special going today. Two Mr. Warners for the price of one."

"Come in," called a voice from inside the room.

Frank opened the door and held it for me. This room was the mirror of Warner's in the other wing, but the furniture here matched the house perfectly. It made it even odder that the windowpanes had all been covered in long curtains blocking the views. It was as though the two Mr. Warners had each chosen to subvert the architect's vision in competing ways.

"Here's Miss Hawkins, sir." Frank's use of *sir* amplified an air of subservience that had been lacking when he'd spoken with Erabelle.

The tall, dark, and handsome man I'd seen earlier looked up from a laptop. "Let's keep this between the two of us, Frank. Until Dad gets better, I'd rather not burden him with needless information."

"Of course, sir." Frank closed the door on his way out.

"Thanks for seeing me." The man closed the laptop, making sure to shield the screen from my view. "I appreciate how busy a professional journalist must be."

"You're the son? The one who lives in New York?"

"Leland Phillip Warner the second, at your service." He stood.

Junior appeared to be in his early forties. An old-fashioned men's sapphire ring sat on his right ring finger. It achieved the almost impossible task of making him look like both a dandy and a thug.

"Please feel free to call me Phillip or even Phil."

I refused to be flattered by his informality. "Home for Christmas or the funeral?"

My tone didn't disturb him. "After our earlier interaction in the hallway, Frank warned me you had no filter." He crossed to a sideboard. "But don't bury Dad yet. He's a tough old goat and may pull through this."

"It's obvious you're taking over. Maybe you're the one who shouldn't bury him yet."

Junior removed a bottle of Scotch from inside the cabinet. "The last thing in the world I want is to take over. Do you know what will happen if my father dies?"

"You'll become one of the richest men in California."

"That's the problem right there." He poured liquor into a highball glass without ice. "I don't want to be one of the richest men in California. I want to be a moderately well-off man in New York, which, thanks to my robust allowance, I already am."

He raised an empty glass. "Have a drink with me?"

"No thanks."

"I know it's early, but I'm on East Coast time."

I waited as he took a sip of the liquor before saying, "You

expect me to believe you'd rather not inherit? That you actually prefer to be a grown man on your father's financial leash?"

"I don't appreciate being compared to a dog." He took another drink and tried to change the tone. "Frank said you're a shooter. That must be a fascinating career." I didn't answer so he said, "Do you mind if I call you Lilly?"

"You'll do better with me if you come right out and say what you want."

He nodded. "Why did you come here today and is it related to my sister in any way?"

"It has nothing to do with Mary or what happened to her last year." Now that I'd spoken with Warner, there was no reason to keep Junior or Erabelle in the dark about my motives. "My uncle was shot this morning, and I think your father is somehow connected to what happened."

He looked surprised, but he could easily have been faking it. "Who's your uncle?"

"Bud Hawkins, although your aunt calls him Allan."

Junior clearly recognized the name, but didn't say so. I forced myself to remain quiet while he considered the matter. I'm not good at controlling myself, and it wasn't easy.

Finally my patience was rewarded. "Someone with that name called yesterday on Dad's direct line, so you're right they must know each other. That number's private."

"What did they talk about?"

"They didn't talk at all. Dad was having an angina attack and the nurses wouldn't put him on. I guess your uncle got very cross with one of them."

That at least explained what the nurses knew and whom Bud had been yelling at over the phone.

The door suddenly opened. Erabelle stormed in despite Frank's attempts to stop her.

"You want to try knocking?" Junior smirked. "I'm entertaining a lady. We could have been doing anything in here."

"No," I said louder than was necessary. "We really couldn't have."

Erabelle didn't even acknowledge me. "You miserable little . . ." Erabelle struggled, but finally decided against completing the insult. "I've just been on the phone with my people. I know what you've done."

Junior reverted to his previous superficial charm. "I'm sure I don't know what you're talking about."

"Don't pretend. You've cut off the funding to my foundation. Do you know how many women are counting on those loans? You're ruining lives."

Her anger didn't rattle him. "With Dad incapacitated, I've had to take a hand in the family finances. You wouldn't believe the people and causes he was sending checks to." Junior shrugged. "Last month I put a hold on all of his discretionary expenses until I can make sure each is legitimate."

"Oh, please. That money's going straight into your pocket. You're trying to sponge off as much as you can to pay off your own debts."

"You should watch how you speak to me. Dad may not get better." Junior didn't raise his voice, but somehow that made him sound even more menacing. "And after the will is read, you're going to need me more than I need you."

They stared at each other. Erabelle didn't even seem to know I was there. Frank, still hovering in the doorway, was similarly invisible to her. I wondered how many scenes like this had unfolded in front of him and if their casual disregard made him angry.

"As lovely as this is," I said, "I need to get back to the subject of my uncle."

Junior jumped on the change of topic. "That's right. How exactly does Dad know this guy?"

Erabelle was still too angry to answer.

"They were best friends," I said, then turned to Erabelle. "But I'm afraid Bud was shot this morning. He's in surgery at Bakersfield Medical Center."

I immediately regretted telling Erabelle so bluntly. Her passion, so provoked by her nephew, wavered, then vanished as though I'd blown out a flame.

Junior either didn't notice her distress or didn't care. "I didn't think Dad had friends—just employees and family."

Erabelle's head stayed down, but her eyes rose to look at me. "How is he?"

"Very bad. They don't know who shot him or why, but I think it has something to do with your brother. Apparently Bud got upset about something and tried to call him yesterday."

She turned for the door.

"Hold on," I called. "We have more to talk about."

She exited without looking back.

"Excuse me," I said to Junior while starting for the door. "Thanks for being honest with me."

He took a seat on the sofa and spread out his arm along the backrest. "You'll keep me informed if you find out anything relating to Dad? I only ask so I can head off trouble if it's brewing."

I stopped at the door. "If you'll do the same for me."

He nodded. "For what it's worth, I only ever heard one reference to Dad having a best friend. I'm hazy on the details, but I believe the fellow walked off with our family heirlooms. I always wondered if that experience was what soured Dad on friendship."

I'd been in a hurry to catch up with Erabelle, but that gave me pause. Was this the real reason Bud and Warner hadn't seen each other in over fifty years? "What kind of heirlooms?"

"Military medals from back in mother Russia. Czar-type stuff. Mom made it sound very romantic, or melodramatic, depending on your point of view. I guess there was a big police investigation when they were stolen."

I shook my head. "Bud might be a little shady, but he'd never rob his best friend."

Junior raised the glass in a toast. "Like I said, for what it's worth."

SIX

I left Junior and hurried to follow Erabelle. I'd hoped that she was on her way to confront Warner and drag the truth out of him, but I was wrong. Frank gestured to a closed door down the hall.

There was no answer to my knock. "Erabelle, you can't just walk out and think I'm going to let it go. What do you know about Bud's shooting?"

I heard the click of the lock, then the door opened just enough to reveal her face. "Whatever Allan and Leland are up to, I'm not a part of it." She started to close the door. "And I don't want to be."

I jammed my size-ten boot in the door. Having large feet sometimes has its advantages. "You said you brought me up to the house specifically because you wanted to know what was going on."

"It was a mistake. I don't want to backslide like this."

She tried to close the door again, but I held my foot firmly in place. "You're going to have to elaborate on that."

"There's a reason I live in Indonesia now. I've spent years trying to make a life for myself outside of this family. I came home for Christmas this year because Leland is sick, but I can't let myself get drawn back into his scheming. It's not healthy."

"Bud is dying. Maybe that doesn't mean anything to you, but I love him." I felt my eyes sting. "You may be done with Bud, but I'm not. I care that someone deliberately tried to end his life."

A slight hitch in her voice betrayed the emotion under the words. "I didn't say I don't care. But there's a reason your uncle and Leland used to be friends. They were both very good at hurting people."

This last statement took me so much by surprise that when Erabelle moved to close the door, I forgot to stop her.

I knocked again, but this time there was no answer at all.

Frank had one of the guards drive me back to my news van at the front gate. Before saying good-bye he passed on Junior's cell phone number and took mine in return. Apparently Junior was serious about the two of us keeping each other informed.

I drove back to the station to regroup and see if there was any news about the police investigation. After parking in the fenced KJAY lot, I decided to call Rod again. I wanted to talk over what had happened at Warner's and get his opinion. The call went immediately to voice mail, which meant his phone was off. I left another message asking that he call me as soon as he was done with the police.

I then called Leanore at the hospital. There was still no news about Bud. I told her to go home, but she offered to stay and call me if Bud got out of surgery. It was a lot to ask of her, and I hadn't asked, but Leanore was the kind of person who instinctively knew what was most needed and didn't hesitate to help.

My profuse thanks were interrupted by a yipping sound outside the van. I hung up and opened the door. At first I thought the thing looking up at me was a possum or giant rat. I instinctively jerked back, but then it barked again and I decided it was just a really ugly dog. I swear, one of the thing's eyes was bigger than the other. Its black hair looked as brittle and unappealing as a porcupine's coat.

The animal shelter's truck sat in a space nearby, but if they thought anyone was going to adopt this thing, even on Christmas Eve, they were nuts.

Despite its small size, it tried to jump into the van. I reached down to pick it up, but it leapt at me and licked my face. Before I could jerk back, a cloud of monumentally bad breath made its way into my nostrils.

"What did you eat?" I held the dog at arm's length while walking to the building. "Poop? Vomit? Vomit made of poop?"

I found the shelter guy in the break room. He had several crates with dogs and cats, and one birdcage.

I held out "Thing" for him to take. "I found this dog in the parking lot. Is it one of yours?"

Right after I said the words, I felt uneasy. What if it wasn't a dog? It would be just like me to casually walk around with some dangerous wild animal that I'd mistaken for a pet.

Fortunately the shelter guy recognized Thing and apologized for letting him get away. The man's manner was edgy and preoccupied. I guessed he was the lowest employee on the totem pole—hence his working Christmas Eve—and probably inexperienced.

By the time I entered the newsroom it was eleven forty-five.

Instead of the scanners and the usual mix of typing, conversation, and cable news channels, I heard the chorus of "Grandma Got Run Over by a Reindeer." One of the writers had brought his guitar to work and was accompanying the celebrants. I guessed most of them were scheduled to leave after the noon show and were coasting through their remaining time on the job.

I picked up three homemade Christmas cookies on my way to the assignment desk. I did a double take when I saw Freddy sitting in Callum's spot.

"Dude," he said when he saw me. "How's your uncle?"

I avoided the question. "Has Rod called in?"

Freddy shook his head, and the mop of curls whipped back and forth. "No, but Callum's here. He shot video at your house and is totally trying to cut something for the noon." Freddy leaned down and lowered his voice. "Don't tell him I said so, but it's not half-sucky. He's got an eye for composition."

"Is there anyone who can relieve you from the assignment desk? You don't even work here anymore."

"Callum's putting me on as a freelancer." Freddy gestured into the newsroom. "Most dudes are saying adios after the noon, so I offered to stay."

Scanning the dry-erase board where the day's stories were listed, I could see he was right about our staffing. Already thin for the holiday, we were now stretched to the breaking point with the sludge crash and Bud's shooting.

"We're lucky you're here." I pointed up at the board. "But you might want to take down that last story."

Freddy turned, read *Grandma vs. Sleigh*, and jumped up. "I can't look away for five seconds." He finished erasing the joke, then yelled into the newsroom, "Not cool, dudes. Some of us are trying to work."

The ten-thousand-year-old demon entered.

Since she was coanchoring the noon with Ted, I thought I should warn her. "The shelter is here with the animals, but the guy's distracted and nervous. You may want to spend some extra time with him going over how the adopt-a-pet segment works."

She gave me a frosty look, probably because of the words we'd exchanged earlier that morning, but thanked me.

After she'd left, Freddy said, "Just saying, dude, think about the old olive branch. It's smart to make friends with the friend of your friends."

I couldn't imagine who'd want to be friends with her, so his argument didn't move me. "Whatever. Is the live shot ready for the noon from the scene of the sludge accident?"

"Totally." Freddy's face lit up. "And rumor's going around that it wasn't sludge that spilled. I'm hearing it was some kind of secret, toxic military waste."

I bit into the last sugar cookie and spoke while chewing. "Weren't you trying to convince me earlier that a giant snake escaped from the same crash?"

"Dude, I hear a lot of stuff. Not all of it's gold, but I seriously got a feeling in my gut about this toxic-waste thing."

"Hey, Lilly." Callum stood in the open doorway of an edit bay. He still wore his casual vacation clothes and the beard. The hair growing out of his ears was longer than normal too. "I uploaded all my raw video from the scene to the server. Be kind when you look at it. The camera work isn't the greatest."

"I'm sorry you had to give up your vacation."

He waved me toward the edit bay. "Come on. I'll fill you in on what I found out. It won't take long."

I followed him in and slid the sliding glass door shut to block out the Christmas carols.

"How about Freddy on the assignment desk?" Callum sat down. "I'm trying to hang back and let him get a feel for it. Don't tell Freddy I said so, but he's not half-bad. He's got a real ear for the scanners."

He reached for the mouse. The edit bays, which previously housed decks and monitors for editing videotape, had been retrofitted with computers. Reporters could now edit their video digitally and push it directly onto the control-room playback server via our network.

"I'm trying to cut some B-roll and a couple sound bites for the noon." He clicked on a file. "It's taking me forever because I have no idea what I'm doing."

He played the raw video from the scene and also what little there was of his going door-to-door on my block, which even by his own admission had been a complete failure.

"There's some drug and gang activity in the neighborhood." I felt awkward admitting it. Rod had wanted to move. Maybe I should have agreed. "The people who aren't involved themselves make a point of not seeing crime for fear of retribution."

Callum nodded. "One of my sources at the Sheriff's Department says it's looking like a robbery gone bad. They figure your uncle walked in on a thief who shot him."

I hesitated. How much should I tell Callum? Could I trust him to keep quiet if it turned out Bud was doing something illegal? "Is that their only theory?"

"I heard they're taking molds of tire tracks from the alley

behind the house. Your uncle's '71 Plymouth Fury was found back there, and they think his attacker parked next to it. Preliminary word from the scene is that they're looking for a pickup."

"Good luck with that. As Bud would say, you can't toss a sack of armpits in this town without hitting a pickup." I waited while Callum laughed, then stepped cautiously out onto the proverbial limb. "I think Bud was meeting someone."

Something in my voice got Callum's attention. "Why? You know something you're not telling me?"

I decided to tell Callum about Bud's visit to the pawnshop and subsequent call to Leland Warner. I finished with the message Bud left on my cell that morning. "I think Bud was trying to make sure the house was empty so he could meet someone there. He needed privacy and even mentioned that the police couldn't know what he was doing."

Callum leaned back in the chair and whistled. "You got Leland Warner, pawnshops, an implication of illegal goings-on, and an actual shooting, all mixed in together. What a rat orgy."

We were each silent for a moment. Finally I couldn't stand it anymore. "It's a great story."

"No need to say the obvious." He tried to pat me on the shoulder. The gesture was actually more touching because of his awkward execution. "You probably need to be at the hospital for the next few days. If at some point you want to investigate this thing for KJAY, all the station's resources are at your disposal."

I shook my head. "I'm starting now while the leads are still fresh, but what about Bud's phone message to me? If he didn't want the police to know what he was doing, then he's probably implicated in something illegal. I may not want to broadcast that on television."

Callum hesitated. "If you change your mind and drop the story, the less I know about your reasons, the better."

Callum's professional ethics would prevent him from suppressing news. Even this Don't Ask, Don't Tell suggestion was probably costing him some self-respect.

Now it was my turn to awkwardly pat him on the shoulder. "Thank you."

Callum, never comfortable with emotion, reached for the mouse again. "After I finish editing this for the noon, is there any background work I can do for you?"

"Yes. I need information on the Warner family. Leland has a son who may need money and a sister named Erabelle. She lives abroad and seems to have some old issues with Bud."

I hadn't wanted to say that Bud might have treated her badly. I'd never thought of him as a settling-down kind of man, but I also hadn't thought of him as a callous womanizer either.

Callum nodded. "I can do basic background-type stuff, run a LexisNexis search, but my contacts are all cops and politicians. We'll need somebody else for society gossip."

I remembered what Junior had said as I was leaving his room. "There's an old story about Warner being robbed of some family heirlooms. Military medals or something like that. Can you see if any of your police contacts remember an investigation?"

I refused to believe Bud would steal from his best friend, but I did have doubts about what soured that relationship. People grew up and apart, as Warner had said, but those two had spent fifty years living in the same city and pretending not to know each other. That rift sounded traumatic and final.

"I've never heard of it," Callum said. "So that means the theft was before my time. For something that old, the cops will be retired. Let me make a few calls."

"Thanks." I stood. "I'm going to call pawnshops. Maybe I can locate the one Bud visited yesterday and find out what upset him so much."

The noon was just beginning so I stopped in the hallway outside the studio. The shelter officer was there waiting with the animals in crates. We each watched Ted and his coanchor through a large glass window.

"I thought I was nervous," the officer said, "but that guy looks like he's going to throw up."

I said a silent prayer on Ted's behalf to God, fate, or whoever might be listening. On a normal day I would have stayed and watched. Instead I found a phone book and retreated to an edit bay.

The calls to pawnshops went quickly. The owners all knew Bud—apparently he was a regular customer—and four of the six reported seeing him the previous day. None could remember anything unusual happening and all said Bud lingered to crack jokes with the men and flirt with the women.

When I'd reached the final listing, I asked the owner if there were any other pawnshops I might have missed.

"You could try Pawn Max. He's retired, but his wife keeps the shop open a couple days a week. Doubt they'd advertise in the phone book. I think she only works to get away from all the craziness at home."

He didn't have a phone number, but the address he gave me wasn't far from the station. I decided to drive over and check it out.

Pawn Max did business in a commercial strip cutting between a neighborhood on the upswing and one in decline. The businesses looked as if they were sliding the wrong way, despite the best efforts of the shopkeepers.

Just as I'd been told, the Pawn Max sign above the storefront was discreet. Less discreet were the plywood and the police tape covering the door and the windows.

They'd been robbed.

SEVEN

I retrieved my gear bag and camera from the van before walking down the block looking for an open business. I hoped to find someone who could get me in touch with the owners of Pawn Max, since they obviously weren't going to be opening the store anytime soon.

I stopped at Kincaid's Pharmacy and Gifts. A blast of air, thick with heat and potpourri, hit me as I pushed open the door. The flowery odor went with the cute teapots, stationery, and tea towels they were selling. It did not go with the security guard sitting by the door.

The female cashier was busy ringing up a customer with a last-minute Christmas gift, so I spoke with the guard.

He was a large man, but probably too old to stop an actual robbery. I guessed he was there more as a deterrent to shoplifters than anything else.

He spoke in a deep bass. "I'd help you if I could, but I only know the Pawn Max lady to say hi." He pointed to a Caucasian man in a white coat behind the pharmacy counter. "But I think Mr. Kincaid is friendly with her."

I thanked him and walked through the aisles of laxatives and deodorants to the rear. As his Scottish name suggested, Kincaid had red hair. It had probably dimmed a little with age, but hadn't gone gray.

"I'm from KJAY," I said. "I'm hoping you might know how I can contact the owner of Pawn Max."

"I can give you the store's phone number."

Despite its not being offered, Kincaid probably had a home

number for Mr. and Mrs. Pawn Max. At the least he'd know another business owner on the block who had it. I tried to quickly size him up.

Pushing fifty, but still trim. Vain enough to make the extra effort to stay in shape. Single, judging by the lack of a ring, but not a player. Probably divorced. Pictures of golden retrievers taped to the register where you'd expect to see kids. It appeared that he made his employees, although there were only two of them, refer to him as Mr. Kincaid.

Instinct told me he'd want to be on TV, want it real bad. His brain would replay fantasies about old rivals and enemies seeing the segment. If he did have an ex-wife, he'd probably call and tell her to watch.

"Can I interview you about the robbery?" This was a twofer. I actually wanted a sound bite for the five o'clock show, but also hoped interviewing him might help me get a home number for the Pawn Max owners.

"I don't know if that would be good for business." Contrary to his words, he straightened the white pharmacist's jacket and ran a hand through his thinning red hair. "Things are bad enough without scaring off the customers we have left."

"I understand. Thanks anyway." I started to turn, wondering how far I'd get before he stopped me.

"Although they say there's no such thing as bad publicity." He took a few steps and tried to see himself in the mirror running along one of the walls. "It might even be good for business."

I positioned the tripod, then set the camera's white balance off Kincaid's jacket. A stained-glass representation of the pharmaceutical arts had been hung on the back wall between the shelves of drugs. I framed my shot so it appeared just over his shoulder.

After he said and spelled his name for me, I asked the most basic question imaginable. "In your own words, can you tell me about the robbery?"

"Happened in the middle of the night."

This was a terrible sound bite—too short and no context at all. After three more tries I finally got something usable about neighborhood crime.

"This is a terrific neighborhood," he said. "It's full of hardworking, law-abiding people. It's a shame that a rougher element is making it difficult for business owners. It drives up our costs when we have to install more security."

"That's great. Thanks." I started to shut off the camera, but he continued.

"Not that you can defend yourself against a backhoe. There's no security system that's going to keep something like that out."

I froze, even as my inner newshound was baying at the moon. "Do you mean the thieves drove a backhoe into the store?"

"Stole it from a construction site the next street over." He gestured down the block. "That's how they got in. Pawn Max had the strongest door money could buy and bars over the window."

My throat went dry, but I still managed to ask in a squeaky voice, "Is there surveillance-camera video of the backhoe driving in?"

"I think so, but you'd need to ask the owner."

Jackpot! Blackjack! Eureka! Video such as that would be a sensation. It could even go viral and get all kinds of attention for KJAY.

I shut off the camera and said honestly what I'd planned to be sneaky about. "I need to talk to the owner of Pawn Max. Can you give me a home number?"

"I'm not sure. Christmas is their busy time at home."

I should probably have asked why this was their busy time, but I was too focused on my own issues. "I need that surveillance video. It's crucial to the story."

He glanced at the shelves of drugs and lowered his voice. "I only have her home number because she's a customer of the pharmacy, which I shouldn't even be telling you."

I decided to apply pressure where Kincaid would probably feel it the most. "If I can't get an interview with the pawnshop owner tonight, the story probably won't air, including your interview."

Kincaid saw his fifteen minutes of fame slipping away and grabbed for it. "She's coming to pick up a prescription later. I can ask her to speak with you."

My phone started vibrating. I checked the screen, told Kincaid I'd only be a moment, then answered, "Callum, can I call you right back?"

"The Sheriff's Department is sending Rod home." Behind Callum's voice I heard the hum of multiple conversations and forks scraping plates. "I said you'd come get him at headquarters, but if you're in the middle of something, I can make other arrangements."

"No, I'll get him. I'm almost done. Thanks for calling."

"If Rod's hungry, come down to the Knotty Pine. I'm here now meeting with a couple retired cops I know."

The Knotty Pine Café was a police hangout a block from the Sheriff's Department headquarters. The thought of their tuna melt made my mouth water. "I'm so hungry. Even if I have to take Rod home first, I'll come back and find you."

I hung up and gave Kincaid my business card. "Please tell the owner of Pawn Max that I'd like to speak with her, even if it's off camera. I'm happy to meet her here when she comes for the prescription."

I paused at the van to shoot quick video of the damaged storefront, then I drove as fast as I could to the Sheriff's Department headquarters. It's in a section of Norris Drive bordered by Airport Drive and, I kid you not, Oil Junction. The airport butted up behind the facility, and train tracks ran directly across the street.

Rod looked completely out of place standing outside in his expensive wool coat, but his face brightened when I pulled up in the van.

He jumped into the passenger seat and immediately reached for me. "You have no idea how glad I am to see you."

"You're glad to see me? This morning I thought you'd been shot."

"I'm so sorry about Bud. I tried everything to help him, but there was so much blood." His arms tightened around me. "And the ambulance took forever. I keep thinking I should have done something. Maybe driven him to the hospital myself."

"Don't be silly. It's not your fault." I kissed him as if it were my last chance. His arms relaxed and slowly wrapped around my back. The feel of his hands and lips sent a jolt through my system despite the day's sorrow.

After a moment I pulled back just enough to look at him. Dark bags hung under his eyes and his usually smooth skin had wrinkles.

"I'm sorry you had to go through all this. We probably should have moved like you wanted to. I really didn't think the neighborhood was that bad."

"It's not your fault either. It's not anyone's fault." He took a breath and asked the question. "How's Bud?"

"They're doing surgery, but it's a long, difficult procedure. At his age . . ." I couldn't bear to finish the sentence.

"Thank you for coming to get me." Rod took my hand. "We can go right back to the hospital now."

"I wasn't exactly at the hospital when you called."

"Oh?" He didn't look judgmental, just confused. "Where were you?"

"I was canvassing pawnshops, but I think I'm free now until Mrs. Pawn Max calls for her drugs."

Now he looked judgmental. "Who's Mrs. Pawn Max and why do you have her drugs?"

"I don't have her drugs. The pharmacy does." I put the van in drive and pulled away from the curb. "Let's get something to eat. Callum's down at the Knotty Pine pumping some retired cops for information."

Rod's voice rose. "What's been going on while I was being interrogated?"

My head jerked from the road to Rod's face. "They interrogated you?"

His tone immediately changed. "No. I misspoke. I gave a statement is all."

"You don't misspeak. Your speak is perfect." Suddenly a lot of things seemed ominous. Why had Handsome Homicide insisted Rod come to headquarters to make his statement? Why had they kept him for so long? Where were the gym shorts and T-shirt he'd been wearing back at the house?

"Did the police confiscate your clothes?"

He shrugged. "They just want to run some tests on them. It's not a big deal."

Bud's blood had been on Rod's clothes, but they'd hardly need a lab to prove that. "Are they testing for gun-powder residue?"

"Yes, but it's procedure. They're just being thorough." He raised a hand as if dismissing the whole thing. "Obviously they won't find any powder because I didn't fire a gun."

I turned the van into the parking lot in front of the yellow building that housed the Knotty Pine Café.

Rod pointed. "There's Callum's car."

I refused to drop it. "Is Handsome harassing you because I wouldn't go out with him? I knew he was a jerk, but this is beyond anything."

"At least it's over now. We can focus on Bud and his recovery." Rod reached for the door handle. "I'll go in and find Callum while you park. This is actually a good idea. I haven't eaten all day and I could use something before going to the hospital."

Rod jumped out and shut the door before I could say anything else. He'd apparently forgotten about Pawn Max, or else he was too exhausted to deal with another complication on an empty stomach.

I parked next to Callum's Ford Taurus and took a moment to change my shirt. Pumping retired police officers for information was something that required discretion. My wearing a big red KJAY polo shirt at a cop hangout would have been a little too obvious, even for me. Fortunately I kept a generic Gap T in my gear bag for just this sort of occasion.

After ducking down between the seats and making the switch, I followed Rod in. On my way to the front door, I passed the trunk of the pine tree that grew straight up and through the veranda's roof. Its green branches sprouted above the building like flowers out of a vase.

Inside, the restaurant buzzed. They were closing soon for the holiday weekend, but plenty of patrons lingered over their lunches. Christmas lights had been strung across the wood paneling covering all the walls. It somehow fit with the old saws and other lumberjack paraphernalia decorating the restaurant.

Callum waved at me from a corner booth he shared with three old men. I approached and noted their empty plates.

"Rod's over there." He pointed to a pine table in the back where Rod sat. "I'll join you two in a minute."

I took the hint and left him alone with his sources.

Rod tried to smile as I approached. "I ordered you Roger's Raving Tuna Melt. I hope that's okay?"

I sat down opposite him. "Perfect."

He'd removed his winter coat, revealing khakis and a gray cashmere sweater his fashion-conscious mother had sent him last month. "I don't understand. Who are those men Callum is speaking with?"

"Retired cops. I asked him to find out some background on Leland Warner."

"You did what?" Rod lowered his voice after an older couple sitting nearby turned to look. "Why would you do that?"

I told him about Bud's phone call to Leland Warner. I also filled him in on the robbery at Pawn Max.

Rod's already tired face lost the rest of its color. "Lilly, you need to let this go. It's not a story. We're not working."

"Actually, it is a story. Callum has me on it."

We each sensed someone approaching and turned to see Callum himself. The men he'd been sitting with were all waiting in line to pay.

"One of my guys remembered Warner getting robbed back in the fifties." Callum pulled a chair over from another table. "And it was a lot more than heirlooms. He thinks the thief got away with jewelry. Diamonds, no less."

Callum paused so the waitress could place our food on the table. In addition to my tuna melt, Rod had ordered catfish and eggs for himself.

When the waitress left, Callum continued, "I guess the thief was a friend of Warner's. He fled town with the loot and was never seen again."

I took a bite of my sandwich and savored the combination of tuna, mayonnaise, and melted cheese. "It's obviously not Bud, although I think he and Warner were still close back in the fifties. Maybe the thief was a friend of Bud's too."

"It's probably unrelated to the shooting today, but I'll follow up." Callum took a fry off my plate and popped it in his mouth. "A cop named Hoyt handled the case. He's a bit of a lone wolf and hasn't been seen much since retirement. They're going to try to contact him for me."

"What about the case file?" I said. "Is there any way we can get our hands on it?"

Rod set his fork down. He'd hardly eaten anything. "Lilly, that's illegal."

Callum shook his head. "It's not illegal for us to ask. I've got a call in to a guy I know who's still on the force and owes me a favor. He's trying to pull the old file right now. If he gives it to us, that's illegal."

"I understand that you'd do anything to help Bud." Rod looked at me with tired eyes. "But digging up Warner's ancient history isn't going to make him better."

"Whoever shot Bud is still out there," I said. "That's not exactly good for his health."

"It was a robbery." Rod reached across the table and took my hand in his. "As horrible as this whole thing is, at least we don't have to wonder if someone targeted Bud. It wasn't personal."

"I understand where you're coming from, Rod." Callum glanced at him. "And you're probably right, but the first rule of good journalism is don't make assumptions."

Rod took a deep breath. A little color returned to his cheeks. "You and the rest of the news department should do whatever you think necessary to cover the story, but Lilly and I need to be at the hospital focusing on Bud's recovery, not working."

I knew I should tell Rod that I didn't expect Bud to live through the surgery, let alone recover, but I didn't seem to be able to say it out loud.

"This might be my guy." Callum pulled his vibrating cell phone off his ample belt and answered. The conversation lasted for less than a minute, but Callum still took out his tablet computer to take notes. "Thanks," he finally said. "I'll meet you at three."

He hung up and opened the browser on the tablet. "Back in 1955 a man named Carter King stole two gold brooches from his friend Leland Warner. One of them had a buttload of diamonds on it. Carter was never caught. The warrant is still open and he's been a fugitive all these years."

Callum paused from his web search to look up. "According to the file, the primary witness against Carter King was none other than Allan Hawkins."

EIGHT

T hat's Bud." I sat forward. "Allan is his real name. If Bud turned this man in to the police, then maybe he held a grudge all these years. King could have shot Bud out of revenge."

"That's a huge reach." Rod shook his head. "King would have to be in his seventies or eighties by now, if he's not already dead."

"My source is making a copy of the police file to slip to me. We'll know a lot more when we see it." Callum held up the tablet. "But according to the county assessor's website, Carter and Mida King are still the legal owners of five hundred acres of land just north of town."

I took the tablet from him and stared down at the map. "This borders Warner's property."

Rod laughed, but his voice was hoarse from the strain of the day and it sounded forced. "That doesn't mean anything. Warner is so rich that almost everything in town borders something of his."

"No," I said. "It borders his original property. The one he inherited from his father. It used to be orange groves, but now it's an oil field."

My cell phone made a noise, followed by Rod's and Callum's. We all silenced them and read our new text messages.

"That's weird," Rod said. "Freddy is texting me from the station. He doesn't even work there anymore."

Callum stared at his screen. "He's filling in on the assignment desk today."

Rod's head shot up. "Freddy?"

I nodded and then read my message: SOS. 911. HLP. XMAS PETS GNE2HELL. CAT8BRD.

Callum leapt from his seat.

"It might not be as bad as it sounds," Rod said, but Callum was already running out of the restaurant. "Maybe Freddy means the animal shelter brought one cat and eight birds."

"Your optimism is the thing I love best about you."

Rod didn't laugh. He didn't even look at me. He took a breath that sounded surprisingly like a sigh. His shoulders hunched and the worry lines on his forehead deepened. "Lilly, I need you to stop working on this story."

"I know you've been through hell today." I got up and transferred to Callum's empty seat next to Rod. "But is there more you're not telling me?"

"The hardest part about how my grandfather died was that I couldn't get to the hospital in time to say good-bye. He asked for me, and I wasn't there."

His eyes were glassing over, but he didn't look away.

"I'm so sorry," I said. "I forgot that you . . . I mean, of course that's on your mind now. We'll go to the hospital right away."

We paid our check and left. I'd eaten half my tuna melt, but Rod had barely touched his catfish and eggs. I wrapped the biscuit, usually his favorite, in a napkin and took it with me.

We were close to the Oildale house so we detoured to pick up Rod's Prius. Neither of us wanted to go inside what I'd once thought of as a safe place—which was good, because we couldn't. Crime-scene tape blocked the front porch and a police seal was on the door.

Rod suggested, and I quickly agreed, that we stay at the house he owned near the bluffs. The repairs that had prompted his moving in with me a year earlier had been completed, and the 1970s ranch-style house would be free and comfortable.

We drove to the hospital in our separate cars. I lagged behind only long enough to put my KJAY shirt back on. Once on the road, my cell phone rang. It was Callum, so I took the call and put it on speaker.

"What happened with the animals?" I said. "Is the bird really history?"

"Yes, but it didn't happen on air." Behind Callum's voice I heard a cat meowing. "The animal control guy took off after the noon show, but he left a couple cages unlatched."

"I thought he looked distracted. What if he doesn't come back for the five?"

"We'll figure something out." Callum paused, and I heard a computer mouse clicking. "I've done more Internet snooping about the man who stole Warner's jewelry. Mida is Carter King's sister. They both inherited the family farm from their parents, who died young."

"Is Mida still alive?"

"Nobody ever bothered to change the title on the land so she must be. The farm is her last known address."

"As much as I'd like to talk with her, I have to go to the hospital first."

"Perfect. I'll call Leanore and brief her on the story." A dog barked, followed by a sharp hiss. "When you're ready, take her with you to the King farm. If you run into anybody, say she's doing one of her local-history pieces on the old robbery."

"What about Rod? He's been through a lot today."

"Then leave him at the hospital or send him home to get some rest. Whatever he needs."

At the hospital I parked and met Rod in the lobby. On the ride upstairs I explained that Callum was sending Leanore and me out to the King farm.

Rod's cheeks were already chalky white, so he couldn't pale any more. "This is a bad idea, Lilly. You need to stay here with me."

We stopped at the entrance to the surgical waiting room, where Leanore and Annette sat together. Three new people waited for news of their own relative on the other side of the room. I imagined myself in their place with hunched shoulders and a listless, miserable gaze directed at the floor.

I glanced inside to make sure the patrol officer was gone before speaking. "I know it's important for you to be here, and I understand why, but we're different. If I sit here and wait, I'll come apart. I have to do something."

Rod looked uncomfortable and refused to make eye contact. "The more you investigate who shot Bud, the more you're going to discover about his life. Not all of it's going to be good." He finally looked at me. "If he does die, don't you want to remember the best of him?"

I laughed. "I have no illusions about Bud. He's a cheat, a liar, and probably even a petty criminal, but I love him. There's nothing I can find out that's going to change that."

"Are you sure?"

I flashed on Erabelle standing in her bedroom doorway. *Bud was good at hurting people.* Was Rod right? Was I going to find out that Bud used women? That he even led them on and treated them badly? He'd obviously treated Erabelle badly. What had happened that she still felt the pain after so long?

"You're right," I said. "There may be some things about Bud that I'd rather not dwell on, but even if the worst is true, it won't change the way I feel about him. He's always been there for me, and my dad before that. If our situations were reversed, he wouldn't rest until the person who hurt me was caught."

Leanore had seen us in the hallway and now joined us. "Rod, you look terrible."

"I'll be okay."

"Poor thing." Leanore hugged him. "Don't worry. Lilly and I will handle this new assignment for Callum. You rest."

We left an unhappy Rod slumped in one of the waiting-room chairs. The only time I'd seen him looking worse was when he'd been shot.

Leanore and I drove north past the city limits. The freeway

was crowded with people ripping through Bakersfield on their way to Fresno or Yosemite for the holiday. On the relatively short drive, Leanore filled me in on what she knew about Warner's sister and son.

Apparently Erabelle had been a fixture in Warner's household until the early seventies. Rumors at the time said she ran away to Europe against Warner's wishes. He'd cut her off, but she hadn't returned. That is, until five years ago when Warner had funded a charity she was running. Leanore thought it helped business-women in developing countries but wasn't sure.

"That must be what Erabelle was talking about," I said. "She had a huge fight with Junior because he cut off all of Warner's discretionary spending, including Erabelle's foundation."

"Junior, as you call him, is well thought of, but rarely seen. He lives in New York, I think."

"He may be in debt. Erabelle accused him of siphoning off money while his father was sick."

I spent the rest of the trip describing Warner's mansion. Leanore was like a kid in a candy store as I detailed the architecture and construction. By the time we'd exited the freeway, I'd resolved to blackmail Warner into finally letting her do a story on the house.

That we were discussing a famous property, whose owner and architect had spent a fortune to perfect it, was ironic consider-ing the property at our destination was a rocky, barren stretch of no-man's-land.

"I thought you said this was a farm." Leanore leaned forward to see out the windshield. "Demeter herself couldn't grow any-thing on this land."

I didn't point out that weeds and scrub brush were growing with abandon. Instead, I looked again at the county assessor's website on my iPhone. "Callum's the one who said it was a farm. Maybe it used to be."

"I'm guessing there's no oil." She glanced at the fence on the opposite side of the road from the King property. A Warner

Petroleum sign cautioned that the fence was electrified. "Otherwise the Kings would have sold the land or dropped their own well a long time ago."

She was probably right. It didn't appear Warner had any actual oil wells nearby. Instead his property housed a massive refinery, processing the crude oil and natural gas coming to it from other locations through a maze of pipes. I guessed that the field I'd seen from Warner's mansion was some distance to the south and probably feeding the refinery.

I pointed to the county assessor's map on my phone. "Supposedly some kind of driveway or road cuts into the Kings' property at this spot. It leads to a house and several other structures." I rolled down the driver's-side window and looked out. "But I don't see anything resembling a road. Is it possible my GPS is wrong?"

"It's more likely that the driveway is so overgrown with weeds that we can't see it." Leanore pointed to a stretch of ground that was slightly more even looking than the rest. "That might be it."

We decided to give it a try. The news van was not a sport-utility vehicle and I had to drive carefully.

After a few minutes, Leanore, who held my phone with the plat displayed on the screen, pointed toward a cluster of trees. "It should be just ahead."

The trees were grouped at the top of a small ridge. Through the branches and trunks several structures were visible below. I stopped the news van so we were at least partially concealed by the pines. Caution seemed in order. Bud had been shot, after all. Not to mention that the house and the land were still co-owned by Carter King, a wanted criminal. Wouldn't a remote farmhouse be the perfect place for him to hide?

"Just a minute," I told Leanore and got out.

I crouched next to a tree trunk and gazed down at the empty, decaying structures. The barn had collapsed inward as though the hand of God had chopped it down the middle. The black, rotting wood stuck out at sharp, unnatural angles the way a broken bone might.

The other smaller structures were in similar states of collapse and ruin, but the main house at least was still standing. It appeared to be structurally sound except for where the roof of the long porch dipped at one end.

Leanore followed me from the van. "There can't be anyone living out here. Is there even electricity?"

"I'd like to check it out anyway, but I don't think I can drive down." I gestured to where the road disappeared at the ridge. It had probably gone down to the house at one time, but growth and decay had removed all traces of it. "Even if the brush were cleared, the drop is too steep."

Leanore looked down at her pretty leather shoes. "I don't think I can make it dressed like this."

I lifted one of my size-ten boots and set it next to Leanore's dainty foot. "I won't have that problem. You stay here and I'll go check it out. It's probably abandoned, but I'd like a closer look anyway."

I took my gear bag with the camera. The hill proved easy going. My boots provided excellent traction, and I was able to grab hold of a large weed the one time I began to slip.

At the bottom, I dusted off my jeans and took stock of my surroundings. It was a cold day, but the trees up on the ridge behind me made it worse by blocking the sun's direct rays. The resulting drop in temperature was unsettling. My unease wasn't helped by a pungent odor I guessed to be the rotting barn.

"Hello?" I didn't really think I'd get an answer, but this was private property, after all. Technically we were trespassing. "Is anyone here? We're from KJAY."

On the way to the house, I passed a large oak tree with a tire swing. Dead winter leaves rotted on the ground below, leaving the tree's branches exposed. I observed that the ground directly beneath the tire had been cleared, probably so someone could use the swing.

If so, it meant either a child or a whimsical adult had been on the property recently. Certainly not an old man such as Carter King.

My attention was diverted by these thoughts and I was not heeding the ground ahead of me as I walked. A sharp increase in the foul odor got my attention just in time to stop.

I cried out and stumbled back as a cloud of flies erupted from the dead animal.

"Lilly?" Leanore yelled. "What's wrong? Are you okay?"

The animal was unrecognizable, but had probably once been a rabbit or large cat. I raised my shirt up over my nose to block the revolting smell. "I'm okay. There's a dead animal in the weeds. Don't come down."

I walked well around the remains, but had to stop again. Another animal's body lay in my way. This one was fresher. The rabbit had been shot—probably recently, since it was still intact.

I found four more small animals, all shot, before I finally made it up to the porch. I dropped my shirt and took a deep breath. The smell was less rank up here, but somehow sharper and more metallic. I wondered if this might be a separate odor coming from the treated lumber I observed in the porch roof. It looked as though a well-meaning amateur had recently tried to make some repairs.

There was also a new, unpainted metal door as well as new plywood up over all the windows. The latter made it impossible for me to see inside. I knocked, then pressed my ear to the door. Dead silence inside. I knocked again with similar results.

I retrieved the camera from my gear bag and rolled off a few shots. If we got permission later from the property owner, the video might come in handy.

When that was done, I walked around to the side of the building. Leanore had been right about the building's not having electricity. I knew because a portable diesel generator was set up in the back. A power cord ran from its base and up into a high, open window. There were fresh tire tracks too. They came and went on a dirt road running out past the barn. Someone had definitely been here recently.

Obviously that wasn't a crime, but what if that someone had been Carter King? He'd grown up here. This was his home until the day Bud's eyewitness testimony had branded him a thief. Where else would he come to hide?

The high window where the generator cord entered the house appeared to be my only way inside. Unfortunately, I couldn't reach the window ledge.

After looking for something to stand on and finding nothing, I lifted a leg and tried putting a little weight on the generator. It held.

This was a bad idea. Entering private property without permission was illegal and a violation of journalistic ethics, not to mention I'd probably fall in the attempt. But this was also personal. If our situations had been reversed, Bud would already be halfway through the window.

I set down my gear bag, took one last breath, and prepared to stand on the generator.

"Don't even think about it, Lillian."

NINE

The term *jumping out of your skin* pretty well describes my reaction. "Leanore, don't sneak up on me like that."

She put her hands on her hips. "We're here as KJAY employees for goodness' sake. We don't commit breaking and entering to get a story."

"I was just going to take a peek," I lied. "I wouldn't have actually gone inside." I suddenly noticed that Leanore's pants were covered in dirt and her leather shoes scuffed. "How did you get down here?"

"I was worried when I couldn't see you anymore."

"So you slid all the way down the hill and wrecked your clothes?" My voice softened and I made a sound like "Aww."

"It's not that big of a deal." She started back around the house. "Walking through that horror of a front yard was much harder than getting down the hill."

I followed. "Do you think it could be a serial killer or something? I heard they start out killing animals."

"It looked like small-caliber bullets to me. I'm guessing it's a little boy with his first rifle."

We reached the front of the house and stopped. "Did you just use the words *little boy* and *rifle* in the same sentence?"

"It's different on a farm. My brothers and I all shot rabbits and coyotes." Leanore took a tissue from her pocket and held it over her nose. "But that doesn't make the smell any more palatable."

I raised my shirt over my nose. "If someone was using animals for target practice, why leave them all here?"

Leanore steeled herself, then marched forward into the field of carcasses. "Laziness."

We climbed back up the short slope. On the way back to the main road, I dropped empty bottles of Mountain Dew out the driver's-side window. Plenty were in the van since Mountain Dew is my caffeine delivery system of choice. Leanore, tracking our progress on her smartphone, didn't notice I was laying a trail of bread crumbs for when I came back.

We reached the public road, but instead of turning back toward the freeway to leave, we decided to follow as the road cut between Warner Petroleum and the Kings' farm. The only break in the electric fence protecting the refinery was a heavily manned gate. We continued past and soon came to a pair of structures on the Kings' side of the road.

"That's not on the plat." Leanore leaned forward. "Are those houses? Maybe the family still lives on the property, just not at the farmhouse."

The closer we got, the more the buildings did look like houses. "If there are people there, do you mind doing most of the talking? To them, I'm just a camera person."

I also thought Leanore, with her sweet grandma demeanor, would make more headway than me with my pit-bull routine.

She smiled. "I assume you'd prefer I avoid talking about how we just trespassed on their land?"

I smiled back. "I wouldn't volunteer it."

The structures turned out to be a pair of matching mobile homes. A paved driveway ran from the public road, divided the buildings, and continued as a dirt road into the property's interior. It presumably led to the abandoned farmhouse.

Someone had put a lot of work into planting garden beds and grass around the mobile homes. Several mature bougainvilleas bloomed in front of each structure. Their red flowers popped in front of the white siding.

Unfortunately, the yard had been overrun with weeds during the previous growing season. Whoever the gardener was, that person had abandoned his or her hobby or moved away.

A woman stood on a ladder hanging Christmas lights from the home on the right, so I parked on that side of the driveway next to a Cadillac Escalade. I spotted a lost-dog flyer taped to the vehicle's window. The word LOST had been crudely written in big letters with a felt-tip pen, but the flyer did include a picture of what it claimed was a purebred Labrador retriever.

Leanore took lead while I stayed inside the van. She kept a hand on the open passenger door. "Happy holidays. I hope we're not intruding."

The woman didn't descend the ladder. It wasn't out-and-out bizarre, but I would certainly have been more interested in the strangers appearing on my remote property.

"Does this look straight to you?" The woman indicated the section of lights she'd already hung. The strand was plugged in, and the rainbow of large bulbs glowed. "I need it to be straight for Christmas."

"It looks perfectly straight," Leanore said. "Much better than at my house."

From my place in the van, I couldn't see the woman well, but she appeared to be pushing the higher end of middle age. Her pear-shaped body was decked out in a sweatshirt, white sneakers, and "mom jeans."

Leanore waited a moment, but when the woman didn't respond, she said, "I'm sorry to interrupt. We're looking for Mida King."

"I'm Sally King." The woman turned fully for the first time and looked at us. "Why do you want to see Mom?"

"It's lovely to meet you, Sally. My name's Leanore Drucker."

Leanore stepped toward the ladder. She offered her hand to the other woman to shake. Sally only stared at her. After an awkward moment Leanore was forced to drop her arm. "I do stories for KJAY about Bakersfield's history. I'd like to interview Mida for one of my pieces."

Sally turned back to the lights. "Why? She's an old lady."

"Most of the people I interview are older. My series is called *Tales from Bakersfield's Past*. Right now I'm doing a story about old unsolved robberies." Leanore glanced back at me. "A man named Carter King was involved in one many years ago. Is he your uncle?"

Sally took a moment to process Leanore's statement. "Oh, that old scandal?" She removed a section of the lights from where it rested on a nail. "I guess I heard some stories a long time ago, but Mom has never liked to talk about it."

I got out of the van and shut the door. "Has your uncle ever been in contact?"

"No." Sally pulled the string as tight as she could and then hung it again. "I don't know why this won't sit right."

I joined Leanore at the base of the ladder and pointed to the lights Sally still fussed over. "I think those are for indoor use. You probably shouldn't put them outside where they might get rained on."

Sally kept her gaze focused on her task. "I have to get ready for Christmas."

"But it could be dangerous," I said.

She turned and looked at me for the first time. "How can celebrating Christmas be dangerous?"

Her thinning hair was up in a ponytail exposing her face. This was where her soccer-mom look went off the rails. She had acne scars and even a few zits that were red from recent picking. If she'd been a teenager or even in her twenties, I wouldn't have given it a second thought, but it looked weird in a woman likely to be going through menopause. Her teeth were in need of a good brush too, which only added to the feeling that Sally was a little out of control.

"I know how you feel," Leanore said. "Christmas is my favorite time of year."

Sally gestured to another handmade flyer taped to the mobile home. "I've been so busy trying to find my lost dog that I missed getting ready this year. I woke up this morning and realized how behind we were, and now I can't get the lights to run straight. Do you think I should put another nail in?"

She already had a nail every six inches, but instead of telling her she was crazy, I changed the subject. On occasion, I can show a little tact.

"Is your mom here right now?" I glanced at the other mobile home. The lights were off, but I thought I saw movement at one of the windows. "We could talk to her and leave you to do your work."

"There's no one else here right now, and Mom doesn't know anything, anyway."

Leanore stayed upbeat. "We'd be very happy if she just talks about her memories of her brother before he left."

"She doesn't remember like she used to." Sally removed the strand of lights and began hanging them again. Her voice rose. "And I told you, Mom's not here."

The words *Stop lying, you lie-faced liar* were on the tip of my tongue. I'd like to say that I was stopped by a mature awareness that antagonizing Sally wasn't a good way to get what I wanted. I'd like to say that, but then I'd be the lying lie-faced liar. Instead it was Sally herself who stopped me.

"Why can't I get this straight?" She jerked the string with such force that one of the nails came out of the siding. She cried just before losing her balance.

Leanore and I each rushed to steady the ladder, but we were too late. All we could do was help her off the ground.

"I want you to leave. You're distracting me." She picked up the lights and tried stretching out the cord. "That's why I can't get it straight. Because you two keep cackling like hens."

"Of course we'll leave," Leanore said. "If that's what you want, but—"

"You should go now before my son gets back. He doesn't like strangers."

Leanore looked at me and raised her shoulders in a silent question. I reluctantly nodded and turned back to the news van. We had no choice but to leave. It was private property and the owner had ordered us off her land.

Leanore gave Sally one of her business cards and told her to call if she changed her mind.

We'd only driven a short distance from the mobile homes before I said, "What do you make of that?"

"I don't know. Something is wrong there, but I'm not sure it has anything to do with Carter King or the stolen jewelry."

We reached the main highway and turned back toward the freeway. "Sally is strung tighter than those Christmas lights."

"I wonder if she might have a mental condition." Leanore looked uncomfortable, as though she were gossiping. "There was something . . . off about her. Something unsettling, but I don't know what."

I spotted a large casing near a power pole on the side of the road. The metal box probably housed transformers or some other electrical equipment for PG&E. It appeared large enough to at least partially obscure the van from view.

"Why are we stopping?" Leanore said. "Is the car all right?"

I drove behind the casing and turned off the engine.

"I want to know why Sally King won't let us see her mother." I grabbed my gear bag and opened the door. "Stay here. If I don't come back, call Callum."

Leanore tried to stop me, but I was too fast for her. I hurried through the brush in a straight line for the mobile homes. It only took me a few minutes to get within sight of them. I crouched down and watched. The empty ladder still leaned next to the dangling string of lights, but there was no sign of Sally. Since the door to her mobile home was opened, I guessed she'd gone inside to get more nails.

I ran as fast as I could to the rear of the other home. I paused to catch my breath, then peeked around the side.

Still no Sally. I hurried around to the front door. Just as I raised my fist to knock, I heard a noise inside.

"You already ate." It was Sally. "How can you not remember? It's crazy."

A light came on inside and the door handle turned. There was no time to run.

I dove behind the bougainvillea and lay flat. The door opened. Footsteps descended the short steps. I tried to keep my breaths slow and shallow, but my heart felt as though it were smashing up against my chest trying to get out.

The door closed and I heard keys in a lock. Was Sally locking the door from the outside?

After a moment, footsteps receded. I heard the door to Sally's mobile home close. I thought this might be my only chance, so I jumped up and knocked on Mida's front door.

"Hello?" a tentative voice said from inside. "Who's there?"

"Are you Mida King?"

"Who are you?"

I glanced over my shoulder. "Can you let me in? I need to speak with you about your brother, Carter."

"Carter has polio."

Despite the urgency of the situation, that gave me pause.

Mida continued, "That's why he doesn't get along with other young men his own age."

I glanced over my shoulder again. "Can you let me in?"

The door handle moved but didn't open. "It's locked. Can you open it? I haven't been to the drugstore in ages and I need more Jean Naté."

I had no idea what Jean Naté was, but I doubted Sally would allow her mother to go buy it anytime soon. I was even beginning to wonder if the older woman was ever allowed out.

"I'm sorry. I don't have the key." I glanced behind me to Sally's mobile home. "Is there a window on the back side of your house where we could talk?"

"Go around to the bathroom. I've tried to climb out there before, but I can't get over the sink. I have osteoporosis, you know."

I ran around back. Being out of sight was a huge relief. I heard a window open so I went and stood underneath.

An old, thin face smiled down at me. Mida's white hair had been cut short by someone who hadn't tried very hard to make it even. Some of the tips were still brunet so I guessed that the hatchet job had been done because Mida had stopped dyeing her hair.

"I'm Lilly."

Her face lit up with a huge smile. "Lilies are one of my favorite flowers, second only to bougainvilleas, which are actually shrubs." She thought for a moment. "The only trick with lilies is to make sure they get enough light. If it's too shady, the stems will stretch and lean toward the sun."

"I didn't know that."

"God plants everything where it needs to be, and we stretch toward the light."

"That's very poetic."

She glanced over her shoulder. "Why don't you come in."

"You mean through the window?"

She nodded. "Yes, please. I'd love to have company."

I judged the distance up to the window and shook my head. "That may not be a good idea."

"I'll make you coffee."

"I don't drink coffee. You don't happen to have any Mountain Dew?"

"You really should come in." She looked into the gray, rocky land behind me as though the bogeyman were out there. "It might not be safe for you."

TEN

Vague threats of danger are a terrific motivator. The window was higher than I would have liked, but at least my being petite made fitting through the opening a cinch. Once my torso was through, I took a breath and had second thoughts. The foul, stuffy air was so thick that I thought I might be able to push it away from me like water. The base of the odor seemed to be mildew, but layered on top of that I smelled air freshener, burnt plastic, and something else I feared was urine.

I knocked over an empty plastic bottle while dragging my legs into the house, but otherwise made it in without breaking anything.

"Thanks for speaking with me, Mida." I picked up the bottle from the pink carpet. The label said Jean Naté by Revlon. "Is this what you're out of?"

"Am I?" She raised the empty bottle to her nose and inhaled the crusty remnants. "I've always used this instead of deodorant. I know vanity is a sin, but sometimes it's nice to feel like a lady. You know, pretty and pampered."

Seeing Mida up close revealed a person far removed from the rituals of physical beauty. Not only had her hair been cut in short, uneven clumps, it was so thin in places that I could see her scalp. In a mean bit of irony, she had an excess of hair growing from her chin. A teenage boy attempting his first beard would have been jealous.

"I'm still a woman, you know." Her eyes stayed locked on the bottle as a ripple of emotion went through her face. "It may sound silly to you, but a person needs these things. Otherwise they start to feel like they're not a human being anymore."

I felt that I was intruding somewhere deeply private. I was in her bathroom, after all, and she wasn't even dressed in real clothes. Her faded pink housecoat was marked with old food stains, as well as recent ones. This was not how a woman, especially one of Mida's generation, would want to be seen by a stranger.

I placed a hand on her arm. Her thin flesh sagged under my hand and I felt the bone. "Do your daughter and grandson help you? Do they make sure you have everything you need?"

"I think I have an aide who helps me."

I didn't know what to say. The Escalade was the only car, so I doubted anyone else was there.

"And if I ever need help, all I have to do is press this emergency button I wear around my neck and an ambulance will come." She reached to her chest, but there was nothing there. "I don't understand."

"Maybe you forgot to put it on today."

"I hope they didn't get mad at me for pushing it by accident. They call before the ambulance comes, and I say *bougainvillea* if it's a false alarm. That's my secret code."

I gestured toward the bathroom door. "Is there somewhere we can sit down and talk?"

Her face lit up. "Where are my manners? I bet you'd like some coffee?"

"I don't drink coffee."

I followed her out of the bathroom and down a hallway. Fakewood paneling covered the walls, and small paintings of butterflies covered that. They were nice, but the gold frames had a layer of dust.

"I'll get you something else then." She glanced over her shoulder as she took uneven steps. "What's your name?"

"Lilly."

She stopped in the kitchen and turned around with a big smile on her face. "I love lilies. They're one of my favorite flowers."

The burnt smell was strongest here. Behind Mida I saw a large swatch of charred wall next to the stove.

"But you have to be sure and plant them in the sun," she continued. "They don't tolerate a lot of shade."

She turned back to the kitchen. "How about I make a pot of coffee?"

"I don't drink coffee."

Mida didn't hear me. She was staring at the stove where strips of duct tape covered the burner controls. "I don't understand. Do you know where the coffeemaker is?"

"Come with me into the living room." I backed up. "I'd like to talk with you about your brother, Carter."

She relaxed and followed. "Carter has polio."

What would it be like to live with and care for someone with dementia? Would I have the endurance to navigate this same treacherous path through mistakes, corrections, and frustration a million times a day? What if it were Rod? If we got married, I'd be making that kind of commitment. Could I do it?

"It must have been very hard for Carter." I stopped in the living room. "Why don't we sit down and have a talk about him."

Mida took a seat on the sofa. The blue fabric, like her housecoat and the rug, was covered in stains. "Carter didn't die like a lot of polio victims, but his one leg is all shrunk and bent back. Mother says it's why he doesn't have any friends, but I think he doesn't make an effort."

I set down the gear bag and took out the camera, but changed my mind. Not only was it unethical to interview someone with a diminished capacity, but putting images of her on television looking the way she did would be heartless.

I zipped the bag up again. "Carter's friends are exactly what I'd like to talk about. Was he close with two men named Bud Hawkins and Leland Warner?"

Given her condition, I wasn't expecting to get much information, but she surprised me. "You mean Cousin Leland and that fellow who worked on their orchard?"

"Warner's your cousin?"

She nodded, but looked uncertain, so I said, "Are you sure? How exactly are you related?"

She fumbled for a moment, then got angry. "I can prove we're family." She pointed to a glass display case at the end of the room. "He gave me all those Hummel figurines. They belonged to his wife, and when she died, he gave them all to me."

The case was empty, but Mida didn't seem to realize it. I decided to change the subject. "What about Warner's friend Bud? The one who worked at Warner's orchard?"

Her anger faded. "I think he only did that when he was young. When Bud became a man, he left to go somewhere. I can't remember where, but it seemed important."

Not knowing appeared to trouble her, so I said, "The war?"

Relief spread across her face. "Yes. The war."

I doubted she knew which war, but then she surprised me.

"I didn't have business with Bud until after he came back from Korea." She nodded again. "You see, Leland knew our farm got into trouble after my parents died. He thought we could use the extra money Bud was willing to pay."

"What was Bud paying for?"

She giggled. "To care for his little boy, of course."

I shook my head. "Bud doesn't have a son."

"I didn't say he did."

"Then which little boy do you mean?"

"His brother, of course. William."

I pulled back. My spine was as straight as it was ever likely to get. She was talking about my father. "How old was Bud's little brother when you took care of him?"

"Not very old, but he was walking and talking." She frowned. "Although he was so quiet all the time. I'd never had a child before so I didn't know that wasn't normal."

It was actually a relief to learn my father had always been that way. A part of me had wondered if the stress of family life had caused him to withdraw from us. That's a nice way of saying I worried he didn't like me.

My curiosity surged. What else could Mida tell me about my father? I'd hardly known him in any meaningful way. Those who had, such as my mother and Bud, rarely talked about him.

But before I could speak, Mida leaned forward and continued her previous topic. "The only time he wasn't quiet was at night when he would cry himself to sleep asking for his mother."

"Ooooo-kayyyyyy." I took a deep breath. The thought of my orphan father crying himself to sleep broke my heart. My curiosity was replaced by anger toward Bud for leaving him. "I thought Bud raised his little brother. When did William live with you?"

"I'm not sure, exactly." She looked around the room as though a clue might be hidden somewhere. "Ten years ago?"

The look on my face must have told her this was the wrong answer. "Twenty?" she asked.

"How old were you and Carter at the time?"

She looked around again, but this time her search appeared more frantic. "How old do you think I am now?"

It's almost always a bad idea to answer this question, but I sensed that it would be more than vanity upsetting Mida if I told her the truth.

"I'm terrible at guessing people's ages." I barely paused before changing the subject. "If Bud's little brother was orphaned, why didn't Bud take care of the boy himself?"

"He was back from Korea and having trouble adjusting. A lot of the young men did." She sounded sympathetic. "He said that going away to fight wildfires would be like being in the army again. I think it gave him structure."

I remembered Warner's words from earlier in the day. He'd said that Bud's decision to go to Alaska was selfish thrill-seeking. The sanctimonious jerk had failed to mention that Bud had post-traumatic stress disorder from the war. The anger I'd just felt toward Bud easily swung to Warner.

Mida continued, "And Bud eventually did right. Came back at the end of the fire season and never left again. Raised that boy all by himself. I always gave him credit for that."

"It sounds as though you liked Bud." I wondered if it was more than "like." Bud as a handsome young war hero would have turned a lot of female heads. "Was it hard when he told the police about Carter stealing?"

"What do you mean?" Her eyes darted around the room looking for an answer. "I don't understand."

"Carter stole jewelry from Leland Warner. Bud was the witness."

She got up and hobbled toward the kitchen. "Would you like some coffee?"

"I don't drink coffee." I followed her. "What happened to your brother after he ran away from the police? Where did he go?"

She reached the kitchen. What she expected to be there smashed into the reality of the empty burnt room. She looked all around as if she had no idea where she was.

"Mida," I repeated. "Has your brother been in contact with you?"

She spun around. "How did you get in my house?"

"You invited me."

Her entire body began shaking. "Why would I do that? You're a liar. You're not my aide. You don't work for me."

"Someone hurt Bud today. When did you last see Carter? Has he been here to the farm?"

"No, no." Tears formed and fell down her mottled cheek. "I don't ever think about Carter. He was a good brother."

"I'm sorry. I know this is painful, but do you know where he is?"

Mida's hands went to her chest looking for the emergency panic button. When she realized the necklace wasn't there, she began screaming. Not weak, little-old-lady requests for assistance. Mida screamed as though Satan were in the room with her.

I turned and ran for the bathroom. I got to the hallway, remembered my gear bag, and had to go back. I got to it just as Mida reached the front door.

"Help, help!" she screamed, and pulled frantically on the knob.

Outside I heard Sally yelling, "Mom? Mom, what is it?"

I reached the bathroom and leapt on top of the vanity. I had to pause to suppress a laugh at the insanity of my situation. How many times in your life do you stand on a bathroom sink? My mind flashed on Bud as I went feetfirst out the window. Somehow the old codger always managed to land on his feet in situations like this. For once I did too.

I sprinted back to the news van. Fortunately no one followed me.

"What happened?" Leanore said as I climbed into the van.

I tried to catch my breath. "Nothing."

"Then why were you running?"

I set my gear bag in the back and buckled my seat belt. "I saw Mida King. She's thin and frail. Mentally, she's even worse. Some kind of dementia."

"Oh, dear."

I started the van and pulled out onto the road. "Thing is, they're locking her inside. She's basically a prisoner in that mobile home."

"If she has Alzheimer's, they may do it to keep her from wandering. Were there signs of elder abuse? We could call the police."

I glanced in the rearview mirror and saw a pair of headlights some distance back. We were still an hour from sunset, but the car's unique LED lights popped in the gray twilight. "It wasn't like I saw bruises or anything, but the setup is unhealthy. It's just a matter of time before something bad happens."

"We can contact the county's elder-care ombudsman," Leanore said. "A social worker should check on her."

I think Leanore might have said something else about how to

help Mida, but I was focused on the car behind us. It had come up fast and now aggressively rode our tail.

Leanore tried to turn around and look. "Who is that?"

The vehicle swerved into the lane reserved for oncoming traffic. A powerful engine roared. I recognized the Cadillac Escalade as it passed us going over a hundred miles an hour.

Leanore checked her seat belt. "What on earth do they think they're doing?"

"I don't know, but I wish they'd quit driving on the wrong side of the road." Suddenly the Escalade cut in front of us. I slammed on the brakes and jerked to the right.

The van dipped off the road, then shot up. I struggled to keep us from flipping as a loud bang came from the front of the vehicle.

We came to a stop a short distance from the road. From the way the van tilted to one corner, I guessed we had a flat tire. The Escalade had spun around and now faced us.

Sally King got out, but it wasn't her so much as what she had in her hands that made me say, "Call nine one one."

Before Leanore or I could get to our phones, Sally was at the window. "Put your hands up."

As I obeyed her command, I said quietly to Leanore, "Is that what a small-caliber rifle looks like?"

"Yes." Leanore also raised her hands. "I guess we know it works."

"Stop whispering in there." Sally banged on the window with the end of the rifle. "Open the door and get out."

We both obeyed. Sally had us each walk to the front of the van.

"There's no need for this." Leanore's voice was the very definition of nonthreatening. "I thought we all got along well earlier."

Sally raised the rifle. "What did you do to my mother?"

"Nothing," I said.

"You broke into her house. Why?"

"That's—"

I was about to say *crazy*, but thought it hit a little too close to the mark and stopped myself. "That's not true. Your mother invited me in and she's still the legal owner of this entire property. I didn't do anything wrong."

"I don't believe you. She was screaming."

Leanore made a noise.

I followed her gaze to a car approaching on the highway. "Someone's coming, Sally. You better put that rifle down before you get into trouble."

She looked frightened, but as the vehicle neared, her expression changed. "I'm not the one who's going to be in trouble."

The lights belonged to a pickup with a camper shell. It looked exactly like the kind of vehicle a seedy, old thief such as Carter King would drive. It pulled off the road next to the Escalade and stopped. For a moment the rough idle of the engine obscured all other noise. Then the truck shut off and the door opened.

ELEVEN

Christmas Eve, 3:58 p.m.

I realized that I hadn't truly been afraid until that moment. If Carter King had shot Bud, would he do the same to us? What was to stop him from dumping the bodies back at the farmhouse with all those dead animals?

But instead of an old man, someone much younger stepped out of the truck. "Mom, what are you doing?"

He looked to be in his early twenties, but unlike Sally had smooth, acne-free skin.

Sally didn't take her focus from us. "Did you get all the holiday stuff I put on the list?"

"Who cares?" He gestured to the news van. "Why are you pointing a gun at TV newspeople?"

"Brandon, you know how important this Christmas is to me. You got a fresh turkey, right? Because there's no time left to thaw a frozen one."

He gestured to Leanore. "Why are you pointing a gun at Leanore Drucker? She's famous. There's an ice cream flavor named after her at Dewars."

The Leanore Drucker was one of my favorite flavors at our local ice cream parlor. It was sweet and mellow with a little bit of a tart aftertaste. Very appropriate.

But Sally didn't seem to care about Leanore's status as a dessert. "They were trespassing and snooping around."

"I was invited by your mother," I said. "She's the legal owner so it wasn't trespassing."

"Stop arguing with me," Sally shouted. "All I wanted was an old-fashioned Christmas, but first my dog runs away, then you two show up and the Christmas lights won't go straight. Now my mother won't stop screaming." Her grip on the rifle tightened. "So thank you very much and merry Christmas."

"Mom, do me a favor and put the gun down." Brandon maneuvered himself so his own body blocked her shot at us. "Someone could get hurt, and that's the last thing either of us wants."

"Listen to your son," Leanore said, again with the soothing voice. "He sounds like a wonderful young man. You should be very proud."

Sally hesitated, then looked at her son. "Did you get a fresh turkey?"

"It's practically still alive."

I managed not to laugh, but I felt my affection for Brandon growing. Not only had he stepped between me and a gun, he also had a sense of humor.

Sally lowered the gun. Brandon quickly took it away from her. He escorted her to the Escalade with instructions to check on Mida.

After she drove away, he hurried back to us. "I'm so sorry."

"We didn't mean to cause so much trouble," I said. "All we wanted was to talk with your grandma about her brother, Carter."

"Let me guess, she invited you in, then forgot who you were and started screaming."

"Exactly."

He looked down at the dirt. "She's sick. It's not her fault."

We continued talking while Brandon helped me change the tire. He said Mida had moved off the farm shortly after the scandal with her brother in the fifties. She married badly, had Sally, and then divorced his now deceased grandfather. When Sally had gotten pregnant with Brandon twenty-two years ago, the two women bought the mobile homes and moved back to the farm. His father wasn't in the picture.

When I asked about Carter King, Brandon said he'd never even met his great-uncle. He'd always assumed the man was dead. By the time we'd put on the spare tire, the conversation had come around to Leland Warner's relationship to Mida.

"They knew each other as kids. The Warner family used to live on that land over there that's now the refinery." He tightened each of the nuts with a cross wrench. "But we're not relatives."

We each stood and I lowered the jack. "She called him Cousin Leland."

"Maybe they used to call him that as a friend of the family and now Grandma can't remember the difference." The tire reached the ground. Brandon knelt again and gave each of the nuts another turn with the wrench. "She gets very confused between the past and the present. In the beginning she only mislaid things. Now it's like she's mislaid herself."

I glanced at Leanore. I didn't want to open this can of worms, but I also didn't feel right about going behind Brandon's back to social services. Once you've changed a tire with a man, you owe him better than that.

"Maybe Mida needs more professional care than you and Sally can give her. Have you considered moving her to a facility?"

"We had an aide that came every day and helped, but Grandma's pension went bust last month. There's no money anymore."

They'd probably been forced to cancel her medical-alert service too. No wonder Mida believed she wore an emergency button around her neck. She probably had until recently. "What are you going to do?"

"I'm using my winter break from classes at Cal State Bakersfield to fix up the old farmhouse on the other side of the property. Hopefully we can rent it out and make a little extra money that way. Until then, Mom is taking care of Grandma during the day."

I started to ask if Sally was a whack job, but thankfully Leanore jumped in before me. "Being a caregiver is stressful enough, but if your mother also struggles with her own issues, the burden might be too much."

He stood up and wiped the grease off his hands with a rag.

He'd been careful not to get anything on his CARTOON NETWORK T-shirt. "You're right. Mom has always struggled with . . . issues, but she loves Grandma very much."

Leanore and I exchanged a glance, but didn't say anything.

Brandon recognized our less than subtle meaning. "I understand it's a bad situation that shouldn't continue indefinitely. If Grandma's pension doesn't resume and we can't rent the farmhouse, we'll go ahead and sell this land if we have to."

Leanore and I said good-bye to Brandon with considerably less concern for Mida. I admired him for taking care of his family. A lot of young men his age would have buckled under the weight of an aging grandmother and a mentally unstable mother.

On our way to the freeway I scanned the side of the road looking for my Mountain Dew bottle. I saw it and recognized the entrance to the dirt road we'd taken to the farmhouse.

I was glad I'd laid a trail of bread crumbs. As much as I liked Brandon, I wondered if he'd been truthful about never seeing or hearing from his great-uncle. A return trip to the farmhouse might be necessary.

I drove back to the hospital so Leanore could get her car. The sun had almost set, so the lights were on in the parking lot. I pulled up next to her Camry and idled.

"Aren't you going to park?" she said.

"I need to go to the station first and check in with Callum. He was going to get a copy of the old police report on the stolen jewelry."

"I know why you're investigating Bud's shooting, especially if you think the guilty party is going to escape punishment."

"But," I said.

She took a breath. "Bud may die. Won't you be sorry if you're not there to say good-bye?"

"That's what Rod thinks too, but I'll be much sorrier if the person who killed him is never caught."

Leanore got into her own car and left for home. I called Rod upstairs. If there'd been news, I'd have stayed at the hospital, but the surgery was still under way.

When I tried to tell him about meeting Carter King's family, Rod again said it was a waste of time. I knew he was tired, but I couldn't help but feel disappointed. I usually went to Rod when I needed to talk things over, and the weird situation out at the King farm definitely needed talking over.

I told Rod I'd meet him at the hospital in an hour and drove to the station. On my way into the building I noticed that the animal shelter's truck wasn't in the lot. Ominous considering the five o'clock show began in ten minutes. I passed the control room, where a skeleton crew prepared for the show, then went into the studio.

Ted and the demon sat at the anchor desk reading over their scripts. The explosion of garlands and poinsettias that covered the set this time of year threatened to swallow them.

I navigated around the robotic cameras run from the control room. "Thought I'd stop by to wish you luck, Ted."

"I'm so glad to see you." Ted wiped his brow with a Kleenex. The sweat there did not come from the studio lights. "The animal shelter guy never came back and we don't have a floor director. Can you bring in the pets and hand them off to us at the end of the show?"

"Isn't there someone better qualified?"

"All you need to do is bring in the crates during the commercial break and take the animals out for us when we ask for them." He lifted some papers. "We have the notes from the noon show, so we know what to say."

"But Lilly will look terrible on camera." The demon must have realized how that sounded because she tried to switch her tone. "It's not just you. I had to veto Freddy and Callum helping as well."

Freddy was wearing shorts and Callum looked like the Unabomber on vacation, so there were real reasons they might not be suitable. What was wrong with me?

"I'll do it." I immediately regretted the words, but Ted looked so relieved that I couldn't take them back. Besides, helping Ted, who'd been such a good friend to me that morning, would only take a few minutes.

I left the studio and walked to the newsroom. Except for Freddy, using one of the assignment-desk phones, the room was empty.

"Dude, I totally don't care if your Christmas is ruined." Freddy's voice was firm, but he wasn't yelling. "I don't care if your mommy and daddy want their precious baby home so they can spoon-feed you turkey and mashed potatoes. You're scheduled to work."

Freddy listened for a moment, then hung up.

When he saw me, he shook his head in disgust. "The kid scheduled for audio tomorrow asked for the day off, was told no, and then called out sick via text message. Millennials, man. And I thought I hated the baby boomers."

I didn't point out that Freddy was himself a millennial. Maybe carping about the fickleness of young people went with the job of assignment manager.

"Callum's in the break room," he said. "Can you tell him about audio sicking-out? I'd go, but I can't leave the scanners."

Freddy was officially down the assignment-manager rabbit hole. Seeing how he'd so completely settled into the job only reminded me how itchy and unhappy I'd been. Whatever my future at KJAY held, it wasn't going to be on the assignment desk.

What then, when everything was said and done, was there left for me to do here? How much longer would they keep paying a chief photog when there were no photogs on staff?

I found Callum sitting among dogs and cats in their pet carriers. An empty birdcage sat to the side. I didn't ask. On the wall above Callum a muted TV played KJAY, but he wasn't watching. Instead he examined dozens of photocopied pages spread out on the round table before him.

"Hi, kiddo." Callum used his foot to kick a chair away from the table for me. "My source came through with the police file. It makes for interesting reading."

Instead of sitting down I fished a dollar out of my coat pocket and went to the vending machine.

I bought a Mountain Dew and popped the top. Between caffeinated sips, I told him about the old farmhouse and the three generations of Kings in their mobile homes. I included Mida's claim that my father had actually lived there and my suspicion that the farmhouse would be a great hangout for a wanted criminal.

"You could tell an amateur had done work fixing up the house, but maybe that was so Carter King could hide there and not for rental income, like Brandon said."

Callum nodded. "Were there any pictures of Carter King around his sister's place? I'd like to have something to put on the air if we eventually do the story."

I shook my head. "No photos at all. The knickknacks and small appliances were all gone too. I think that stuff is either dangerous or likely to upset her."

He picked up one of the photocopied pages on the table. "There's also no picture in the police file, but there is a description." He read aloud from the sheet, " 'Five-eight, a hundred and seventy pounds, brown hair, brown eyes, walks with a limp.' "

"Mida said he had polio as a child." I took the sheet from his hand, but paused when I noticed the news had started. "How far into the A block are they? I have to help with the animals at the end of the show."

Callum offered to enlist Freddy's help in moving the crates so I could skim the report. Freddy spent most of what he termed Operation Orphan Critters trying to convince Callum that the sludge spill earlier today was actually toxic waste. Callum rolled his eyes, but Freddy kept pitching the story.

When they were almost finished, the door flew open on the final crate.

"Dude, this lock is broken." Freddy tried to grab Thing as he hobbled out, but somehow the dog escaped his grasp.

Callum also made a grab, but despite the tiny dog's slow pace, he was remarkably adept at avoiding capture. "Is this the dog that peed earlier?"

Freddy nodded. "Right after the noon the little dude let rip all over the animal control guy."

"Why is he going into my gear bag?" I paused from reading long enough to scoop Thing up. "He tried to get in my van earlier today too."

"Dude, you should totally adopt him. Rod's always saying how he wants a dog."

I got a whiff of its breath and jerked my head away. "Just put it back in the crate."

They did and took him to wait with the others. I continued to read the police report while keeping an eye on the show.

Junior's original account, that the heirlooms were military medals, had been correct. The stolen items were officially listed as *The Order of St. Andrew*. The first part, described as *the badge*, was a gold brooch in the shape of a double-headed eagle with a blue St. Andrew's cross. The second, described as *the star*, was a diamond starburst with a miniature of the badge at the center, surrounded by Russian Cyrillic letters.

Warner had taken both pieces out of a safe in his office to show them to his friends Allan Hawkins and Carter King. He'd left the jewelry out on his desk when called away to take a phone call. In his sworn statement, Allan Hawkins had said that while they were waiting for Warner to return, Carter suddenly grabbed both pieces and ran out.

Hoping Carter would have a change of heart, Warner and Bud had waited several hours before contacting the police. King had used the time to get a head start out of town.

Mida had also been interviewed. She'd stated that her brother returned home to the family farm in a rush to retrieve some personal items before fleeing. While packing he admitted what he'd done, but said this was his only chance for a better life.

The Bakersfield police had several leads on King over the years. The better life he'd hoped for had never materialized. Instead, he'd slipped into a pattern of shady schemes and confidence games. Every few years there was a new entry in the file leading up to an actual arrest in El Centro, California, in 1984. Authorities there had detained him and a female accomplice for selling stolen Bibles. He'd posted bail and disappeared before the outstanding warrant from Bakersfield had come to light.

Mida appeared to have cooperated with the authorities. She'd alerted them each time her brother made contact and even turned over several letters and postcards.

I got out my phone and dialed the number Frank had given me for Warner's son.

"Lilly." Junior's fake charm sounded even more hollow when it was just a voice. "Thank you for calling. Have you discovered something?"

"Maybe." I didn't quite trust him, so I decided to keep my cards close to the vest. "Remember telling me that story about Warner-family heirlooms being stolen?"

"Yes."

"I'd like to speak with your father about it. Can I come to the house tomorrow?"

"I doubt he'll see you, but don't worry. After you left, I got the details from Erabelle."

"I didn't think she was in the mood to talk to you."

The slightest of giggles came through the phone. "I may have twisted her arm a little."

I pictured Junior literally twisting her arm. "What did she tell you?"

"Your uncle wasn't the thief."

"I know. Bud would never steal from a friend." I paused. "A stranger, no problem, but never a friend."

Junior laughed and took a drink of something—probably more Scotch. "Technically, it wasn't actually Dad who was robbed. It was Erabelle. That's why she knows about it."

"The police report says the brooches belonged to your father."

The second after the words came out, I regretted them. So much for keeping my cards close to the vest.

"The police report?" he said. "You have been a busy little reporter."

TWELVE

I 'm a shooter, not a reporter."

He didn't seem interested in the distinction. "The medals belonged to Erabelle, not Dad. My great-grandmother smuggled them out of Russia when she fled the communists. It was the only thing Erabelle inherited when her parents died. Dad got all the land and property."

If the diamonds had really been Erabelle's only asset, it might also have been her only chance for financial independence. I suspected that a woman such as Erabelle would have felt that loss more than the monetary one.

I said I still wanted to see Warner, if circumstances allowed it, then we said good-bye. Just as I was hanging up, I had a thought and called out to him.

"I'm still here," he said.

"The man who stole the jewelry was named Carter King. His sister, Mida, still lives on the family farm adjacent to your refinery."

Silence.

"Is there any chance the King family is related to you?"

"Why would you say that?"

"Mida King called your father 'Cousin Leland.'"

Silence.

"Hello?"

"I'm here." He cleared his throat. "What name did you say?"

"Mida King." Silence again. "You going to tell me how you know that name?"

He laughed. "Nothing to tell. Never heard of her." He barely paused. "I've got to go now, but I'll call you if I learn anything."

He hung up. Obviously, Mida's name had meant something to Junior—something I doubted he would ever willingly share with me.

I thought again about Bud's visit to the pawnshop the previous day. Something he'd seen had upset him enough to call Warner.

Pawnshops sold jewelry.

I called Kincaid, the pharmacy owner. He had the prescription ready, but the owner of Pawn Max wasn't returning his calls. He promised to let me know if or when she did.

It was almost time for the pet segment, so I gathered the file and went into the newsroom. Callum sat with Freddy on the assignment desk.

I handed Callum the pages. "There's no sign of Carter King since '84. Where do you think he's been?"

Callum shrugged. "He could have gotten sick and died. Or maybe he made a big score and retired."

"Did any of his known associates have ties to Bakersfield? If Carter's in town his old friends might know."

I could tell Callum liked the idea. "Good thinking. I'll run the names and see if I find anything."

Callum pulled out those pages from the file. They'd been converted from microfilm. It reminded me how ancient some of this history was. "I wish I could talk with someone who knew Bud back in the fifties. Maybe fact-check what Warner and Mida King have told me."

"Your uncle was in the army, right?"

I nodded. "Paratrooper toward the end of the Korean War."

"Doesn't he have any old army buddies who knew him back then?"

"You would think, but Bud's never talked about friends from the war or been involved with any veterans groups."

"When I'm running King's known associates, I'll poke around your uncle's military service. See if any names come up with his." Callum gestured back to the police file. "And I'm expecting to hear from Kelvin Hoyt within the hour."

"Who?"

"The retired cop who handled the King case for a couple decades. His name is all over the file and I'm hoping he'll talk to us even if it's off-the-record."

Freddy, who'd been watching Ted with the volume low, spoke before I could thank Callum. "Commercial break."

I hurried into the hallway, picked up two of the crates, and carried them into the studio. Ted and the demon were already moving to the interview set. I set down my load, then Ted and I went back outside for more. When we returned, the demon had taken a tabby out of its crate.

She placed it on a table draped in red cloth. "This is the docile one. She'll stay here during the entire segment with no problem."

Ted was helping me carry in the largest crate, containing a chocolate-colored Lab. "This one keeps moving around inside. He seems totally spooked." Ted caught his slip and corrected himself. "I mean *very* spooked."

"Let's not use him." I set down my end and the Lab began scratching at the crate. "The last thing you want is an agitated dog around a bunch of cats."

The demon stroked the tabby on the table. "No, there's only one other dog, and he peed right after the segment at noon." She pointed at Thing in his little crate. "That's the one we don't want to use."

I jerked back as the Lab barked. "I think this is a mistake."

"Stop being so negative and work on keeping him quiet."

Ted joined her on the set. I gave the Lab a dog treat, which seemed to quiet him down. He looked similar to the dog on Sally King's flyer so I checked the paperwork. The Lab had been surrendered by the owner and wasn't a stray, but if I needed another excuse to visit the farm, I could always pretend I thought they were the same dog.

The segment went smoothly. The tabby behaved perfectly as it lounged on the table. Two other cats were quickly rotated through as Ted read their information. I hoped they'd end it there, but the demon had other ideas.

"For our final little blessing today, we have a darling chocolate Labrador retriever." She turned to me off camera and waited.

I unlatched the crate. The Lab ran right to her.

She pretended to be surprised, but her remark sounded planned. "Well, you're my number one fan, aren't you?"

For a moment she savored the perfect clip she'd be adding to her audition reel. Then the Lab tried to stick his nose in her rear end.

"Oh, my." She tried to shoo him away. "No, doggy. Sit. Sit."

I hurried in and clipped the leash on him.

He reared up and barked.

The tabby hissed, so Ted moved to calm it with a few gentle pets. "That's okay, sweetie. Everything's okay."

The cat hissed again and leapt at Ted's chest. He shrieked and jerked back with the animal hanging off him. He tried to pull her free with his hands, but the cat sank its claws deeper into his flesh.

"Ted, hold still." To her credit, the demon rushed to help, but in her haste she tripped over the Lab's leash. Her weight ripped the strap from my hand as she fell to the floor.

With Ted screaming as though the monster from *Alien* had jumped out of his chest, I made a split-second decision to help him first.

Unfortunately that left the Lab free. He went nose-first straight up the demon's skirt.

"Bad doggy." Still on the ground, she struggled to push it away. "No. I said no, doggy."

I had both hands around the cat and was trying to dislodge it from Ted's bleeding chest, but I managed to tell her, "Get him by the collar."

I lifted the cat's midsection. The animal hissed, but the claws remained firmly embedded.

Ted tried to remove them one by one, but the cat sank its teeth into his hand. He cried out, but then remembered he was on TV. "Don't try this at home, folks."

Meanwhile, the demon, on her back on the floor, had followed my instructions and grabbed the Lab by the collar. She managed to hold it back from her crotch, but the two seemed to have reached an impasse in which neither could shift position without giving the other leverage.

That's when I saw Thing. He'd got out of his broken crate and hobbled all the way to where the demon was locked in her stalemate with the Lab.

I couldn't drop the cat and help her. All I could do was watch as it lifted its leg.

"No, doggy," she yelled, but it did no good. As the control room rolled the closing credits a stream of yellow liquid hit her like a heat-seeking missile.

After the show, Ted and the demon locked themselves inside gender-appropriate bathrooms. Ted had the excuse that he was cleaning his wounds. The demon was just crying. As the only woman in the building, I was nominated to go in and comfort her. I demurred on the grounds that I was probably the least likely to actually make her feel better.

"Fine, I'll go in there," Callum said. "You go interview Kelvin Hoyt."

"He called?"

Callum started toward the ladies' room door. "During the show. Says he won't go on camera, but see what he'll tell you off-the-record."

Kelvin Hoyt probably knew all kinds of juicy details that weren't in the police file, but I had something far more pressing.

"Rod is pushing himself to exhaustion and my uncle may be out of surgery soon. Before I do anything else, I need to go check on them at the hospital."

Callum stopped at the door with the generic female stick figure. "Then it's a good thing I told Hoyt you'd meet him at the hospital."

I drove as quickly as I could, but once I'd parked in the hospital lot, I stayed in the car. I had a call to make before going upstairs. I'd been putting it off all day.

She picked up on the third ring. "Hello?"

"You have caller ID, Mom. Why are you pretending you don't know it's me?"

"Because I'm polite, sweetheart." She made a sound I knew well, a slight clearing of the throat signaling disgust for her offspring. "I clearly failed you as a mother since I didn't pass that trait on."

"Excuse me for having a low bullshit tolerance."

"Lilly, language!" She lowered her voice. "You could at least use the initials."

"I'm sorry, but my previously mentioned low tolerance prohibits me from referring to it as BS." This was a complete lie. My mother had programmed me against any kind of swearing from an early age. Ironically, the only time I ever broke free and went blue was when speaking to her.

"It's Christmas Eve," she said, playing the holiday card. "Did you call just to start a fight on this holy day?"

Tomorrow's the holy day, I started to say, but guilt stopped me just in time. I had started things off badly with the caller ID comment and then the swearing, which I knew she hated. I really was a jerk.

"You're right. I'm sorry, Mom." How was it possible to feel so guilty and so angry at the same time? "I actually called with bad news. I should have done it sooner, but it's been a crazy day."

Her voice rose with panic. "Did you and Rod break up?"

"No."

Hooking up with Rod was the only thing I'd ever done that made my mother proud. She was even willing to overlook that we were living together while not married.

"It's much more serious. Uncle Bud has been shot. He's in surgery right now."

"Oh" was all she said.

"You sounded more upset at the prospect of my breaking up with my boyfriend. I know you don't like Bud, but that's a bit much."

"I love Bud as much as anyone," she said with absolutely no feeling. "He helped us after your father died. I don't know how I would have paid the mortgage."

She paused. I waited for the inevitable but.

"But there's no denying he associated with some shady characters. There were times I was ashamed to be seen with him, all those tattoos and never shaving."

Her tone reminded me of Warner's when he'd also been talking about Bud. "Did Dad ever mention Bud being friends with Leland Warner?"

"The billionaire?"

"I don't know his exact financial status, but, yes, the rich guy."

"What would a man like that have to do with Bud?"

Her tone, more than the words, made me angry. "Is there anyone else in the family I can ask? Any random relatives I don't know about?"

"Bud was the only family your poor father had."

I flashed on a surprise birthday party my mother had thrown for my father on one of his weekends home. She'd invited neighbors, coworkers, and friends from church. It had been a big success. The sun had shone on our modest backyard. The breeze smelled like clean sheets instead of the usual Bakersfield dairy-cow odor. We ate fried chicken off paper towels soaked with grease and drank Kool-Aid in Styrofoam cups.

Bud had not been invited. Maybe that was why my father had stayed in the kitchen performing useless tasks, absent from his own party. Maybe without Bud there he felt alone.

"What about friends?" I said into the phone. "Bud was in Korea. Did he talk about army buddies?"

"None that lived."

We finished the call with the appropriate promises and good-byes. Mom said she wanted to know the minute there was news about Bud. She even offered to help pay for the funeral, but even that felt like a dig. The implication that Bud wouldn't have left enough money to pay for his own funeral hung in the silence after her offer.

I signed in at the front desk, slapped a hospital visitor badge on my coat, and walked to the bank of elevators I'd used earlier in the day. The doors opened on the surgical floor and I made my way to the waiting room. Annette sat alone looking about as bad as I'd ever seen her. She was pretty, but this day was aging her in a way she'd probably never fully recover from.

On the other side of the empty room, Rod sat with her sleeping daughter, Bonnie. An open children's book rested in his lap as though he'd just been reading the little girl to sleep. I didn't cross the threshold.

"Rod," I whispered.

He glanced up. Relief spread across his face and down through the rest of his body. It was as though stress and worry had bound him into a tight package and seeing me had cut the strings.

He carefully stood without waking the sleeping child. Annette came with him out to the hallway.

I kept my voice low. "Is there any word, yet?"

They each shook their heads, but Annette looked ready to cry. "I don't know how much longer I can stay."

"You should go." Rod gestured toward her sleeping daughter. "You need to take Bonnie home. Lilly and I will stay until Bud's out of surgery."

The assurance in Rod's voice made it that much harder for me to say, "I'm sorry, but I have an errand to run on another floor of the hospital."

Rod stared for a moment. "What kind of errand?"

"I'm really sorry." I looked at Annette. "I have a lead on what happened to Bud this morning. It has to be followed up."

The tension returned to Rod's body. "We should let the police handle this."

I looked him square in the eye. "We both know there may be aspects to this that Bud wouldn't want the police to be aware of."

He started to argue, but Annette said first, "It's okay. You two go, but when you get back, I may take Bonnie home."

She started back into the waiting room, but I stopped her. "Did Bud ever mention any old army buddies? Maybe friends he might have still known right after Korea?"

"No. You wouldn't even know he was a veteran from how little he talks about it."

Annette returned to the waiting room, and Rod and I walked to the elevators. As soon as we were out of earshot, he said, "Where are we going?"

"To see Kelvin Hoyt." I pushed the down button. "He was the police officer in charge of finding Carter King after the robbery."

"He's in the building?"

The door opened and we got on the elevator. It was huge to accommodate stretchers and rolling beds.

I hit the button for the third floor. "He's getting chemo in oncology."

"We shouldn't bother him at a time like this."

"I agree, except it was his idea. Hoyt actually called Callum after hearing we were looking for him."

The doors opened and I exited.

Rod caught up with me. "Leanore told me what happened at the King farm. That crazy woman might have shot you."

"If it's any consolation, Leanore said it was a small-caliber rifle."

He forced me to stop by taking hold of my arm. "It's not."

He kissed me full on the lips until my toes curled and I forgot about everything else. Then he pulled back. "Promise me you won't go out there again. It's not safe."

THIRTEEN

This put me in what Uncle Bud would have called a tighter spot than a cat's butt in winter. You see, I'd already decided to go back out there again that night. I wasn't going to have any peace until I knew if Carter King was using the farmhouse.

Instead of lying to Rod, I deflected by walking to the nurses' station and explaining whom we were looking for. The man behind the counter said the department was about to close for the evening, but we could go in and sit with Mr. Hoyt while he finished his treatment.

Rod did not continue our previous conversation. Chemotherapy rooms aren't good places for arguing or kissing.

An old Caucasian man was stretched out in one of the many La-Z-Boy recliners spaced at discreet intervals. He was the only one in the room and his eyes were closed as he listened to the spa music playing overhead. In that way some people do, Kelvin Hoyt sensed he was no longer alone and looked up.

"Hi." I crossed the room, followed by Rod. "I'm Lilly Hawkins from KJAY. I think you spoke with our assignment manager."

"Sure did." Hoyt brought the chair up to sitting and offered his hand. The rubber tubing from his IV moved with his arm. "Sergeant Kelvin Hoyt, Bakersfield PD, retired. At your service."

We shook. I could feel the bones in his hand. Hoyt had to be in his early eighties, but all of the usual ravages of age were heightened by the chemo. Instead of thinning hair or a bald strip across the top of his head, he was completely hairless. Sitting in the large chair, he looked shrunken. Even the pair of thick, black-framed glasses slipping down from the bridge of his nose looked too big for him.

Rod shook after me. "Pleased to meet you, sir. My name's—"

Hoyt laughed. "No need to introduce yourself, Mr. Strong. Terrific reporting you did last summer on that fire."

"That's very kind of you, sir." Rod always shrank a little into his shell when recognized. "Please call me Rod."

"I'm a big fan of KJAY. You're the most professional operation in town. That's why I was so eager to talk when I heard you were working on the old King case."

Obviously he'd missed the five o'clock show. "I am working on a news story, but there's a personal angle for me as well." I pulled up a stool and sat down next to him. "My uncle was shot this morning. He was the chief witness against Carter King in the theft of Warner's jewelry."

"And you think King might have shot him, out of revenge or something?"

I decided not to mention the pawnshop, since I only had a hunch how it fit in. "Something like that."

Hoyt glanced at each of us. "This is all off-the-record, you understand?"

Rod nodded. "If that's how you want it."

"I doubt it will matter because I doubt Carter King had anything to do with what happened to your uncle."

I tried not to let my disappointment show. I was probably only mildly successful. "Why's that?"

Hoyt smiled. "Besides the fact he waited an awfully long time to get his revenge?"

I smiled back. "Yes. You could drive a dump truck through that hole in my theory, but humor me. Besides that."

"King never was the kind of man for murder."

"Why not?"

Kelvin Hoyt shifted his weight in the chair, as though trying to get comfortable before starting a long story. "You have to understand, I inherited the case in the early sixties. Leland Warner was turning into a real big shot about that time. The powers that be wanted to impress him so they reopened the case."

Hoyt pushed the chair back so he was more comfortable. "I worked at it for the next twenty-five years. Not full-time, you understand, but I kept feelers out there, trying to get information on where King might be and what he might be doing. That's a long time to be shadowing a fellow, and I got a pretty good feel for him."

Hoyt looked at me. "King was shady, but he never was the type to cross the line into murder. And most of his schemes weren't even illegal, just unethical."

I glanced at Rod, who was being uncharacteristically quiet. "Not only does that not sound like a murderer, it doesn't sound like someone who'd commit a high-profile jewelry robbery. Is it possible King was framed?"

Hoyt laughed. "No way. Even if your uncle hadn't witnessed the theft, King's own sister said he confessed to her before running away. She even described the two brooches."

"What about Mida?" I said. "Did she know more about Carter's whereabouts over the years than she let on?"

"You mean the sister?" I nodded, and Hoyt continued, "Doubt it. She got married and moved off the family's land. I think she was trying to put everything behind her."

"She's back there now."

"I heard something like that right before I retired. Her daughter got herself pregnant, no father in sight, so they all moved back to the farm to raise the baby." Hoyt shrugged. "I never was one to believe the country was better than the city. Kids go bad because they go bad, not 'cause the city messes them up."

Rod turned and I followed his gaze to the plump nurse entering the chemo room. "Do you remember any local friends or contacts that King might be staying with if he came back to town?"

"Nah. He'd be an idiot to come here, even after all these years. The man is probably sitting in a condo in Florida, if he isn't dead."

"How we doing in here?" The nurse was Latina, but her hair had been dyed an intense red. It fit her bright personality.

It was obvious Hoyt liked her from his smile. "Better than some and worse than others."

Rod and I stepped back so she could check the IV bags and speak with him.

When she left, I asked my last question. "Were you ever able to trace the brooches? Russian antique military medals must be pretty rare. Did King sell them?"

"No, but that's not unusual." Hoyt took a sip of the soda the nurse had got for him. "Back then there wasn't so much interest in antique jewelry like that. The star, with the diamonds, was probably broken up for parts, like a stolen car."

Rod had been silent through the entire interview, so I said, "Is there anything you want to ask?"

He shook his head and relaxed his arms from where they'd been crossed in front of him. He looked like a man who'd been waiting for something bad to happen, but had somehow avoided it.

Hoyt and I exchanged contact information. Rod and I thanked him and started to leave.

"By the way," Hoyt said as we neared the door. "How's your uncle? You said he'd been shot."

"He's in surgery upstairs."

Hoyt smiled. "I'll say a prayer for him."

We left, but at the door I glanced back for a moment. The smile had vanished from Kelvin Hoyt's face. He no longer looked jovial or wry, just alone.

In the hallway the redheaded nurse stopped us. "Are you Mr. Hoyt's family in for the holidays?"

"No. We just had a few questions relating to his old job."

Her face fell. "Oh. That's too bad. You're the first guests he's had for a treatment. Most people bring someone along at least some of the time."

Rod glanced back toward the empty room. "Is it normal to schedule these things so late on Christmas Eve?"

She shook her head. "Mr. Hoyt actually rescheduled for our last appointment before the holiday. I think he's all alone and wanted something to do."

I always volunteered to work holidays. What happens to workaholic loners who retire? Would a person actually schedule chemo so he'd be too busy throwing up on Christmas to notice he was all alone?

What was I saying? That was exactly what I'd do.

When Rod and I returned to the surgical waiting room, Annette was just ending a conversation with the nurse at the reception counter.

After checking on her still sleeping daughter, she joined us near the doorway. "The surgery is over. Someone will be out to speak with us soon."

The upswing of her words telegraphed hope. It was there too in her face and nervous hands. She actually thought the doctor might have good news.

The instinct to run erupted like a volcano. Wasn't this moment exactly what I'd been trying to avoid all day?

Rod put his arm around me. It gave me more comfort than any words. It also trapped me.

Annette continued in her upbeat tone, "I remembered something too. Last summer, when the wildfire broke out up in the mountains, Bud mentioned an old army buddy."

The fire had been big news, and Rod and I had covered it along with the evacuation of several mountain communities. Bud had been there selling doughnuts to the army of fire-suppression personnel, which had been a lucky break for Rod and me. Bud's knowledge of wildfires had probably saved our lives.

"I didn't want him to go." Annette heard a noise and took a quick glance at her daughter in the waiting room. "We had a fight about it. Bud said he had to go help the wife of someone he served with. She owned a doughnut shop and needed another set of hands in the kitchen. Bud said he had a responsibility to help her on account of her husband."

I remembered the woman and her granddaughter but not their names.

"He never mentioned it again," Annette said. "Sorry I don't know more."

"No, this is great." I felt my phone vibrating and checked the screen. I didn't recognize the number, but given all the leads I was pursuing, that didn't mean anything. "I'm sorry, I have to take this."

Rod and Annette took seats while I stepped out into the hall-way. "Hello?"

"I got this number from the pharmacy." The voice was low, almost furtive. "Are you a reporter?"

I had visions of Woodward meeting Deep Throat in a parking garage. "I'm a shooter, but a lot of the time there's no reporter available and I do interviews by myself." I paused. "Are you the owner of Pawn Max?"

"My husband and I own it together," she continued quietly. Behind her I thought I heard the rumble of an engine or a blower. "I know you want to meet me at the pharmacy, but I can't leave home right now."

"Can we make an appointment for tomorrow? I can come to your house."

"I'd rather do it tonight, but I have a favor. I worked it out with the pharmacy so you can pick up my prescription and bring it to me. They close at seven."

I glanced at Rod inside the waiting room. "I'm not free tonight. Tomorrow would be much better."

"Please. I need that prescription." A train whistle blasted in the background. "You have no idea how stressed-out I am. I'm begging."

I tried to make sense of the different sounds. "Are you at home?"

"Yes, but don't let anyone see you." She paused for emphasis. "Please be discreet. I'll meet you in the shed out back."

She started to hang up, but I stopped her. "Wait. I may not make it to the pharmacy before it closes. I'll try, but I'm not promising."

"Do your best." She sighed again. "And while you're there, pick up some Pepto-Bismol."

She hung up. Pepto? Prescriptions for stress? What exactly was going on in her life?

Before joining Rod and Annette inside the waiting room, I called information. Only one doughnut shop was listed in the city of Elizabeth. I immediately recognized the name Double Down Donuts and dialed the number.

On my third ring a man answered, "What?"

"Can I speak with the owner? My name's Lilly Hawkins. My uncle was there working last summer during the wildfire."

"I am the owner. I just bought the place a couple months ago."

"What happened to the lady who used to own the store? I think she was Korean."

"Retired to a warmer climate. Arizona or New Mexico or something."

"Do you have a phone number?"

"No." He hung up.

I called again. No answer. I let it ring.

After a minute he picked up. "Lady, unless you're calling to buy doughnuts, I don't have time to talk to you."

"You want me to go away, then I suggest you help me. Otherwise, I'm going to keep calling you all night. Tomorrow I'll come up there in person."

He almost growled, but then relented. "Paik's got family still in town. Call them and ask where she is." He gave me the number, but hung up before I could say thank you.

I dialed. Voice mail picked up, and a generic electronic voice told me to leave a message. I wondered if I'd been given a wrong number, but went ahead and left a message anyway.

Afterward, I joined Rod and Annette inside the waiting room. We sat in silence until a doctor entered through the double doors marked SURGERY. She wore clean scrubs, but her face was damp with perspiration.

We all stood and introduced ourselves.

"The surgery went well." Despite the positive meaning of the words, her face and tone looked grim. "It was very long, but that's not unusual for this kind of extensive damage to the abdomen. We had to remove his spleen and left kidney, but we thought he'd made it through as well as could be expected for a man his age."

Her expression further darkened. "We excavated him in the recovery room. Things were going well, but then suddenly he went into respiratory failure and cardiac arrest. Basically, he had a massive heart attack."

I couldn't speak, but Annette said, "But he was in the hospital when it happened, so you were able to help him, right?"

"Mr. Hawkins had no Do Not Resuscitate order, so we spent fifteen minutes trying to restart his heart. We succeeded, but he's intubated now and breathing off a respirator. I'm sorry, Mr. Hawkins is showing signs of severe brain damage."

"Is he conscious?" I managed to say.

The doctor's face gave nothing away, but her silence told me how ridiculous my question had been. Finally she said, "I'm sorry, but when a brain is deprived of oxygen for that long, it's almost impossible to recover. We'll watch him overnight for signs of brain activity, but it's very unlikely there'll be a change."

Annette started crying. She was quiet, so as not to wake her daughter, but it created a chain reaction of emotion. Rod and I each tried to hold it together, but it was almost impossible.

"I know this is painful," the doctor said. "But I suggest you all go home tonight and think about what Mr. Hawkins's wishes might be. If there's no improvement, we can discuss taking him off the ventilator tomorrow. In that scenario, he'd probably die very quickly. With no brain function, Mr. Hawkins won't have the ability to pump air in and out of his lungs."

"Can we see him?" Rod said.

"Yes. He's in the ICU now."

I took Rod aside.

When I told him I wanted to go to the pharmacy, he was understandably upset. "Come with me to the ICU. Bud would want you there, and on a night like this you and I need to stay together. We need to support each other."

"Please don't make me go in there. You heard what they said. There's no brain function. Bud isn't in that room anymore. It's just an empty body." I finally lost control and started crying. "I'll fall apart if I go in there and then I won't be any use to Bud."

Rod put his arms around me and I hugged him. I found that it was easier to be honest with Rod if I wasn't looking at him. "I have to know that I did everything possible to find out who hurt him. I can't let this be like my father's accident. I can't still be wondering about it in fifteen years."

I pulled back and wiped tears from my eyes. "I'll meet you at your house later, I promise."

FOURTEEN

I had to take a few minutes in the van to pull myself together. Kincaid's Pharmacy had closed by the time I got there.

The security guard recognized me and unlocked the door. "Sorry, I can't let you in. Mr. Kincaid is counting out the register and getting the deposit ready."

"I tried to get here sooner, but I had a personal emergency."

"Don't worry." The guard reached back inside and returned with a bag. "All paid for with a credit card over the phone. Address is on the bag."

It felt heavy, but I asked anyway. "Is there Pepto—"

He smiled. "It's in the bag, along with some bath salts and spa stuff."

Mrs. Pawn Max didn't live far from the store. The address sounded familiar, but I couldn't remember what story I'd covered there. It could have been anything from a grisly murder to an interview with a homecoming queen, or both at the same time.

I followed the GPS, but about two blocks before the actual house I had to stop. Cars were backed up in a single line all the way down the street. The one in front of me held a family of five. The children were dressed for the holiday, and everyone was singing a joyous Christmas carol.

I suddenly knew why the address was familiar. I'd done this story two Christmases ago.

I parked and walked. I couldn't tell you what the actual house looked like because little of the physical structure was visible. The entire property had been turned into a G-rated version of Christmas on the Vegas Strip.

I stopped at the curb and stared at the spectacle of color and light. The display had expanded considerably in the two years since I'd seen it. The reds, greens, and blues overwhelmed me. I shook my head, afraid I might have a seizure.

A man carrying a sleeping child passed on his way to his car. "Can you imagine what their electric bill is like?"

I didn't answer. The sound of a train whistle had drawn my attention.

"Best Christmas ever," a child screamed. His fellow passengers on the miniature train agreed as they chugged their way around Santa's Village—also known as the left half of the front yard.

I elbowed my way through the adults gathered on the sidewalk and set up the tripod. I got some nice footage of kids having a snowball fight courtesy of a shaved-ice machine. They chased each other around a blue, neon menorah, then took up defensive positions behind animatronic reindeer.

When that was done, I packed up my equipment. A big part of me wanted to leave. The entire setup here was weird and off-putting. Who instructs journalists to bring their meds to a utility shed? A crazy person, that's who.

I made my way to the backyard not because I wanted to, but because the series of events that had led to Bud's shooting seemed to have been started in motion at the pawnshop. This was my chance to speak directly with the owner. I might not get another.

I turned the corner into the backyard and almost ran into a life-size snow globe. Frosty the Snowman was inside waving. A fan continuously stirred Styrofoam peanuts as though someone had just shaken the globe. That and a North Pole bouncy castle had attracted fifteen to twenty kids and their parents, none of whom noticed me crossing the edge of the yard.

I found the shed, despite its being camouflaged in strings of icicle lights, and knocked. The door opened a crack and an eye peeked out at me.

"It's Lilly from KJAY." I didn't bother whispering. There was so much background noise, I could have screamed and no one would have noticed.

The door, and its lights, swung open and I hurried in.

"I thought you'd stolen my Ativan." A woman locked the door behind me. She wore a red Mrs. Claus dress and a gray wig that sat slightly askew on her head.

The air in the shed was a mixture of cinnamon, chocolate, and potting soil.

"Sorry. I got delayed with a personal emergency." I took the pharmacy bag from my gear bag. "Here you go."

She grabbed it like a drowning woman reaching for a rope. "You have no idea the state I'm in. Between the store getting robbed and all this Christmas insanity, I'm at the end of my rope." She sat down on a box in the corner and dug into the bag.

There was nowhere for me to sit so I knelt. "I'm not actually here about the robbery. Did a man named Bud Hawkins come into your store yesterday?"

She nodded. "He's a regular customer. Kind of a southern hippie."

From within the pharmacy bag, she removed a light green candle with the word SERENITY etched into the wax.

"That's him." I waited while she raised the candle to her nose and took two long breaths. "Did something unusual happen yesterday?"

"The police asked me the same thing." She lowered the candle. "And the answer is a giant yes."

"When were the police here?"

"Two of them came to the house earlier tonight." She removed the cup from the top of the Pepto-Bismol and poured herself a dose. "But they didn't say anything about not talking to the press, so I figure it's okay to tell you the same thing I told them."

I reached for the camera. "Can I record this?"

She froze with the pink liquid halfway to her mouth. "Absolutely not. You think I want to be on TV looking like this?"

"Then how about giving me the surveillance video of the robbery last night? It's a different story, but I'd still love to have video of a backhoe driving into your store."

"The first set of cops took it." Her face screwed up into a grimace as she drank the thick, pink liquid. When it was all gone, she used the back of her hand to wipe away a pink mustache. "The ones who responded to the robbery last night. They were different from the ones who came this evening and asked about Bud."

I guessed Handsome had sent the latter officers. I gave him credit for interviewing Annette and following this lead. "What did happen yesterday when Bud came to the store? Was he upset?"

"He saw a piece of old Russian jewelry and went nuts. He wanted to know where I got it." Mrs. Claus straightened and her overall tone became more dignified. No easy feat considering how she was dressed. "But if someone pawns something, they have an expectation of privacy. We only give that kind of information to the cops. It's part of the ethics of the business."

I leaned forward. "Was it a brooch? Maybe part of a set that was awarded as a military medal?"

"How did you know that?"

What would Bud have done if after all these years he'd seen one of the pieces Carter King had stolen? Of course he'd demand to know where it had come from. "Don't worry how I knew. What happened when you refused to tell Bud who'd pawned it?"

"He got real insistent. Offered me money to tell him. Finally crossed the line into making threats, and I told him he'd have to leave."

"Did he?"

"Not before buying the brooch. Paid full price on a credit card."

My mind quickly sifted through possibilities of where the brooch was now. Had Bud left it at Annette's house, or maybe his attacker had stolen it?

That's when I realized I had no idea which of the two medals it was. "Can you describe it for me? Did it have diamonds?"

She shook her head. "No diamonds, but it was real gold in the shape of a two-headed eagle. It was part of a set that used to be worn on a ribbon back in the time of the czars."

"How do you know?"

"I researched it before I bought. The owner had no idea how valuable it was." She shrugged. "I paid five thousand, which was a fair price for our kind of business, but it was worth twice that on the collector's market. A set of both brooches could have gone as high as fifty thousand at auction."

"A set with diamonds?"

She whistled. "Those would be worth a small fortune. The market for that kind of historical jewelry has gone through the roof."

There was a knock on the door. Mrs. Claus's hand shot out and covered my mouth.

"Sweetheart? Sweetheart, are you in there?" The voice belonged to a man—a man I was pretty sure had a long, white beard. "People are asking for you. The kids want to meet Mrs. Claus."

She didn't answer.

The handle jiggled and then we both heard a key.

"Don't come in." She jumped up and grabbed the handle.

"Sweetheart, what's wrong?"

"You know exactly what's wrong. I can't do this anymore. All year long. It never stops. You're either planning, doing, or cleaning up after."

"Sweetheart, you're overwrought."

Some boiling point was reached, and instead of holding the door shut, she tore it open. "You're an addict. You have no control over yourself. Every year it gets bigger. You're going to bankrupt us just like a crack addict chasing his fix."

Santa looked over his shoulder to see if anyone had heard and then entered. If it had been cramped before, the space was now claustrophobic. I held my camera close to my chest and tried to stand, but ran into Santa's round belly.

The man himself had to stoop because of the low roof. "Sweetheart, where's your Christmas spirit?"

"I'm Jewish."

I sucked in an accusatory breath. It was one thing to love Christmas, but another thing to shove your religion down your wife's throat.

He responded to my scorn with overwhelming good cheer. "She's not Jewish." A jolly laugh. "Her father married us in his Lutheran church."

"I converted." Her voice was defiant. "Last year I studied the Torah, met with Rabbi Shulman every week, and had a bat mitzvah. You can't prove I'm not Jewish."

"Maybe I'd better go." I tried to get up, but his stomach still blocked me.

"Sweetheart, I love you whether you're Christian or Jewish or Muslim, or whatever you want." His good humor refused to be diminished. "Didn't I put the menorah in so you could give out chocolate coins to the children? But you don't want to do that either."

"That's how sick you are. I converted to another religion so I wouldn't have to celebrate Christmas, and it hardly even fazed you." She reached for the candle and inhaled. "I married you in sickness and health, but I thought that vow was referring to cancer or alcoholism. I should be so lucky."

Meeting Mida King had made me wonder if I had what it took to stand by Rod if he got sick. Now that looked like a relatively mundane worry. What if he started dressing like Batman? What if he decided to only eat orange-colored food? If I married him, I'd have to trust that over a lifetime his personality wouldn't go off the rails in some unexpected way.

"Maybe I better go," I said again. This time I forced my way up. Santa stumbled back against the closed shed door, but kept talking to his wife. "You can't honestly wish I was a drunk instead of providing all this joy and happiness."

I reached around him and got the door open. Just as I was escaping, I heard her say, "At least then I could go to a support group or something. There's no help for a woman whose husband is addicted to Christmas."

FIFTEEN

I returned to the station. It had been two and a half hours since our final show of the day, but I hoped Callum would still be there. I needed to tell him what I'd learned from Kelvin Hoyt and the pawnshop owner.

Inside the newsroom, Callum and Freddy sat together on the assignment desk fielding ringing phones.

"KJAY, we're on your side." Callum paused to listen. "I'm glad you thought it was hilarious, but we're not putting it on the website." He hung up and took another call.

I'd forgotten about the pet segment.

I turned and looked through the rows of empty desks all the way to Ted's, in the back. I didn't see him at first. He slumped low in his chair. Without moving the rest of his body or changing his facial expression, he raised a hand in greeting.

I walked straight down the aisle between desks. I reached Ted and hugged him. "I'm sorry. It's my fault. I booked the animal shelter."

"No, it's not. You were great."

I knelt beside him. "I know it seems bad now, but it's really not that big of a deal. Hardly anybody watches on Christmas Eve."

"It's already on YouTube." He looked down at the remains of his tie on the desk in front of him. The silk fabric was bloody and shredded.

I was tired and emotionally strung out but seeing Ted moved me. I wanted so badly to help him. "I'm usually the one people are giving heartfelt life-lesson-type pep talks to, so excuse me if I get this wrong."

He smiled, and I continued, "You're a fundamentally decent person. You're loyal and kind, and you're going to be okay. This is a bump in the road that you'll be laughing about one day."

"If only I hadn't reacted so badly when the cat first jumped at me."

"It was ripping holes in your chest. It's hard to ignore that." I looked around. "Where's your coanchor?"

"I don't know. Home I guess. She's not speaking to me."

Indignation pushed me to stand. "None of this was your fault. Where was the animal-shelter guy? That was the real problem, you having to do the segment without him."

"I don't know. He still hasn't come back. The animals are all locked up in the break room." Ted thought of something and looked down at the floor around his desk. "Except for that little dog. He's out again, but nobody wants to find him since he keeps peeing on whoever tries to pick him up."

"This is outrageous. The shelter may be broke, but they can't just abandon animals at the TV station."

Ted pulled himself out of his slouch. "I'm a total jerk for feeling so sorry for myself while your uncle is lying in a hospital bed." Ted gestured toward the assignment desk. "Do you need Callum? I can relieve him from the phones."

"Are you sure you're ready to interact with viewers?"

He didn't answer, which meant he wasn't, but that didn't stop him from walking through the empty newsroom and right up to the assignment desk. When Callum hung up, Ted said, "I'll take over for a little bit. Lilly needs to talk with you."

Callum hesitated, but then got up. "Okay, here's the game plan. They're going to try and hook you into an extended conversation." He took his finger and hooked it in his mouth like a fish-hook. "Don't get stuck debating facts or small details. You need to get on to the next call as soon as possible."

Ted sat down. "I'll keep it generic and polite."

Freddy, a few feet down the assignment desk, finished a call. The line immediately began ringing again.

Freddy looked at the device as though it were a snarling dog. "I totally can't stay much longer. I'm already late to my yuletide merrymaking, and I'm bringing the plates and cups. My bros are going to be eating and drinking with their hands." Despite his words, Freddy picked up the receiver. "KJAY, we're on your side."

Callum sighed. "Maybe we should think about putting the pet segment on the website, or re-airing it tomorrow. Sometimes embracing something like this is the best way to handle it. Show everybody you have a sense of humor about it."

The phone rang. Ted looked at it with dread, but picked up. "KJAY, we're on your side."

Callum and I retreated to an edit bay.

I set my gear bag on the floor and fished out my tape. "This is holiday video of a decorated house. I thought you might want it for the web."

While Callum imported my video onto the computer's hard drive, I quickly related what Kelvin Hoyt and the owner of Pawn Max had told me.

Callum listened to my ramblings and then, like the experienced newsman he was, broke the story down to its essentials. "Your uncle sees a gold brooch at a pawnshop and recognizes it as half of a pair stolen by Carter King. After trying to learn who pawned it and failing, Bud buys the brooch himself. He then calls Leland Warner, the original owner, who was too sick to talk to him."

I nodded. "We don't know who else Bud might have called or gone to see after that. The next morning he left me a voice mail saying he was meeting someone at my house and didn't want the police to know."

"You know what's bothering me?" One side of Callum's unibrow raised. "The pawnshop getting robbed last night. It's too much of a coincidence."

"I agree. Someone could have been after the brooch thinking it was still in the store. Maybe they tracked it to Bud and shot him to get it back."

"If that's true, then the shooter probably has the brooch now." Callum got up and exited the edit bay. I followed.

On the assignment desk, Ted seemed to be staying focused, but Freddy had gone decidedly off-script.

"Dude, I totally agree," Freddy said into the phone. "It's taking way too long to clean up. Probably toxic waste or something."

Callum waved his hands like a base coach telling a runner to stop. "Are you out of your mind? You're speaking for the entire news department now."

Freddy sat up. "I mean, not that there's any proof," he said into the phone. "It's probably just sludge. No conspiracy."

Callum turned back to me. "I drew a blank on your uncle's army buddies, but I did find a known associate of Carter King with ties to Bakersfield."

He handed me a printed page from a LexisNexis search. "He and a woman named Laurie Bogdanich were caught peddling stolen Bibles down around El Centro back in '84."

I took the page and glanced over the information. I remembered the arrest from the police report because it was the last anyone had ever seen of Carter King. "What's Laurie Bogdanich's tie to Bakersfield?"

"In the nineties she was co-owner of the Booby Hatch."

The Booby Hatch was an old strip club on Union Avenue. It had closed and been replaced by another strip club called Stallions ten years ago.

I returned to the edit bay and grabbed my gear bag. On my way out to the van I paused at the assignment desk. Callum had relieved Ted, but instead of retreating back to his desk, Ted had chosen to stay and continue answering calls. It was a good sign.

I returned to my van and dialed Kelvin Hoyt. I immediately regretted it, since he sounded groggy and disoriented.

"I'm sorry. Did I wake you?"

"No," he lied. "You think of another question?"

"The last lead anyone ever had on Carter King was an arrest

for selling stolen merchandise down in the southeast part of the state. They picked him up with a lady named Laurie Bogdanich."

"Was that the thing with the stolen Bibles back in '84?"

"That's right." I looked at the LexisNexis search. "Laurie Bogdanich later moved to Bakersfield and owned half of the Booby Hatch over on Union Avenue."

Hoyt hooted. "The old strip club?"

"That's right. Any chance King and Bogdanich were lovers? Maybe she's hiding him while he's back in town."

"Nah. That's a dead end. Even if it's the same lady and she's still in Bakersfield, she wouldn't hide Carter."

"Why's that?"

"The SOB ran off on her. Posted bail and left her holding the bag."

I thanked him and hung up. Despite Hoyt's pessimism, I was still curious.

My final errand of the night was something I wanted to do as late as possible. A detour now would be perfect, even if it was to a strip club on Christmas Eve.

When Los Angeles was still young and freeways didn't exist, Union Avenue in Bakersfield had been part of the main road up to Northern California. When Highway 99 had been built, and then Interstate 5 after that, Union Avenue slid into skid row like a silent-film actress put out of business by talking pictures.

The section where the strip club Stallions made its home, and the Booby Hatch before that, was actually on the nicer end of the faded boulevard. It bordered an industrial area, but with no by-the-hour motels or hookers standing on corners.

The bouncer, dressed in a tuxedo and a Santa hat, eyed my news van as I pulled into the large parking lot. Since I'd been made, I didn't bother changing my polo shirt.

Before leaving the van I reviewed Callum's LexisNexis search for the name of Carter King's known associate. Keeping straight the various supporting players in this drama was getting harder, and my fatigue wasn't helping.

Before becoming chief photog, I'd used nicknames to differentiate people. Over the last year, I'd made a conscious effort to stop reducing people to clichés. I didn't count the ten-thousand-year-old demon because I knew what her name was and only used the nickname privately, in my head, for spite.

I resisted the urge to call Carter King's friend Booby Hatch Bible Thief and repeated Laurie Bogdanich several times out loud, so I'd remember it.

The bouncer turned out to be even bigger than he'd looked from a distance. The man loomed over me. Despite the tux, I could see the muscles bulging as he crossed his arms. "No reporters. Sorry, but it's bad for business."

"I'm a shooter, not a reporter," I said before realizing that was not the right tack to take. "But it doesn't matter because I'm not here on the job. This is personal."

He smirked. "You're here to see pretty, naked girls rubbing themselves on a pole?"

"Not personal like that." I officially hated him. "Maybe you can help me and I won't even have to go inside. Did you work here back when it was the Booby Hatch?"

He shook his head. "How old do you think I am? That was over ten years ago. I was . . ." He paused trying to do the math.

Apparently working as a strip-club bouncer required more muscle than brain. I know, shocking.

"I get your point," I said. "You didn't work here then."

He finished the calculation. "Seventeen, which isn't even legal."

"Maybe there's somebody else around who did work here then. I'm trying to find one of the old owners, Laurie Bogdanich."

His eyes glanced down and then up again quickly. "Never heard of her."

"Can I at least go inside and ask some of the other employees if they remember?"

"The last thing our customers want is for their pictures to be broadcast on the news."

I opened my coat like a flasher. "I don't even have a camera."

He mimicked me by opening his tux jacket. "Answer's still no."

I mustered as much quiet dignity as possible, which wasn't a lot, and returned to the news van.

It was earlier in the evening than I would have liked, but I decided to go ahead and run my final errand of the night. I texted Rod my plans in case something went wrong. I would have called, but I knew what his reaction was going to be.

As soon as I passed the city limits, fog crept into the beams of my headlights. It wasn't nearly as thick as the infamous tule fog that can smother California's Central Valley in the winter, but it did concern me. Fog usually gets worse before it gets better.

I reached the freeway exit and, for the second time that day, followed the highway to the King farm. Light from the refinery warmed the sky on Warner's side of the road.

In contrast, the other side had no light for the mist to soften. The King family's useless land kept its secrets. I eventually found my Mountain Dew bottle by the side of the road and headed toward the farmhouse. I didn't even need the trail of bread crumbs. The van had crushed a trail through the weeds earlier in the day. I just followed the path.

As soon as I saw the trees, I stopped and cut my headlights. Leaving my door open so the interior light would stay on, I walked around to the rear and retrieved my Maglite flashlight, camera, and gear bag. As I lifted the gear bag, I heard a small noise from inside, but foolishly ignored it. I closed the rear hatch, walked back to the open driver's side, and quietly shut the van door. The vehicle's interior light died.

When you live in a city, even one the size of Bakersfield, you take light pollution for granted. I wasn't prepared for complete darkness. I rushed to turn on the Maglite. Water particles from the fog appeared in the thick beam. I used it to find the trees, then quickly shut it off again. I crouched next to a tree trunk and looked down where I expected the house to be.

Nothing. I couldn't even see where the ground dropped off. If a light was on inside the house, the plywood over the windows blocked it completely. I would have assumed the place was deserted except for one thing: hammering heavy-metal music. The aggressive thumping of the bass jolted me, even from a distance.

Someone was in the house, although given the nature of the music, it seemed unlikely to be an old man such as Carter King.

I wouldn't make it down the ridge carrying both a flashlight and my gear, so I reluctantly decided to leave the latter behind. I opened the gear bag, intending to store the camera inside, away from the moisture in the air.

A pair of odd-shaped eyes popped out. Thing must have climbed in my bag when I'd left it unattended at the station. Ted had warned me that the dog was loose, but I hadn't actually thought it would try to stow away with me.

"Dog!" I said. "Don't you have sense enough to know I don't like you?"

It burped and a cloud of foul breath floated up.

I zipped it back inside the bag and left it along with my gear at the top of the ridge.

At the bottom, I kept the flashlight low and navigated my way through the dead animals. The stench was definitely mixed with something more industrial. It had a sharp chemical quality that was different from natural decay.

The music got louder with each step I took toward the house. I avoided the front porch and continued toward the back. At the corner, I stopped, shut off my light, and peered around the side.

A faint light came from the open back door. In contrast, the music blasted. It easily overpowered the rumble of the generator, which unlike on my previous visit was now running at full power.

I crept to the back steps and peeked into the former kitchen. It was hard to tell in the reduced light, but it appeared the old iron stove had fallen through the floor. The top rose out of the splintered wood like the head of a partially submerged body.

The generator cord snaked a path on the still intact portion of the floor. It disappeared into a wall of opaque plastic sheets backlit by a bright light.

I stepped up, testing my weight on the rotting wood, and slowly entered the kitchen.

I froze. A shadow appeared against the sheeting, then disappeared. Someone was around that corner. After waiting to be discovered and realizing it wasn't going to happen, I crept to the doorframe. I found the seam in the plastic and peered inside.

A figure in a protective suit and goggles stood with his back to me working over a table. The plastic sheets covered the entire room like a cocoon. The only other visible objects were a powerful light on a stand and a speaker blasting the heavy-metal music. Without those violent rhythms, the figure would surely have heard my approach.

My breathing slowed. Disjointed memories of horror movies—chain saws, bloody limbs, and the idiot girl who walks right into the serial killer's torture chamber—all flashed before my eyes. Despite the cold, a bead of sweat fell from my bra line and down my abdomen.

Then I glimpsed a pile of Sudafed boxes in the corner. Nearby, the empty foil blister packs had been dumped along with bottles of bleach and antifreeze. My head shot back to the figure as it bent over the table working.

I took a deep breath and let it out. The good news: this was not a serial killer's den. The bad news: it was a meth house.

SIXTEEN

I slowly lowered the sheeting back into place. I turned, planning to make a quick exit, but something small and dark jumped up the steps into the kitchen. The animal was followed by a man with the hurried pace of someone in pursuit. He didn't pause at the steps. Instead he swooped down and grabbed the animal and rose triumphantly into the light.

It was Rod. Thing rested in his firm grip and gave me a lopsided dog smile. Seconds later it began peeing. As Rod jerked the dog out to arm's length, he saw me.

I hurried forward and cupped my hand over Rod's ear so he could hear me above the music. "We have to get out of here before anyone sees us. They're making meth."

He pulled back in disbelief, but then he saw the plastic sheeting and inhaled the chemical smells.

He nodded and stepped toward the exit just as a set of headlights passed through the open back door. I glanced out long enough to see Sally King's Escalade coming down the dirt road from the mobile homes. I hadn't heard the car's approach over the music, and now it was too late. We couldn't go outside without getting caught. We couldn't retreat inside without getting caught. My eyes darted from place to place in the kitchen looking for somewhere to hide.

The headlights died. Sally must be getting out of the car. We had seconds before she walked in. Thing barked and leapt from Rod's arms. It darted along the floor like a rat and disappeared into the hole made by the fallen stove.

I grabbed Rod and followed. My foot hit dirt and we scrambled into the crawl space under the house.

We ended flat on our backs looking at the underside of the kitchen floor. Light streaked between the rotting planks of wood in the makeshift lab, but the crawl space was dark enough that I couldn't see Thing.

Someone shouted, but I couldn't understand them over the music. The planks above me moved. Dirt fell straight down as two sets of feet walked across the kitchen.

I covered my face, but still had to cough. I froze, listening to see if I'd given myself away.

More shouting I couldn't understand. The music abruptly stopped. The only sound came from the generator rumbling outside.

"I said get out of here." I recognized Brandon King's voice. "You idiots are going to contaminate this entire batch."

"Sorry, dear." It was his mother, Sally. "Why don't you take that work suit off and we'll wait for you outside."

Two sets of footsteps returned to the kitchen. Who was the third person with Sally?

"He didn't mean to yell like that," I heard her say. "He's under a lot of pressure. My mother and I are both completely dependent on him now."

"He needs to watch his mouth. I'm used to a little more respect than that."

It was a man. His self-important tone seemed just as familiar as his voice, but I couldn't place him. I glanced at Rod, but he showed no sign that he'd recognized the voice. Instead he was peering into the darkness, trying to locate Thing.

Brandon, presumably now divested of his protective suit, walked toward the kitchen. I heard the plastic sheeting move. "Okay, what do you want?"

"How can you work with all that music?" I absolutely knew this man. I strained trying to listen to his voice. "If you screw this up, we're out all the ingredients with nothing to show for it."

Brandon was on the far end of annoyed and teetering into

angry. "If you're so worried about my concentration, why are you here interrupting me?"

"Don't get smart. Your mother placed another order." An image of a white coat and red hair flashed in my mind. "Since I drove her fix all the way out here, the least you can do is give me a progress report."

Kincaid? Could the fiftysomething pharmacist with two beloved golden retrievers actually be standing above me in the old King farmhouse? I sat up and tried to see through the slits in the floor, but they were too thin.

"You need more?" Brandon shouted. "What happened to the stuff you just got?"

"The holidays are hard," Sally said matter-of-factly, as though she were talking about taking an extra nip of eggnog. "I'm still trying to get the lights straight, and thanks to you I'm going to have to stay up all night trying to thaw that frozen monstrosity. I told you to get a fresh turkey."

The puzzle pieces fell into place and I felt stupid for not seeing it earlier. Sally's pockmarked skin and brown teeth, which Leanore and I had taken for bad grooming and OCD, was good old-fashioned meth addiction. An addiction serviced by Kincaid, who owned a business just down the block from where the brooch had been pawned.

If Sally had visited Kincaid to buy drugs, then Pawn Max would have been a convenient place to pawn the brooch. Or she might have traded it to Kincaid directly and he'd pawned it. Either way, the trail led back to the King family.

"How's your progress?" Kincaid said. "Are you still on track for tomorrow?"

"If I don't get any more interruptions." Judging from Brandon's still unblemished good looks, he was not an addict like his mother. How long would that last now that he had his new job as a meth cooker?

Sally tried to make up for her son's hostile tone with a surplus of deference. "Brandon will have it all ready, we promise. You can come pick it up and stay to eat with us. I'm making turkey and stuffing and mashed potatoes and cran—"

"Your drug dealer doesn't want to stay for Christmas dinner, Mom."

Kincaid's voice dropped. It had that quality men's voices get just before a bar fight breaks out. "I'm not a drug dealer. I only do this because I have to."

"What exactly are you, then?" Brandon escalated the tension. "You sell illegal drugs. Isn't that the definition of a drug dealer?"

I glanced at Rod. In the dim light coming through the slits, our eyes met. The prospect of violence breaking out above us was growing more likely and we each knew it.

But fortunately Kincaid backed down. Maybe his business sense told him not to get in a fistfight with his meth cooker. "There's no need for either of us to get sore. We're both trying to make a living, and neither of us likes how we're having to do it."

I heard a noise.

Kincaid heard it too. "What was that? It sounded like it came from under the house."

"Probably just an animal. The house is infested." Sally started toward the door. "But don't worry, I've got the gun in the car."

"Mom, that's not a good idea."

My hands shot to my face. I managed to deflect the falling dirt and dust as Sally quickly walked out.

Rod rolled over on his stomach and began crawling toward where the noise had come from.

Sally had only been gone a few seconds before Brandon said, "How much meth did you give her?"

"Too much for her to be handling a loaded gun. I didn't even feel safe with her driving down here from the mobile homes."

Both men ran out after her. I took advantage of their absence to turn on the flashlight. Thing appeared near the sunken stove base. Rod was only a few feet away, but each time he moved, Thing moved too. I began crawling with the intention of cutting the dog off from the other side, but I heard voices and had to shut off the light.

"I won't use it unless I have to." Sally must have been outside standing by the generator because I had a harder time hearing her. "But I feel better having the gun with me. I think a coyote may have killed my dog."

Brandon was louder. "Will you both please go away and let me work."

"Sure we will," Kincaid said. "Just let me take a look around your lab and make sure things are going as well as you say."

"I've taken chemistry classes at school. I'm premed, remember? Compared to some junkie cooking on a hot plate, I'm Einstein at this."

"Then you won't mind me looking around." Kincaid stepped back into the house and crossed the kitchen to the lab.

After a few moments of silence, Brandon whispered, "Why did you bring him here? Did you leave Grandma alone?"

"Don't worry, I gave her cough syrup to sleep." Brandon must not have reacted well. "Spare me the lecture, and Mr. Kincaid has every right to check up on you. You're using all his Sudafed and this is your first time. If you screw it up, he's in big trouble."

"Mom, you know I hate this."

"Yes, but we're counting on you, Grandma and me. Her ten thousand isn't coming in every month like before. What will we do for money?"

Brandon had said that Mida's pension had gone bust, but ten thousand a month sounded like a lot more than a pension.

Sally continued, "I know you don't like Mr. Kincaid, but we need every penny we can get right now."

I heard a noise from a few feet away.

Sally heard it too. "What was that?"

"Mom, put the gun down."

I turned on the flashlight long enough to see that Rod had

grabbed Thing. Rod lay flat on his back near the stove holding the dog to him with both hands. Unfortunately, Thing was
growling.

Sally pounded on the planks above me as she walked toward
the stove. "It's a coyote. I'm going to shoot straight down."

"Don't be silly, Mom. You're high and you're not thinking
right. How could a coyote get under the house?"

Thing continued to growl. I didn't know what to do. Rod
needed to let go of the dog and get as far away from it as possible.
Why hadn't he already done that?

"I can hear it taunting me." She stopped directly above Rod.
"See how it likes this."

"No, Mom!"

I had one of those moments of clarity that people talk about.
Rod would never let go of the dog. He wasn't made that way.
He'd never abandon something helpless or dependent on him to
save himself. He'd go down with the ship or, in this case, get shot
by a whacked-out drug addict who thought he was a coyote.

And all because he'd followed me out here trying to help.

I kicked up with my knee, hit the plank above me, and rolled.

"It's moving." Sally pulled the trigger. A plank splintered as a
shot tore through the decaying wood floor. The bullet hit the dirt
where I'd been seconds earlier and ricocheted into the darkness.

"What the hell?" Kincaid tore through the plastic sheeting.
"Why are you shooting?"

All three began talking over each other. Brandon wanted them
both to leave. Sally wanted Brandon to give her back the rifle. I
think Kincaid just wanted to feel as though he was in control. Finally, Sally handed the car keys over to Kincaid so he could drive
them back to the mobile homes.

Brandon stood alone at the kitchen door watching their lights
disappear. After a few moments he sat down on the floor with his
back against the wall.

I thought he might be listening for more sounds from under the house. I was terrified to even breathe. Thank goodness Thing had gone quiet after the rifle had shot through the floor.

Then all at once I heard it. Soft crying. The sounds were muffled as though Brandon was ashamed of this moment of weakness. Just as I had with Mida, I felt as though I was intruding on something deeply private. Brandon was breaking under the weight of his family.

He tried to collect himself. He stood and crossed the kitchen, careful to avoid the new hole in the center. I heard the sheeting move and then he entered the lab. After a minute or two the music resumed.

We waited a few minutes before crawling out the hole by the old stove. Rod held Thing as we ran around the side of the house and up the ridge. I clawed at weeds and roots to speed my climb.

At the top I turned on the Maglite. "Did you get my text?"

"Yes. I came immediately to try and stop you, but all I found was your gear bag by this tree. Something moved inside, so I made the mistake of opening it." Rod lifted Thing in his arms. "This little dog jumped out and I chased it down the hill and around the house."

I turned on my camera and checked the settings. "But how did you know where to drive on the property? This road is almost impossible to find in the dark."

When he didn't answer, I looked up from the camera.

"I used your phone's GPS signal," he admitted. "As senior producer I have access to the station's cell phone accounts."

I returned to prepping my equipment. "That's a little creepy, but I'm glad you came." Rod didn't say anything, so I continued, "You call the police. I'm going to get the camera in position so I can shoot their arrival."

I was so giddy with the thought of filming an actual police raid that it took me a few moments to notice Rod wasn't moving. "Don't you have your phone with you?"

"I have it." Rod set Thing down inside my gear bag and zipped it up. "But we're not calling the police. We're getting out of here."

"I feel bad for Brandon too, but they're running a meth lab down there." I fished my own phone out of my pocket. "Of course we're calling the police."

"You don't understand." He grabbed the phone out of my hand before I could dial. "We can't turn them in."

I stared at him in disbelief, partly for what he was saying and partly for the violence with which he'd taken the phone. "Why not?"

"We just can't." The flashlight highlighted his cheeks as he took hard breaths. "We shouldn't talk about this here. Come back to the house."

I continued to stare.

All at once he looked self-consciously down at the phone. "I'm sorry. I know this must sound crazy to you." He handed it back to me. "But please, trust me."

SEVENTEEN

When the man you love asks you to give up exclusive video of a meth-lab bust, well, I'm sure we can all agree that is a bitter pill to swallow. Rod's refusal to involve the police was also unsettling for moral and ethical reasons, but I decided to trust him. It was Rod after all.

He'd parked his Prius next to my van, back far enough from the ridge so it wasn't visible from the farmhouse. We each got in our own vehicle and left. He got ahead of me at the light just before the freeway entrance.

While I waited for it to turn green again, I let Thing out of my gear bag. It wandered into the van's back cargo section and out of sight. I spotted one of Sally King's lost-dog flyers at the gas station next to the freeway. I made a quick detour to where the flyer was taped on a pole by the free air. The dog really did look exactly like the chocolate Lab we'd had on the show. It even had the same white spot over its eye.

I got on the freeway and drove back to Bakersfield. It would've been easy to work myself into an emotional state wondering why Rod had refused to call the police. Instead, I tried to focus on Bud and what I'd learned.

It seemed likely that Sally, Carter King's niece, had traded the gold brooch to Kincaid for drugs. Kincaid had turned around and pawned it at the store near his own, where Bud had later bought it. So where was the more valuable diamond-star brooch and how had Sally obtained the gold one?

Had her uncle held on to it all these years? If Carter had given the gold brooch to Sally, I doubted he'd planned for her to buy drugs. More likely, it had been intended to finance Mida's care after the termination of her pension.

That termination must have triggered all the family's financial problems. Ten thousand dollars a month was an enormous sum. Not many people still actively working made $120,000 a year.

I wondered if there was a way to look at Mida's bank account. It would be illegal, and certainly nothing that Callum or any good journalist would be a part of, but if the money had been coming from Carter, I might be able to trace him that way.

I reached Rod's house and parked the van next to his Prius in the driveway. Thing romped in the back underneath the tarp I use to cover equipment and emergency supplies from view. I fished the little guy out and tucked it back into the gear bag. It actually was a pretty decent pet carrier.

Rod opened the front door shortly after I rang the bell. "You could have come right in. This is your house too." He took a key off the table in the entryway and gave it to me.

He barely shut the door before I said, "Please explain why we just walked away from a meth house."

He took a breath and steeled himself. "No, I can't explain. You have to trust me."

"What does that mean? We pretend it never happened?"

"It means that we get some sleep. In the morning we go to the hospital and do everything we can for Bud. If he doesn't recover, we mourn him." He looked me in the eye for the first time. "It means you forget about the Kings and the Warners and whatever ancient history boomeranged back around to destroy Bud."

"You expect me to forget that someone shot my uncle? If he dies, it'll be murder." I walked toward Rod, but that only started his moving into the kitchen. I followed. "I owe Bud better than that. He would want justice."

"No, he wouldn't."

"How could you possibly know that?"

Rod stopped at the tile counter and turned around. "Because he told me."

"How is that even possible? Bud was in surgery all day. He never . . ."

I got it and stopped cold. The ramifications—the lies Rod had told to both me and the police—were enormous. "You said he was unconscious when you found him this morning."

Rod didn't say anything. His silence served as a passive confession.

I took a moment to try to steady myself. I felt like someone who'd just got off a boat and couldn't get her bearings. "I thought Handsome was being a jerk for questioning you, but he was right. You were lying. Bud was awake when you found him."

"Let it go, Lilly. Stop turning over these rocks. It's going to change things in ways you won't like."

"Why do you think I haven't gone to the police? The odds are pretty good that Bud did something bad—maybe now, maybe a long time ago." I shook my head. "Whatever it is, I love Bud, and nothing is going to change that."

Rod reached out and put his arms around me. For a moment I thought everything was going to be okay.

But instead of telling me the truth he said, "That certainty is exactly what I'm trying to preserve for you."

I had a terrible thought. "Are you keeping this secret because Bud asked you to, or because you've decided it's what's best for me?"

"Both."

I jerked away. "You don't get to make those kinds of decisions."

I picked up my gear bag with Thing and walked out. I got in my van and didn't even think about turning around. I've never been that angry at someone I loved before. My hands shook so badly that I dropped the car keys trying to put them in the starter.

Who was Rod to decide what I should and shouldn't know?

Did he really think I was this fragile? True, I had a history of poor judgment and broken relationships after my father's death, but that was a long time ago. The gall, the arrogance, of his making that kind of decision enraged me.

In short, I was in the mood for trouble and I drove to the one place I was guaranteed to find it.

A new voice answered the intercom at Warner's gate, but the rigmarole was the same. After going several rounds with the unseen guard I was angry enough to plow my van straight into the copper door.

Fortunately, my cell phone rang. I recognized the Lake Elizabeth number. I'd called it earlier in the evening.

"I'm going to take a call," I said into the intercom. "While I'm doing that, get on the phone with your supervisor and tell them that Lilly Hawkins isn't leaving without seeing Mr. Warner."

The call was from Mrs. Paik's daughter, responding to my earlier message. Unfortunately, Annette's lead turned out to be a dead end. Bud may have told her that he was going up to Elizabeth to help the wife of an old army buddy, but that didn't mean it was true. Mrs. Paik's dead husband had been Korean, never served in the American armed forces, and never even met Bud.

Bud had gone to help in the doughnut store during the wildfire because the money was good and he wanted to. He'd lied to Annette because she hadn't wanted him to go.

After we said good-bye, I rolled down the window and pushed the intercom button. "Have you talked to your boss?"

My answer came not through a garbled voice on the intercom, but in the opening of the copper doors. A young man in a Valsec Security uniform walked up to my car window. "Please unlock your passenger door, ma'am. I'm going to escort you to the house."

I noted his choice of words, as though his escort were the only thing getting me inside the gates. The posturing continued in his tone of voice, which was meant to sound authoritative and in command. The entire act only made him look less in control.

He got in, but before driving onto the property I texted Callum. I wanted someone to know where I was just in case this went badly.

We didn't talk on the ride. As I suspected, the view at night was even better than during the day. When we came over the hill, I almost hit the brakes. The concrete parts of the house appeared black, but the columns of windows glowed, and the greenhouses on each end were lush and bright. Behind this, the oil field continued this contrast. The artificial lights twinkled and glowed, but in other places fire shot straight into the air in a kind of primal defiance of technology.

Frank, still in his uniform despite the late hour, met me at the front door. He told my escort to wait by the car and led me inside. I checked my cell phone and was glad to see I had reception. I wasn't expecting to be in danger, but it was still nice to know I could call for help.

He led me inside and up the staircase in front of the glass wall.

When Frank reached the top of the stairs and turned toward the left, I stopped. "I'm here to see Warner senior."

"You can come with me now or I can have my men throw you back out on the street. Your choice."

Frank was a fairly straightforward kind of guy, so I knew he meant it. The guard who'd escorted me from the gate would love nothing better than a physical confrontation.

I followed Frank. "Junior it is, then."

Leland Phillip Warner II waited for me in his bedroom, but this time there was no offer of Scotch. Maybe it was because Erabelle was also there, looking as if she'd been stabbed in the gut.

"Miss Hawkins. It's late for an unannounced visit." He stood in the center of the room as though he'd been waiting for the door to open and for me to enter.

"It is, but I notice you're both still dressed."

Junior glanced at Erabelle before attempting a mournful frown. "Dad had another episode."

I nodded. "I'd like to see him anyway."

"The doctors would never allow it."

Erabelle spoke for the first time. "How's Allan?"

"He can't breathe without a respirator," I said. "And by the way, Carter King is back in town."

Junior didn't even blink, but Erabelle covered her mouth.

"You mentioned him on the phone earlier." Junior continued to act nonchalant. "Of course we'd like the man caught, but I can't believe he'd be stupid enough to come back to Bakersfield."

"One of the two brooches he stole from your family was pawned here in town. Bud saw it yesterday. That's why he called your father and tried to speak with him."

"So you think King pawned it?"

I didn't want to share everything I'd learned, so I said, "Or someone in his family."

"Isn't it more likely that the brooch was sold shortly after it was stolen and has passed through many different hands?"

I almost told them about Sally's buying her meth down the street from the pawnshop, but decided to keep things vague. "It's possible, but unlikely considering that I've found a very recent connection between the pawnshop and the King family."

Junior's smile stayed plastered in place as he nodded, but his tightly controlled breathing telegraphed panic. "I know that earlier today I might have encouraged you to keep looking into this—"

I interrupted. "I wouldn't say encourage, but you definitely wanted to know what I was doing and what I found out. Maybe you were just keeping tabs on me."

"Nothing like that, I promise." He stepped toward the desk. "But you have been very good to come and tell us this news about the jewelry. We'd like to be good to you in return."

He picked up a piece of paper and handed it to me. "I was going to contact you about this tomorrow, but since you're here now . . ."

It was a letter of instruction telling the family's law firm to set up a charitable trust in Bud's honor. Bud would have called the endowment "more than walkin' around money."

"Ten million dollars?" I looked at Junior, who easily returned my gaze, and then at Erabelle, who stared at the floor. "I was under the impression that neither of you had this much money to spare."

"This was Dad's idea." Junior glanced at Erabelle. "He's feeling very sentimental about his old friend, probably because of his own health problems."

When I didn't say anything, Junior continued, "We thought you could come on board as director. There would be a substantial salary, of course."

"How substantial?"

He considered for a moment, but this had obviously already been decided. "An endowment of that size could easily support a salary of six figures a year."

"And you'd be making a difference in people's lives." Erabelle spoke quietly, but with feeling. "The Allan Hawkins Foundation can do a lot of good."

"The Bud Hawkins Foundation," I corrected.

Erabelle laughed.

Junior did too, even though he didn't seem to know why. "Of course. We'll call it whatever you like."

I handed the paper back to him. "And I assume you'd like me to focus on building Bud's legacy instead of finding out who shot him?"

My blunt tit for tat made him uncomfortable. "I wouldn't put it exactly like that."

For a moment I relished what I was about to do. How often do you get to throw money back in the faces of rich jerks? This was literally a once-in-a-lifetime opportunity to feel morally superior.

But then an instinct for self-preservation took over. Whatever had led to Bud's shooting, whoever had pulled the trigger, the Warner family was desperate to make it go away—and not just a little desperate. We were talking $10 million desperate.

Since my last visit, something had changed in a fundamental way for Warner, Erabelle, and Junior. Had one of them shot Bud and the other two just discovered it? Regardless, the family was circling the wagons.

And people that rich and that desperate are not above resorting to violence to protect themselves. Was there a plan B if I didn't take the money? Was Frank waiting outside the door to make me disappear? So what if Callum knew I was here? So what if there would be suspicions or even an investigation. I would still be dead.

"Please take the money." Erabelle's voice sounded frailer than when I'd met her earlier in the day. "It's what Bud would want."

I noticed she'd called him Bud for the first time and wondered if it was calculated to win me over.

"It's a very generous offer, but I'd like to sleep on it." I had no intention of being bribed, but despite the hotheaded ambitions I'd arrived with, it now seemed wiser to retreat. "Quitting my job is a big decision."

"Of course." Whatever doubt Junior had about my corruptibility didn't amount to much. He clearly believed you could never go wrong assuming the worst about people. "I'll expect to hear from you soon, though."

We shook hands, and then Frank, who had been waiting outside the door, walked me back to the van. I didn't get an escort to the gate this time. The money was considered enough to guarantee my good behavior.

EIGHTEEN

I wasn't sure where to go. The Oildale house was a crime scene. I'd sleep in the van before returning to Rod's house. Leanore would take me in, but she'd want to know why and I didn't want to talk about it.

I needed to find a motel, but on the way to the freeway where most of them operated, I made a quick detour to the strip club Stallions. The emotion of my encounter with Rod, not to mention the bribe attempt, had me keyed up and I knew I wouldn't be able to sleep.

This time I parked a block down from Stallions so my van wouldn't be recognized. When I got out, I noticed a pickup pulling in behind me. Its motor shut off, but no one got out.

At Stallions the shifts had changed. The new bouncer hadn't seen me driving the news van and let me right through. I kept my coat zipped and paid the cover charge.

Inside, no one paid me any notice as I walked to the bar. Normally, a thirty-two-year-old woman, alone in a strip club, and wearing a bulky jacket she refused to unzip, would probably have drawn some attention. I credited everyone's zombielike interest in the dancer's anatomy to my being able to fly under the radar.

The woman in question wore a Santa bikini and danced to "All I Want for Christmas Is You." The pole had been decorated in red and white stripes like a handcrafted STD candy cane.

I shouldn't be so harsh. Money had been spent on the zebra-striped carpeting and red velvet club chairs. All the men appeared to be clean and respectable. There was even something empowering about the command and athleticism in the dancer's movement.

But, you know, ick.

"What can I get you?" The bartender had to shout to be heard over the music. "We've got a special on peppermint martinis for the holiday."

"Because nothing says Christmas like cheap liquor at a strip club."

He laughed. At first I thought he had a sense of humor about his job, but then I realized he hadn't been able to understand me over the music. He probably just laughed at everything customers said and hoped he'd get a bigger tip.

"The peppermint thing sounds good," I yelled.

He went to work mixing the drink, which included crushing a candy cane to sprinkle on top. When he finished, I set a twenty on the bar for him.

The song had changed to "Santa Baby," which seemed a little on the nose to me, but also allowed us to hear each other better.

"I'm curious. When in the year do you guys break out the Christmas decorations and costumes?"

"Just today."

"I thought maybe it was like the radio, where they start playing Christmas songs in November."

He laughed, but then something behind me caught his attention. His frown made me curious. I turned and saw a man sitting alone in a chair by the wall. He wore a Santa hat and cradled his head in one hand. His body moved back and forth in an odd way.

"Just what we need." The bartender removed a cell phone from his belt and used the instant-talk function. "We've got a code five on the left side of the stage."

A voice replied, "I'm on it."

I refused to turn around. "A code five . . . That's not, you know, a guy . . . touching . . ."

"No. That's a code nine." He returned the phone to his belt. "Code five is a crier."

I started to ask what the codes between five and nine were, but instead said, "You mean 'crying' crying?"

He nodded. "I'm sympathetic, but it's bad for business. We have to get him out of here before he upsets the other customers."

"Does this happen often?"

"More often than the code nine, actually."

The bartender waited while the crier was escorted out, then took the twenty off the bar and opened the register.

"Keep the change," I said.

He glanced back. "Really? On a twenty?"

"It's not actually that nice. I'm looking for someone and hoping you'll be able to help me."

He grinned, but I noticed he kept the money. "Let me guess, a guy?"

"Not exactly." I tried to remember the name of Carter King's known associate—the woman he'd been arrested with back in the eighties—but all I could think of was Booby Hatch Bible Thief. "This is embarrassing, but I can't remember the name."

I glanced at the door. Was I going to have to go all the way back to the van just to get Callum's LexisNexis search? "It starts with a *B*. It's like Erin Brockovich."

"You're talking about one of our bouncers. His name is Bogdanich."

I started to tell him that I was looking for a woman, but stopped myself in time. "That's right. Is he working tonight?"

"He was on the door, but left early to go to a party."

No wonder the creep hadn't let me inside the club. "That's right. He told me about his mom when we met. Didn't she own this club, back when it was called the Booby Hatch?"

The bartender nodded. "I think that's how he got the job, but it's worked out. He's a good guy."

"You said Bogdanich left early. Do you know where he went?"

"You're barking up the wrong tree." I hadn't heard the woman approach over the music. She set down an overnight bag and a purse on a bar stool near me.

"Why's that?" I said.

The young woman wore skintight jeans with high-heel boots and a bright red winter coat. Her blond hair had been teased and cemented in place with buckets of hairspray—just like that of the dancer currently onstage.

"You're not his type."

At first I thought she might be an ex-girlfriend acting jealous, but then I noticed the bartender.

He smirked. "Bogdanich is gay."

The dancer took a handful of coins from her coat pocket and placed them on the bar along with a pile of bills. "Can you change these for me?"

I guessed she was swapping her tips for higher bills, but wondered about the change. I leaned in as the bartender counted them out, and I recognized Sacagawea dollars. "Did a guy actually tip you in coins?"

"Idiot threw them up on the stage." She rubbed her thigh. "I'm going to have big welts where he hit me."

The bartender deposited the money in the cash register and returned with larger bills.

She placed the money in her purse. Before leaving she said, "If Bogdanich had been inside instead of on the door, I never would have gotten hit with coins. He may be gay, but he's chivalrous as all get-out. Best bouncer we've ever had."

When we were alone again, I gave the bartender another twenty. He wouldn't give me the bouncer's home address, but he did let slip that he'd left work early to attend a Christmas party at Bakersfield University, where he took classes.

I left the club as quickly as I could. Back in the van, I took out my smartphone and opened the Internet browser. The temperature had dropped even more, so I turned on the van's engine and cranked up the heat.

Bakersfield University campus was closed for the winter break, but I did find one club hosting a Christmas party tonight. Bakersfield Pride invited all LGBT students whose families were hostile or prejudiced to celebrate the holiday together. The address listed belonged to the only gay fraternity on campus.

I fastened my seat belt and put the van in drive.

That's when I heard the high-pitched bark. I'd been so wound up since leaving Rod's that I'd forgotten about Thing. He gleefully played underneath the tarp in the back. I was going to have to take him back to the station, but since the Pride party was on the way, I decided to go there first.

While en route, my cell phone rang. The area code was for Lake Elizabeth, but with a different number than before.

I pulled over and answered, "Hello."

"Is this Bud's niece?" The voice was low, as though whispering, but I thought I recognized it.

"Yes. My name's Lilly. I think we met last summer at the doughnut shop. Are you Mrs. Paik's granddaughter?"

"That's right." She still spoke quietly. "I heard my mom talking to you on the phone earlier. Is it true Bud got shot?"

Someone called in the background and then the girl yelled, "I'll be there in a minute. . . . No, I'm watching TV."

There was silence for a moment, then I heard the TV switch on.

"Sorry," she whispered. "I don't want my mom to know I'm calling you."

"Why not?"

"Because Grandma doesn't want her to know the truth."

Maybe I was still bristling from Rod's lying to me, but this bugged me. "Your mother is a grown woman. She doesn't need protecting like she's a little girl."

"Grandma's not protecting her. Grandma's ashamed."

In my business shame usually equals newsworthy, so even without the issue of Bud, I would have been curious.

But before I could ask what there was to be ashamed of, the girl jumped in. "Can you come meet me? My parents will be asleep by midnight and I can sneak out."

"You shouldn't be sneaking out. How old are you?"

"Seventeen." Her voice rose. "Don't act all judgmental. Bud said you used to do all kinds of bad stuff when you were my age."

I had no answer for that. She was right.

A voice called in the background, "Who are you talking to?"

"I have to go," the girl rushed to say. "Meet me at the THINK SAFETY signs at one thirty." She hung up.

Driving up to the mountains, although only a forty-minute trip, was an unattractive prospect. Not only did I want to be near the hospital in case Bud's condition changed, but I was tired and didn't think this lead was important. Mrs. Paik's granddaughter might be able to tell me new things about Bud, but I doubted she'd be able to tell me why he'd been shot and by whom.

I decided to go for one reason: Bud owned a mobile home at the lake. His girlfriend, Annette, even suggested he might have stayed there last night, since he hadn't come home to her house. He might have left evidence behind or even the gold brooch he'd bought at the pawnshop. At the least, Bud's mobile home would give me a free place to spend the night.

I reached the address for the Bakersfield Pride party near the BU campus. I left my unwanted passenger in the van and knocked on the house's front door. No one answered so I tried the handle. It was unlocked.

Inside the air was warm and smelled of cinnamon and ham. Michael Bublé singing jazzy Christmas standards played. The party was in full swing with young men and women talking, sipping drinks, and munching on food. Nobody asked who I was, but I got enough curious glances to make it clear I stood out from the crowd.

I made a full circle of the house and stopped in the dining room. A potluck of holiday food covered the table, and people were filling plates. I took a closer look and saw the KJAY logo disappearing under a helping of potato salad. All the paper plates and cups were from KJAY.

"Lilly, dude, what are you doing here?"

I turned. Freddy had come up behind me.

"What are you doing here?" I said.

"I've been pretty active in Bakersfield Pride since I enrolled at BU last spring. I was going to run for club treasurer next semester, but now that Callum's offering me work on the assignment desk, I may not have time for that and classes."

"But, how long have you been gay?"

Conversations stopped. Heads turned. Michael Bublé's singing was the only sound.

"Since I was born." Freddy's voice turned cold. "It's totally not a choice."

"I know." I looked around the room. "I'm sorry. I didn't mean it like that."

Freddy crossed his arms. "Then what did you mean?"

"How long have you been out of the closet?"

"I've never been in it." Freddy stared at me, then realization flashed across his face. "You didn't know I was gay?"

He started laughing. Between snorts he pointed at me and said to the others, "I've known her for, like, five years. I even told her I liked dudes."

The others joined his laughter.

"That's not fair," I said. "You call everybody dude, even me. How was I to know that this one time you were using it in a gender-specific way?"

They laughed even more.

Freddy put a hand on my shoulder. "Lilly, dude, I totally love you. You're one of my favoritest people, like, on the entire planet, but you do not know what you do not know."

"I know you're my friend." I couldn't help but feeling a little defensive. "I couldn't care less what your sexual preferences are."

This was not a calculated move on my part, but the room's attitude toward me softened and the party resumed.

Freddy walked me back out to the van so we could talk privately. Standing on the curb, my coat zipped up to fight the cold and Freddy stubbornly still in his shorts, I explained I was looking for the bouncer from Stallions and why.

Freddy didn't know the man well, but thought Bouncer—I'd started dropping the *the* by then—had been at the party earlier. Freddy offered to ask around and text me if anyone knew where he lived.

"There's something else." I stepped closer and lowered my voice. "Are there any students at BU who are good with computers? I'd be willing to pay."

"What do you want them to do?"

I looked over my shoulder to make sure the block was empty. "There's a bank account I want to hack into. It may have to do with why my uncle got shot."

I hoped to trace the origin of Mida's pension by gaining access to her financial information, but Freddy actually laughed at me. "That's mondo-serious stuff, Lilly. You're not going to find that at BU, or probably anywhere in Bakersfield. You'd be better off trying to get the log-in and password."

I thanked Freddy and started to say good-bye, but he had other ideas. "Dude, I have a favor to ask."

"What's that?"

"Put me on the clock as a shooter tonight. I'm jonesing real bad to ask questions down at the sludge spill. The city is totally covering something up. I've heard a ton of rumors about toxic waste and—"

I cut him off. "You also heard rumors about a giant snake, and three weeks ago it was aliens landing down by Weedpatch. How about the time you were convinced flu shots were designed to make marijuana less potent?"

"This is a totally different dealio. I drove by the crash on my way to the party and they've still got the streets blocked off. You can't get within five blocks of the sludge spill."

That gave me pause. When I'd been running the assignment desk that morning, authorities had said it would be cleared by the afternoon.

Freddy pointed. "See, your news sonar just pinged. It is suspicious."

I could have been in a Cold War sub the pinging was so loud, but I still hesitated. When Freddy had been a shooter, he'd been irresponsible and childish. Was this just more of the same?

"It's not like you're hiring me as a new employee," he continued. "Callum's already offered me part-time work on the assignment desk. Giving me a couple hours as a shooter tonight is no big deal."

He was right, and it was odd they hadn't finished cleaning the sludge spill. "Okay. Go on the clock and check it out. I'm driving up to my uncle's house in Elizabeth and spending the night there. I'll have my cell on if you need me."

I waited while he whooped with excitement. "I'm glad you're so enthusiastic, but if you're going to work on the assignment desk, you have to give up all these weird conspiracy theories. You can't be hours late to work or come in hungover. Callum's going to look bad."

Freddy retreated into his usual, snarky posture, but then seemed to make a conscious decision to lower his guard. "I get it. The desk is Callum's baby and he's trusting me with it." He paused. "I totally haven't had to live up to anyone's expectations since my dad figured out I was gay and kicked me out. Now Callum believes in me and I don't want to disappoint him."

I remembered now that the Pride party was for people who didn't have family welcoming them home for the holidays. I'd shrugged off my not knowing Freddy was gay because it simply didn't matter. What that attitude ignored was the prejudice that one felt when being gay. I'd never supported him through any of it because I'd never even known he might be hurting.

I reached out and hugged Freddy. The suddenness of it took him by surprise, but after an initial awkward moment he hugged me back.

"That was totally cool what you said in there about not caring if I'm gay or straight, but you know, all the same . . ."

"Say it." I pulled back. "I have it coming."

"You might try and get to know your friends a little better."

"Is Teddy . . ."

"Gay?" Freddy laughed. "He's dating his coanchor."

"What?" I shouted, but then lowered my voice. "The ten-thousand-year-old demon?"

"For two months. They're trying to cruise under the radar." Freddy paused to laugh at my agony. "She's not that bad if you get to know her, which you haven't. Maybe after the holidays . . ." Something caught Freddy's attention behind me. "Dude, is something moving in the back of your van?"

"That little dog that pees snuck into my gear bag." I opened the rear hatch and pulled back the tarp. Thing was batting around an empty Mountain Dew container. "And now that you're on the clock, guess who gets to take him back to the station."

I handed the dog to Freddy, who held it at arm's length waiting for the inevitable urination. Nothing happened.

Freddy shrugged. "Little dude must be dehydrated."

NINETEEN

Christmas Day, Midnight

I drove east out of town toward the Terrill Mountains. The black horizon ahead of me gave nothing of the geography away. The farmland, the peaks rising from it, and the sky above both formed a single dark monolith. It seemed to be a visual representation of something Freddy had said.

You don't know what you don't know.

I'd worked hard over the previous year to make friends and know people better, but I clearly had more work to do. What else was I clueless about? Was I missing something obvious about Bud's shooting?

I reached the entrance to the canyon road and began my ascent. The temperature dropped as I climbed. Half an hour later, when I'd neared the top, snow lined the side of the road. It reminded me that it was after midnight and officially Christmas.

I'd made good time on the way up, so I had almost an hour before the meeting. Bud's mobile home is in one of the many parks near the lake catering to middle-class retirees or people looking for cheap vacation homes. I'd actually lived here when I was nineteen and in the middle of a downward spiral begun after my father's death. I hadn't hit bottom yet. Mostly I was drinking and partying with strangers.

Winter is the low season, so only the hardscrabble year-rounders were in residence. Judging from the number of mobile homes decorated for the holiday, I guessed the park was about a quarter full.

I found the key where Bud always hid it—in the bag of empty beer cans next to the motor oil. Despite a new coat of exterior paint, Bud's mobile home had only gotten older in the years since I'd been there. The same green shag carpet covered the living room and hallway.

There was no sign that anyone had used the place in months. The toilets and pipes had been winterized. It seemed unlikely I'd find anything here relating to the shooting.

I sat down in Bud's favorite living-room recliner. He'd worn a groove in the old thing that I fit nicely into. I thought of him in the ICU and wondered if I should have gone in with Rod to see him.

I phoned the hospital to ask for an update. The ICU said there hadn't been any change. Bud's monitors continued to show no sign of brain activity.

I switched on the TV so I wouldn't have to be alone with my thoughts. After staring at the KJAY Yule log for a few minutes, I got out my cell phone and opened the web browser. If I couldn't hack into Mida King's bank account, maybe I could get in using her own password.

When I'd spoken with her earlier in the day, Mida had said *bougainvillea* was the password to cancel her emergency-response service. Maybe like most people, Mida used the same password for multiple things. During her illness's acceleration, she'd probably needed to keep things simple.

I began checking websites of the four biggest national banks trying to find the one Mida used. Since many people's e-mail addresses also served as log-ins, and older people were fond of AOL, I used *midaking@aol.com* in combination with the password *bougainvillea*.

When that failed, I attempted another round with just *midaking* as the log-in. I'd tried two banks and failed, then the third accepted me. Within seconds I was looking at a joint account shared by Mida, Sally, and Brandon. I started to click it open, but stopped.

Just below was a second link for a mortgage account in Mida's name. It had been opened just two weeks prior. Someone had mortgaged the farm for $300,000.

There was no sign of the money. The regular checking account was actually overdrawn. It wasn't easy on my phone, but I scrolled back through the weeks. Mida's Social Security at the beginning of December was the last deposit. I saw a check written to Kern Home Health in November and guessed it was for the aide Mida used to have.

Then I reached the second bombshell. It wasn't the $10,000 deposit on November the second, or the similar deposits on the second of every month. That's what I'd expected to see. It was whom they were from. The deposit was described as "ELECTRONIC/ACH CREDIT Warner Co., Inc PR PAYMENT."

Cousin Leland had been taking care of Mida.

The $10,000 a month and Mida's Social Security appeared to be the family's only monthly income. Mida, Sally, and Brandon were all living off that money. The utilities, groceries, even Brandon's college tuition, were all paid from this account. How desperate had the family been when the December deposit hadn't come through?

I'd got cold and sleepy sitting in the chair, so I stood. A nap sounded seductive, but I knew if I went down, there'd be no getting up until morning. Canceling the meeting would have been my first choice. I'd sought out Mrs. Paik hoping she or her husband would be able to corroborate or contradict things that Warner and Mida King had told me about Bud's past. How could her granddaughter do that? She hadn't even been alive in the fifties.

Still, the girl had been sure of herself and her information on the phone. The least I could do was meet with her.

I found a bedroom used entirely for storage and decided to fill the remaining time looking through boxes. Anything newer than the fifties I ignored, which it turned out was everything.

Disappointed, I glanced at my watch. Fifteen minutes before I needed to leave for the meeting.

I did some jumping jacks to ward off the cold. The tips of my fingers were tingling and I wanted to go back to the van and blast the heater. Instead I slid open the closet panel. Inside were more boxes and a dresser. I opened the top drawer.

Living in Bud's house in Oildale, I'd often wondered why there were no pictures or memorabilia of my father. He was in group photos with my mother, sister, and me, but there was no proof that he'd ever existed as a child.

The proof was in this drawer. There were report cards, the program from his high school graduation, and a postcard he'd sent Bud from his honeymoon with my mother. I reluctantly put it all aside for another day and continued to look for things that might help me understand what had happened to Bud.

The chest's second drawer was full of sweaters and marijuana. Not a large enough amount to sell—the pot, not the sweaters—but still enough to be a crime. I put on a scratchy wool crew neck that felt hand knit. The material was incredibly warm and smelled like Bud. It wasn't exactly a good smell, but it brought tears to my eyes.

I opened the final drawer and felt a rush of excitement. A jacket with Bureau of Land Management patches from Bud's time in Alaska sat on top. Underneath the aging fabric were documents and other memorabilia from the same time. Old black-and-white pictures of the wildland firefighters taken in what were probably rare off hours sat with a survival handbook and a small ax. I moved the book and the ax to the side and froze.

Letters bundled up with old twine. If they were from the same time in Bud's life as the rest of the contents of the drawer, then I may have hit pay dirt.

I didn't have time to read them there, so I took the bundle and left to meet Mrs. Paik's granddaughter.

I was five minutes late to the meeting, but that was okay. She was late too. A thin layer of snow had accumulated in the dirt clearing beneath the THINK SAFETY signs. Their purpose is to warn vacationers about water safety, and they make their point by keeping a running tally of drownings. This time of year the area around them is deserted.

I stayed in the car with the heater running and read the letters. The cream-colored paper had probably been expensive in the early fifties. Something about the weight of it was romantic and couldn't be duplicated today.

They were all from Erabelle and sent to Bud in Alaska. Her feminine cursive matched the feel of the paper. It sounded as though they'd begun an affair shortly after his discharge from the army. Erabelle, only eighteen at the time, believed herself to be deeply in love. She began the first letter by asking Bud to return to Bakersfield and marry her.

Her brother, Leland, did not approve. He thought Bud was good enough to be his best friend, but not good enough to be his brother-in-law. Erabelle didn't care. She offered Bud the jewelry, saying they could use it to start their life together. It was her legal property, and she would use it to chart her own destiny away from Leland's meddling.

The final letters were hard to read. Not because I felt guilty for invading her privacy—the woman had lost her moral authority when she colluded to offer me a bribe—but because Erabelle abandoned pretense and even pride. She wrote of her love, her devotion, and her faith in the only man she'd ever loved.

None of Bud's replies were there, but judging from Erabelle's exuberant final letter, he must have written to say he was coming home to marry her. Joy was evident not just in her words, but in the wild, sloppy lettering. Leland was still going to be difficult, but what did it matter?

Except they hadn't got married. They hadn't even seen each other in fifty years. Had Bud returned only to end the relationship for good? Was he that heartless that he'd raise her hopes only to crush them?

I started reading them again from the beginning, but wasn't disappointed when the girl arrived and I had to stop.

I lowered the window. "Are you okay? You're late."

She rubbed her nose with a gloved hand. "My mom and dad wouldn't go to sleep."

She rubbed her nose again, as though it had lost feeling. That's when I noticed she was on a bike. "You rode a bike here in this weather?"

"It's no big deal." She tried to shrug, but her bulky winter jacket muted the gesture. "I'm practically eighteen. I know what I'm doing."

I had the wisdom not to contradict her, despite that the entire clandestine meeting felt like an immature lark. "Why don't you get in the van with me? I've got the heater on."

She left the bike and climbed into the passenger seat. "Is Bud going to get better? I only knew him for a couple weeks, but I really loved the old guy."

"The doctors will know more tomorrow."

She would probably have noticed I'd dodged her question if she hadn't been so desperate to get her gloves off. "I hope they catch whoever did this to him. If it helps you to know about Grandma, I'll tell you, but my mom can't find out."

"I doubt it's even important." I shifted all the air vents so they were pointing at her. "I heard that your grandfather served in the army with Bud. I thought he and your grandmother might know details of Bud's life back in the fifties, after the war."

She held her fingers directly in front of the hot air. "My grandfather's dead, but even if he were alive, he couldn't help you. He didn't serve in the army or know Bud."

"That's what your mother said."

"But she doesn't know what I know about Grandma." She obviously relished this reversal in the parent-child balance of power. "Grandpa Paik was her second husband. It's the first who was friends with Bud."

"Why is that secret?"

She rolled her eyes. "Because it's different in Grandma's

generation. Being divorced was really bad. Even if your husband went out for a pack of smokes and never came back."

That got my attention. "Her first husband disappeared?"

She nodded. "Deserted her a couple years after the war ended."

"Can you be more specific?"

"Not really. Grandma said it was right after he and Bud got back from Alaska."

"This guy was a smoke jumper too?"

She nodded. "I think he and Bud met in the army, then signed up for firefighting together. Sort of like they were brothers-in-arms."

"Do you know his name or what happened to him?"

"You don't get it." She started to roll her eyes again, but stopped herself. "Grandma doesn't like talking about this stuff. She only admitted the first marriage existed because I was doing a report for school and noticed some of the dates didn't match."

I wondered if this man might have been involved with Carter King and the robbery. Both men knew Bud and both men skipped town around the same time. "I need to call your grandma in Arizona. I have to find out her first husband's name."

"Why?"

"Because he might still be alive and I need to talk to him. I think he might know something about what led to the attack on Bud."

"She'll just hang up if you call. You should talk to her in person."

"I can't go all the way to Arizona right now."

"Duh, it's Christmas." She lost the battle and finally rolled her eyes. "Grandma's flying in to Bakersfield tomorrow."

We put the bike in the rear on top of the tarp and I drove her home. The romance of our secret rendezvous had worn off and she seemed eager to get to bed.

I returned to Bud's place with the intention of spending the night. I parked in the carport, then found the propane tank out back. Before turning on the heat and going to bed, it seemed wise to make sure everything was in working order. I was brushing old snow off the rounded metal top when a powerful flashlight beam hit me full in the face.

"Hello?" I raised my hand to shield my eyes. "Who's there?"

"I'm the park manager." It was a woman's voice. "I got a call about someone inside Mr. Hawkins's house."

"It's okay. I'm Bud's niece."

She pulled her coat tighter over her robe. "He didn't tell me anyone was using the place."

I showed her my ID. After I explained about Bud's being in the hospital, she apologized for coming on so strong.

"Another resident called from down the street and said there were lights on in Bud's place and a pickup truck was circling the park." She gestured behind her to my news van. "If he'd said you were driving that, I'd have known who you were right off."

"Why's that?"

"Bud couldn't be prouder of you. He brags all the time about how you work for the news."

I was so moved that it took me a moment to realize what she'd said. "Who said a pickup was here?"

"Sam, who lives down the street." She pointed toward the lake. "He saw lights on half an hour ago, then a pickup truck was driving around the park."

Had someone followed me from Bakersfield? The police were looking for a pickup in connection with Bud's shooting. Was his attacker now following me?

"Do you mind helping me check the doors and windows?" I said. "I want to make sure no one broke in while I was gone just now."

We finished quickly. There were no signs of forced entry, but the locks were cheap and flimsy. Despite the late hour, it seemed prudent to drive back to Bakersfield. The idea of sleeping alone here gave me the creeps.

"Has anything else unusual happened?" I said after locking up the mobile home. "Anyone hanging around?"

"No," she said, but then reconsidered. "Just, well, someone called for Bud yesterday at the park's general number. That's hardly sinister, but it was unusual."

"Called you?"

She nodded. "They had his address, but no phone number."

"Who was it?"

"A woman. Didn't leave a name. When I said Bud wasn't staying at his place, they hung up."

"Do you have caller ID?"

"Sure, but it didn't show a name, just a number."

We drove in our separate vehicles to her office. It was in the first mobile home as you drove in the park. The air inside was warm and smelled of fresh paper and printer ink, with an undercurrent of home cooking. I guessed the one interior door led to her personal living space.

She gestured to the standard multiline office phone on the cheap metal desk. "I took the call right here. Should still be in the memory."

She found the call. It had come from an area code I didn't recognize. What really interested me was the timing: roughly two hours after Bud had bought the brooch at the pawnshop. I wrote the number down and thanked her.

"You don't owe me any thanks. I'm always happy to help Bud. He got me out of a jam a couple years ago." She shook her head. "Tricky thing down in Yuma."

"He's good at getting people out of jams. I only wish he'd gotten himself out of this one."

On my way out of town, I stopped at an open gas station to fill up and use a pay phone. I glimpsed a car following me, but it was so far back that it might have been unrelated. One of the many things I keep in the back of my van is a baseball bat. I moved it up to the front seat and made sure the Mace was in my coat pocket.

The gas station's pay phone was attached to the outside of the building and I was glad to be wearing Bud's sweater underneath my jacket. I would have used my own cell phone, but I didn't want Bud's mystery caller to see KJAY on caller ID and not answer.

She answered on the third ring. "Who is this?"

The voice hit me with a jolt. I had to take a breath before speaking. "Hello, Erabelle."

TWENTY

S ilence. Was Erabelle debating hanging up on me?

Finally she said, "Lilly? How did you get this number?"

I thought of my first meeting with Erabelle yesterday. She'd told me it had been over fifty years since she'd last seen Bud. Now it turned out she'd called him the day before.

I wanted to accuse her of lying, but knew that over the phone I'd be at a disadvantage. If she didn't like what I said, she'd simply hang up. "Let's talk in person."

"You can come to the house tomorrow, if you'd like."

No way was I meeting on Warner-family territory. I also wasn't in the mood to wait for answers. "Zingo's in one hour."

"You want to meet now?" Her voice rose. "It's the middle of the night."

"We're both awake and it's fitting. Zingo's is one of Bud's favorite places to eat."

"Is it even open?"

"It's a truck stop. They're open twenty-four/seven, even Christmas." I paused. "There are things we need to discuss that you probably want kept private."

She agreed to the meeting, which in itself was suspicious. If Erabelle had nothing to hide, she would have told me to call back in the morning.

I drove back down the canyon road to Bakersfield. Now that I knew to look, it was obvious I was being followed. The headlights never got close enough for me to tell if it was a pickup. Eventually, I lost them on local streets. Either they weren't good at tailing cars or they were so good that I'd been suckered into believing I was free.

I stopped at KJAY and ran in to make copies of Erabelle's letters. I still managed to arrive on time. Despite the holiday several big rigs were in the lot, their drivers probably sleeping in the cabs. I avoided them and parked next to the only other car. Erabelle had driven a black SUV, instead of the pickup she'd been in when I'd first met her. Undoubtedly both vehicles were from Warner's vast fleet.

Inside, the only waitress had seated her in one of the black vinyl booths and was taking her coffee order.

"Mountain Dew, please." I removed my coat and slid in opposite. "And the chicken-fried steak with extra biscuits, no gravy."

Erabelle waited for the waitress to leave before speaking. "How can you eat like that?"

"It's Bud's favorite thing on the menu." I set the bundle of letters on the table. "I guess I'm feeling sentimental."

At first she didn't recognize them. Then she sucked in a breath. "Where?"

"Bud still had them."

She reached with one hand. The other she kept pressed against her abdomen. "I didn't think he kept them a day, let alone all these years."

Great tenderness was on her face, but then it turned to horror. "You didn't . . ."

I nodded. "Oh, yeah. I read all of them."

Despite her already heightened anxiety, despite her skin's being old and wrecked from too much sun, despite that it had been over fifty years since she wrote the letters, despite everything, Erabelle still blushed. "You shouldn't have done that."

"Under the circumstances I think it was exactly what I should have done." The waitress returned with my soda and her coffee. As soon as she left, I continued, "Don't try and make me feel bad because it won't work."

"You could at least say you're sorry."

"I'd be lying." I took a drink of the soda. The green caffeine felt good going down. "And that really would be something to feel bad about."

"You have a very idiosyncratic moral code. It reminds me of your uncle."

"We're a lot alike." I looked her in the eye. "Which is part of the reason I'm not taking that bribe you offered me."

She flinched. "That wasn't my idea."

"I didn't see you objecting."

She remained silent. I got a sense that colluding with her brother and nephew to buy me off had cost her. Erabelle had got her hands dirty and could no longer sit outside the family circle in judgment.

"Why did you go along with it?"

She took a deep breath. It lent gravity to her words, but it might also have been a stalling tactic. "Because Allan would want you to have the money."

"Did Bud take a bribe all those years ago? Did your brother pay him to stop seeing you?"

"I always thought . . ." She was in danger of crying and paused to compose herself. She even took a drink of the coffee before continuing. "I always thought that it was the jewelry being stolen."

I followed Leanore's and Rod's interview technique and stayed silent.

"The brooches were my only asset. The only money or property I had. Without it, I was either penniless or completely dependent on my brother. Allan didn't want me like that."

I took a deep breath and let it out. "So Bud only wanted you for your money?"

She wiped the back of her hand across her cheek where a tear had fallen. "I don't know."

Her uncertainty made me wonder. "Did something happen to change your mind? Something you're not telling me?"

"Don't be melodramatic." She tried to pull herself together. "I just don't know. And never will, I guess. All that's over."

I wasn't sure I believed her. "Then why did you call Bud yesterday?"

"What makes you think I did?"

"I got your number from the caller ID at the mobile home park."

She nodded. "I wondered. I didn't remember giving it to you."

"Why did you try to speak with Bud the day before he was shot?"

"It's nothing sinister, I promise." She took another sip of the coffee, frowned, then added two creamers. "I heard he called for Leland. He made a big ruckus on the phone. I was curious, so I asked Leland's secretary if anyone named Hawkins was in the Rolodex. She gave me the address in Elizabeth, but there was no phone number."

I didn't know if I could believe her. She was no longer the eighteen-year-old girl who'd worn her heart on her sleeve in those letters. She'd lied when we first met, she could be lying now.

The waitress brought my food. Erabelle winced when the smell of the chicken-fried steak reached her.

I picked up the steak knife and fork. "Are you a vegetarian?"

She nodded. "For forty years now."

I pushed the plate of biscuits toward her. "Maybe that's why you're in such good health."

"Thank you." She pushed the biscuits back. "But I don't have much appetite tonight."

I cut into the steak. "You know who isn't in such good health? Mida King."

Erabelle didn't say anything.

I wasn't sure if she was upset by my eating a dead cow in front of her or the name I'd just said. "Do you know Mida?"

"No," Erabelle said.

"She's Carter King's sister. Her family lived on the property next door to your father's."

"I think I remember a girl. She was older than me."

"Mida calls your brother 'Cousin Leland.'"

Erabelle laughed. "You wouldn't believe the number of people who claim to be relatives. When you're as rich as Leland has become, it draws them out of the woodwork."

"If Mida's not a relative, why does your brother send her money every month?" Erabelle didn't answer, so I continued, "Why would Leland give ten thousand dollars a month to the sister of the man who robbed him?"

Erabelle's smile didn't waver, but it was held in place by fear. "Where are you getting your information?"

"Mida told me," I lied.

"But she's . . ." Erabelle stopped herself, but the damage was done.

"Sick?" I took another bite of steak. "Yes, she is. We can get into how you knew she was sick later. It should be an interesting conversation considering you don't know her."

"Don't put words in my mouth." Anger, which I now realized she'd been fighting to contain all along, broke through. "I was going to say, but she'd have to be in her eighties."

"Sure you were." I winked, which made her even angrier. "What I really want to know is why the money stopped coming last month."

Erabelle appeared to suffer through an internal battle. Finally she waved her hand as though giving up. "My nephew took control when Leland had his heart attack. He cut everything personal or charitable. My own foundation lost its funding too."

"You accused Junior of siphoning off the money to pay his own debts. How desperate is he for cash?"

"I don't know, but if Phillip is involved in this, you should stop asking questions." She wrapped both hands around her coffee mug as if fighting a sudden chill. "Don't underestimate him. He's even worse than Leland."

So far, Junior had slithered through this sad story in a fairly obvious way. His self-interest was neither subtle nor particularly frightening. But what if Erabelle was right and I had underestimated him?

"Thanks for the warning." I took out some money and put it on the table. "And thanks for meeting me this late." I picked up my coat and began to slide out of the booth. "If I don't see you again, merry Christmas."

"You're not going?" Erabelle's eyes widened and she looked worried. "You haven't finished your food."

Was she this reluctant to go back home? I felt bad for her, but not enough to stay. "I was never that hungry to begin with."

I started to leave, but stopped and turned around. "I'm sorry for the way Bud treated you."

A strange look appeared on her face. "You feel sorry for me, but you're not angry with him."

I didn't know what to say except the truth. "You're right. I wish Bud had been a better man, but it doesn't change the way I feel about him."

"That's because you're not the one he hurt. Could you forgive him so easily if the damage had been done to you?"

"Not so easily, but I would forgive him." I walked out and left her sitting by herself in the empty restaurant.

I got back in the van and started driving. Down the street from Zingo's, I passed the Crystal Palace, Buck Owens's upscale honky-tonk. It was closed for the night, but the Christmas lights strung along the cheesy Old West balconies made the phony place look warm and fun. Who wouldn't prefer this clean, attractive, and safe version of the truth over a real Old West saloon?

Despite what I'd said to Erabelle, her question disturbed me. Was it easy to forgive Bud's crimes, trespasses, and sins because none of them had hurt me personally? If that was true, did my forgiveness amount to a lack of empathy for those Bud had hurt?

Instead of finding a motel I decided to return to Rod's house. My anger had cooled and I hoped Rod might also have rethought his position. For me at least, nothing was broken between us that couldn't be fixed by his being honest about what he knew.

Half a block from my destination I passed a parked pickup. Its dark paint blended into the shadows at that end of the street, making it almost invisible. A reindeer could have been inside and I wouldn't have been able to see.

I wondered if it was the same truck that had been following me earlier. This would have been a natural place for the driver to come and wait after I'd lost the tail. Then again, this was Bakersfield, and pickups were the vehicle of choice. Everyone either had one or knew someone who did.

I parked in the driveway next to the Prius and used the key Rod had given me earlier. I took off my blue jacket and walked to the master bedroom. If memory served, this was the only one with furniture in it. I flipped the light switch on the wall. I felt bad waking Rod up, but I didn't want to startle him by crawling into bed.

Except Rod wasn't there.

I called his name. I searched every room. Fear didn't enter the equation until I dialed his cell phone and heard it ringing in the kitchen. An uneaten delivery pizza sat next to it on the kitchen counter.

Either Rod had decided to spontaneously leave the house on foot and without his phone, or . . .

Or what? He'd been kidnapped? Who would hurt Rod? The answer was obvious: the same person who'd shot Bud.

TWENTY-ONE

I told myself to calm down. The house had almost no furniture in it and hadn't been lived in for months. Rod could easily have decided to sleep somewhere else. He had no reason to expect me back tonight, and given how we'd left things, he wouldn't have been likely to call and tell me his plans.

Despite those rationalizations, I would have called the police. What stopped me was Rod's own admission that he'd been lying. If I told Handsome that Rod knew more than he'd said, which was the main reason Rod might now be a target, Handsome wouldn't hesitate to charge him with obstruction of justice. Rod might return after spending the night at a hotel only to find Handsome there to arrest him.

I called Ted, who'd been asleep, then Freddy, who was down at the site of the sludge spill. Neither had heard from Rod.

Freddy did offer me an update on the cleanup. He hadn't been able to get beyond the roadblocks, but judging from the trucks and other vehicles he'd recorded coming and going, a lot of manpower was working there tonight.

Just before hanging up, Freddy said he hadn't been able to get any contact info for Bouncer, but he'd try again tomorrow. The only thing he'd learned at the party was that Bouncer's mother owned a religious bookstore in the Rosedale neighborhood.

I offered Freddy my enthusiastic thanks and explained that Bouncer's mother had been an old accomplice of Carter King's. She was the one I was trying to find.

I was way too anxious to sleep, even if I'd felt safe enough in Rod's empty house to do so. I was also reaching the stage where my body stopped fighting my desire to stay awake and started pumping me full of adrenaline to combat sleep deprivation. A nervous energy coursed through me like that of a kid on a sugar high.

I used the Internet access on my phone. Bakersfield had three Christian bookstores—one more than we had strip clubs. I easily found a listing for the one in Rosedale.

I left a note for Rod telling him to call me if he came home and drove to Rosedale.

The store belonging to Bouncer's mom projected respectability, tucked as it was between a Supercuts and a vitamin shop. The simple lettering on the large window read CHRISTIAN BOOKS AND GIFTS. Looking through the glass into the dimly lit interior, I saw the stock was low, probably from the holiday season.

More important, a light was on in the back office of the store. I parked at the end of the strip and walked along the alley behind the shops. A van was parked near an open door spilling light from the bowels of a store. I cautiously approached and peeked inside the van's back window. Several boxes with the label LUTHERAN CHURCH OF THE REDEEMER were stacked inside.

I heard voices and walked toward the open door of the building. This back room, like the alley, was never meant for the public to see. The plain white walls had been scarred and nicked by the flow of inventory passing through. A pile of flattened cardboard boxes, marked with the same lettering as those in the van, sat in a pile by a utilitarian steel bookshelf.

"I'm just saying, should it be this much work?" Bouncer unloaded black books from another cardboard box. He'd changed out of the tux and into jeans and an LA Lakers sweatshirt. "I mean, if you're going to put so much effort into it, why don't you do something legit?"

He spoke to a woman sitting at a plain metal table. More black books—probably Bibles—rested on each side of her.

She took a book from the stack on her left, cut out the first page with a razor, then placed it on the stack to her right. "If I can get product at bargain-basement prices, I'm going to do it. Why should I care which truck it fell off?"

I couldn't see the page she'd cut, but I guessed it had a PROPERTY OF LUTHERAN CHURCH OF THE REDEEMER stamp. This explained why they were working in the middle of the night. Buying, transporting, and altering stolen merchandise is best done under cover of darkness.

Bouncer added more books to the pile on her left, then flattened the empty cardboard box. "But I worry about you, Mom. One of these days you're going to get caught, and you've already got two strikes."

The woman had to be Laurie Bogdanich—yes, I'd consulted the paperwork in the van and tried really, really hard to memorize her name.

If I walked right in and introduced myself, I'd officially be a witness to what they were doing. I figured Laurie would be more inclined to speak with me if things stayed friendly.

I backed up and waited out by the van. A few minutes later, Bouncer came out for more books.

I made sure to approach from a distance and make noise as I walked. "Hi. Remember me?"

His head shot up.

"Don't worry, I'm not here to cause trouble. I just want to speak with your mom."

He dropped the box in his hands.

"Maybe you can go tell her I'm here. It's not for a news story. It's personal."

All at once he lunged forward and grabbed me. It was such an unnecessary thing to do that I was completely unprepared.

"What are you doing?" I struggled as he easily dragged me inside. "Seriously, what are you doing?"

His left hand let go of me long enough to grab a roll of duct tape from a shelf.

That's when I got worried. "Let go of me, you idiot." I raised my knee and kicked backward into his shin.

He was ready for it and jerked his leg out of the way. He was a bouncer, after all.

"I said I'm not here for a—" The duct tape went across my mouth in a crooked vertical line.

I hit at his face. I got one good scratch, but then he knocked my legs out from under me.

"What's going on?" Laurie appeared. Her face contorted as she watched her son grappling with me on the ground. "What are you doing?"

"It's that girl from the news." He ripped off another piece of duct tape, but because of our struggling it ended up over one of his eyes. "The one who was asking about you at the club."

"Why are you fighting with her?"

"Because he's an idiot," I yelled through the corner of my mouth that wasn't taped.

"Because she's going to do a story about you." He had me on my back, but couldn't get ahold of my arms. "It'll be three strikes and they'll send you to jail for the rest of your life."

He tried again to rip off a piece of tape. I took advantage to send my elbow shooting into his ribs. He cried out and dropped the roll.

I ripped the tape off my mouth. "I'm not here to do a story." All at once the pain registered in my brain and I shrieked. "Are my lips still there?"

Bouncer rallied and knocked me on my back again. I raised my knee and tried to kick him.

He intercepted my boot and held it in both hands. "How big are your feet? You're like some evil little pixie with boulders in your shoes."

I reached up and ripped off the duct tape that was still attached to his face. Most of his eyebrow came off with the tape.

He cried out, but grabbed my wrists. "Help me tape her hands, Mom."

Instead, his mother collapsed into a chair and took out a cigarette.

Bouncer looked up from attempting to pin my arms. "You know what the doctor said about smoking."

"Sweetheart, it's Christmas, and you've kidnapped and assaulted a reporter—"

"Shooter," I corrected while landing a punch across Bouncer's jaw.

"Sorry." She exhaled a cloud of smoke. "You've kidnapped and assaulted a shooter, whatever that is. Point is, I'm having a smoke."

"I'm not here to do a story," I said. "I don't care about your business or where you buy the stuff you sell."

Bouncer let up on me a little. "Then why are you here?"

I looked at his mother. "Carrie, you got arrested in 1984 with—"

"Laurie," she corrected. "My first name's Laurie."

"Sorry, I've met a lot of people tonight. It's hard to keep them all straight."

"Remembering people's names is the only talent that matters." She took a tall devotional candle from a box and used it as an ashtray. "Doesn't matter if you're a CEO or a . . . What did you say you were?"

"A shooter. I shoot video for the news."

"Whatever business you're in, remembering people's names will make you successful."

I wasn't in the mood to get lectured. "Did you sell stolen Bibles with a man named Carter King back in 1984?"

"I sold Bibles." She grinned. "They may have been stolen, but the police never proved I knew that."

"I'm looking for Carter."

She shook her head. "When we got picked up, he made a

couple phone calls and had bail there lickety-split. Took off and never looked back."

"Did you ever see him again?"

She took another drag on her cigarette. "Why you looking for him?"

I paused to think. She clearly knew something, but didn't want to get Carter in trouble. "I think he's in town. He and my uncle have some old business, and I think Carter's revived it."

She gestured to Bouncer, who let go of me and sat back.

"He may be in town"—Laurie paused to take a drag on the cigarette—"but I don't think he'd be likely to stir up trouble. The one time I met up with Carter again, he looked like he'd pretty well settled down. Going the straight and narrow."

I sat up. "When was this?"

"Back five or six years ago. Ran into him at Valley Plaza."

I stood and walked to her at the table. "You saw Carter King at the mall, here in Bakersfield?"

She nodded. "Said he lived here. Had family in town." She waved the hand with the cigarette at me. "His niece was a mess or something."

"She's a meth addict," I said. "And her mother, Carter's sister, has Alzheimer's."

"He may be gone again. I don't know." Laurie crushed the stub of the cigarette into the candle. "But he seemed settled, back when I saw him. Said trying to help his family was all that mattered now."

"What did he look like?"

"Same old Carter. Older, but still that same smile. I swear he could sell sunscreen to a crocodile with that smile."

The fondness in her words made me wonder if they'd been romantically involved, but it seemed awkward to ask in front of her son.

My hesitation left an opening for her to try to end the conversation. "Is that all? Can I consider us square?" She stood up. "Or am I going to have a problem with you knowing about my business?"

"No. We're square."

Back in the van, I called Callum to tell him I'd found Laurie Bogdanich, as well as to ask if he'd seen Rod. I'd avoided doing it so far because Callum is notoriously grumpy when woken.

"Sorry to wake you," I said when he finally answered.

"I was dreaming that chief meteorologist was an elected position in Kern County." Callum's voice sounded groggy and slow. "No problem because our weather guy is so popular, except in my dream some other jerk with the same last name decided to run and confuse everybody."

I told him about Laurie and that Carter King had been living in Bakersfield for years. Then I told him about Rod.

His voice changed. "What do you mean you don't know where he is?"

I explained everything—all the reasons he was probably fine as well as all the reasons I was worried.

When I'd finished, he said, "You're right, there's nothing to really indicate Rod is in danger, so wait until morning. He'll probably turn up at the hospital or the TV station and you'll feel silly for worrying."

Collum paused. "Unless you want to try an end run around Handsome. Maybe go direct to a cop you trust who'll be more sympathetic."

Only one cop might be considered sympathetic to me. I'd first met him a year ago at the same time as Handsome Homicide. We'd helped each other again last summer when I'd tried to prove an accidental drowning was actually murder.

Despite the late hour, I found his cell phone number and dialed.

"What the hell, Hawkins?" Detective Lucero's usually playful voice sounded strained and hoarse. "It's four thirty in the morning, and Christmas morning, no less."

Note to self, people will forget they like you when woken in the middle of the night.

"I'm sorry to bother you, but I can't find Rod and I'm nervous."

He said a swear word I'd never heard before, and I'd heard some doozies.

After I explained that my uncle had been shot, Lucero's voice changed. "Your uncle? The old guy?" He waited for me to say yes, then continued, "He's a character. I'm sorry, I didn't hear. I'm off all this week for the holiday."

I told him about how I'd come home and found Rod's car and cell phone at the house. He took notes, then put me on hold.

Finally Lucero's voice returned. "Sorry to keep you waiting. I'm getting dressed and heading in to Sheriff's Department headquarters. Can you meet me there in an hour?" Lucero was actually a detective with the Rural Crimes Investigative Unit. He wouldn't normally work from headquarters, but this wasn't a normal situation.

"Thank you. I can't tell you how grateful I am."

When I hung up, I saw that I'd got a text from Freddy asking that I call him.

"Dude," he started. "I've got sort of a situation-type thing going on."

"What's that?"

He hesitated. "So, it's possible I lost that little dog."

"It's possible? You don't know?"

"Calm down, I know." He took a breath. "I definitely lost him."

"How?"

"I took him back to the station, like you said, but after I geared up to go back out, the little dude kept trying to get in the van. He's like a newshound, literally."

My voice rose. "You brought him with you to the sludge spill?"

"I totally figured he'd stay in the van, but, like, a couple minutes ago, he jumped out when I had the door open."

"Can you find him? On those stubby, little legs he couldn't have gotten far."

"I'm trying, dude."

At this time of the morning, it would take an easy ten minutes to reach the Sheriff's Department headquarters. Instead of the fifty-minute nap I'd been planning to take in the news van, I decided to go help Freddy and Thing.

I drove to where Highway 178 emptied out onto Seventeenth Street. Almost twenty-four hours earlier a tanker truck carrying sludge had crashed into a car. Five more cars and a smaller truck had crashed behind it. The injuries had been relatively minor, but the tanker had spilled its load of sludge. The cleanup had been expected to be finished by midafternoon. Now, almost twelve hours later, the roadblocks had actually been pushed out from the crash site, not in toward it.

I drove to the roadblock where Freddy had said to meet. I quickly removed Bud's sweater so my logo shirt would be visible under my coat and got out.

Freddy's news van was still parked next to the sawhorses, but there was no sign of him or the officers who should have been stationed there. I heard a noise from inside the restricted area. Two Bakersfield PD cops were chasing someone. I couldn't see who the fugitive was, but then I heard, "Dude, I'm totally sorry."

I jumped back in and drove the van up onto the curb. By the time I'd got around the sawhorses, the pursuit had turned into an alley. I stopped at the entrance and jumped out. I left the engine running and my door open, but I figured that inside a police barricade the van would be safe.

Down the alley, the officers had Freddy cornered at a Dumpster.

"Dude, you don't understand." He was kneeling with his back to us.

The officers had their hands on their weapons, but hadn't drawn yet. "Put your hands where I can see them," one of them instructed.

Freddy didn't obey. "But my dog is under the Dumpster."

"Never mind," I shouted. "Do what they say."

The officers saw me and freaked out. Now two journalists were inside the restricted area.

"Freddy, stand up and turn around," I said. "You're going to get yourself shot."

He finally obeyed. "He's totally under there, but good luck getting him out."

"Dog," I called. Thing appeared from under the metal bin. He walked slowly, but with purpose, until he was standing right in front of me. His crooked face looked up and curled into a dog smile.

The officers had already called for backup. After a surprisingly short lecture, we were let go. I had the feeling that they were actually concerned for our safety. It helped that Freddy had the dog to prove his story that he'd only entered the restricted area chasing Thing.

We returned to my van. I'd let a lot of the heat escape by leaving my door open so I turned the heater up to full blast. I drove Freddy back to the other side of the sawhorses with instructions to return Thing to the station and contact Callum about the sludge story.

At the Sheriff's Department, I parked in the small lot where I'd picked up Rod yesterday. I remembered those first moments in the van, how grateful I was that he was safe.

I took a moment to call the hospital and check on Bud. Still no change. It wasn't a surprise, but that didn't make it easier to hear.

Because of the early hour, I had to walk to a side door near the rear, gated parking lot. I picked up a phone receiver mounted to the wall and gave my name and whom I was there to see. After several minutes of waiting I heard a noise. Through a thick glass window I watched a uniformed officer appear at the end of a long hallway and start toward me.

When the officer finally reached the other side of the door, he entered a code into a push pad, waited for a buzzing sound, and let me in.

He held the door while I passed inside. "If you'll follow me, Detective Lucero is waiting for you."

The door swung shut with an intimidating thud. I followed him through a maze of fluorescent-lit hallways and corridors. After four or five turns and a flight of stairs, I realized I'd never be able to find my way out again.

We passed a man in handcuffs being led by another uniformed officer. The man looked up from his shackled feet. His eyes found me through strands of long, stringy hair, black with filth. "You're a tiny little slut."

"If you're going to name your junk, you shouldn't say it out-loud."

He suddenly cut toward me. The officer escorting him was taken by surprise. His delay made it that much harder to rein the man in. I stayed back as both officers working together took the man down to the floor.

"You had to be a smart-ass."

I turned and saw Lucero. I immediately relaxed. "Yeah, yeah. I say stuff I shouldn't, blah, blah, blah."

He smiled at me, then looked at the officer. "Thanks for bringing her in. I got it from here."

"Come on." He led the way toward the end of the hall.

We reached a door and he held it open for me. "Thanks for coming, Lilly."

"Are you kidding? I'm the one who's thankful that you're help-ing me." I entered the room and stopped short.

Handsome Homicide sat behind an industrial metal table. That wasn't even the worst. Lucero had brought me to an interrogation room.

TWENTY-TWO

Christmas Day, 6:05 a.m.

M y head spun around just in time to see Lucero shut
the door behind us. "What is this?"

"We'd like to ask you a few questions." Handsome
gestured to a single chair placed opposite him. "Would you please
take a seat?"

"No." I walked around Lucero and reached for the door.

Handsome didn't get up. He didn't even lean forward. "I understand you're afraid the same person who shot your uncle may be
after your boyfriend. If that's true, then you walk out of here and
he's as good as dead."

I turned back. "Is junior-high bully your only interview technique? I'm starting to think terrifying people is all you're good for."

"He put it a little bit strong," Lucero said in sympathetic tones.
"But the basic sentiment is true. Let us help you."

"I'm surprised you haven't already left," I said to him. "You did
your job and got me here."

Lucero started to say something, but Handsome cut him off.

"I've agreed to let Detective Lucero sit in on our interview."
Handsome and Lucero exchanged a look. It wasn't exactly hostile, but it wasn't friendly either. "I can bring in a female officer if
you'd prefer that."

"No, I would not." I turned to Lucero. "I came here to speak
with you. Get him out of here."

"My hands are tied. It's his case."

Even I had to see the truth in that. Lucero wasn't even a homicide detective.

Lucero must have sensed I was weakening. "Tell us both what

you know and we'll help you. That's everyone's goal here. What could be more important than Rod's safety?"

Nothing, of course. I reluctantly took the seat opposite Handsome. I figured I'd play this out as far as I could without implicating Rod or Bud in anything illegal.

Lucero leaned against the back wall since there was no third chair.

"This interview is being video-recorded," Handsome said. "Do you consent to that?"

I unzipped my jacket. "No."

He scowled and got up. After being gone for a few moments he returned and sat back down. "Will you say and spell your name for me."

He took notes on a laptop while I answered basic questions such as my Social Security number and age. Then he started in on Rod's relationship to Bud, Bud's history of small-time offenses, and what scams or deals Bud might currently be involved with.

Finally I lost my temper. "You haven't asked me a single question about Rod being missing. All you care about is trying to nail my dying uncle with some kind of trumped-up charge."

Handsome turned the laptop so we could all see it. After a few clicks, a piece of grainy video began playing without sound. At first I didn't know what I was looking at. That's when the backhoe burst into view. Glass shattered and wood splintered. Almost as quickly as it appeared, the machine backed up. It only got a few feet before the snarl of debris forced it to stop.

"Is this Pawn Max last night?"

Handsome turned. "You know about that, do you?"

I didn't answer. Instead I watched as two men in black entered through the hole left by the backhoe. They even wore ski masks to hide their faces. One smashed jewelry cases and threw the contents in his bag while the other hurried behind the counter.

Handsome pointed to this second man. "He's taking the records."

He was right. As soon as the man had the binder in his bag, they both left.

Handsome stopped the video. He pointed and clicked a few times and brought up a still image. "This is a blowup of the second man's arm as he reaches under the counter."

A small section of wrist was visible between the man's black sleeve and glove. He appeared to be wearing a watch.

"And?" I said.

Handsome clicked again and zoomed in closer. That's when I realized it wasn't a watch. It was a tattoo of a watch. I'd only ever met one man with that design inked on his wrist. Bud Hawkins.

This was unnerving, but I still managed to say, "I have no idea what I'm looking at. It could be anything."

"It's your uncle, and you know it."

I waved a dismissive hand. "This grainy, blurry image will never hold up in court."

"It won't have to since he's not going to live long enough to be charged with felony burglary."

Lucero pushed off from the wall. "A little respect for her loss."

Handsome gave him a dirty look, but downshifted from mean to merely hostile. "Let's say for the sake of argument that I've identified suspect number two as one Bud Hawkins."

I didn't say anything, but by not denying it, we all knew I was agreeing.

He clicked a box and the original video returned. "My first question has to be, who is suspect number one? Who's helping him?"

Handsome's head turned from the monitor. His eyes stared into mine with an intensity that both challenged and accused.

"It wasn't me." I pointed to the monitor. "That guy is both slower and taller than I am."

Lucero laughed. "That describes the entire male population of Bakersfield."

Handsome ignored the joke. "I know it's not you. I can tell the difference between a man and a woman."

"Glad to know the Sheriff's Department is training you for that. Is there a special remedial class or did they get you a tutor?"

Lucero walked to the table and sat on the edge. "Remember that thing we talked about in the hall. You know, where you say things you shouldn't, and the blah, blah, blah." He smiled, but his height relative to mine felt intimidating. "Maybe try and control that."

I stood. "That was the controlled version."

Handsome followed me up. "Where was your boyfriend last night?"

"In LA. He drove back early yesterday morning." Then I got it and had to laugh. "No way Roddy helped Bud drive a backhoe into a pawnshop. You are so off base."

Handsome didn't let up. "You and your boyfriend are up to your necks in something with your sleazy uncle, and we're not leaving here until you tell me what it is."

Lucero continued his role as good cop. "I understand how you might have felt obligated if your uncle got into trouble and asked for help. Blood is thicker than water and all that."

"Or maybe it was the other way around," Handsome countered. "Maybe you're the one who asked your uncle for help. Is all this some news story that got out of hand?"

"We don't drive construction equipment into buildings." I smiled. "It's not even a ratings period."

"Fine, Lilly," Lucero said. "We're totally off base and chasing our tails."

Handsome didn't like the sound of that, but he managed to stay quiet.

"But you're obviously sitting on a bunch of information. If you're truly worried about Rod, then you need to start sharing. Otherwise this will end badly."

They didn't seem to have any idea about Carter King and Warner's stolen brooches. For a moment I thought about telling them everything, even about Kincaid and the meth.

"I know you sent officers to interview the owner of Pawn Max," I said. "I know she told them Bud was very upset when he saw a certain piece of jewelry in the store." I pointed to the monitor. "I suggest you find out who pawned the brooch and talk to them."

Handsome bristled. "I intend to interview that individual later today."

"Good." I waited for him to add something more, but he only stared at me. "So what are you going to do about Rod?"

"Absolutely nothing." Handsome shook his head. "By your own words, he's only been gone for a few hours and there's no sign of violence at his house."

Lucero tried to intervene. "Maybe we should—"

Handsome cut him off. "You know what I think happened? I think he's gotten sick of being your adorable, half-grown German shepherd puppy and left you."

I turned to Lucero. "Get me out of here right now before you have to arrest me for assaulting an officer."

Handsome protested, but Lucero could tell I was serious. As he walked me back out the maze of corridors, I thought about the video from the pawnshop break-in.

It couldn't have been Rod. Years spent as a wimpy teenager getting picked on for his geeky hobbies had left him with a passion for physical fitness. He rarely skipped his daily trip to the gym. If Rod had been the first man in the video, he would have been notably faster and stronger than Bud.

Which gave me an idea. The two figures had been fairly well matched. Was the second man as old as Bud?

What other friends his own age did Bud have? Mrs. Paik's husband—Bud's loyal comrade through war and fighting fires—had disappeared fifty years ago. Leland Warner was in bed with a heart condition.

That's when I remembered Carter King. He'd have to be roughly Bud's age. Given his history, he'd have no moral scruples about robbing a pawnshop. Had he and Bud partnered to discover who'd pawned the brooch?

Or had they partnered long before that? Was that the nasty truth Rod was attempting to shield me from? Had Bud conspired with Carter King to steal Erabelle's jewelry?

I started the news van and did a U-turn with the intention of returning to Rod's house. I passed a pickup just cranking its engine. I almost slammed on the brakes, but managed to control myself.

I got to the light and made a right over the train tracks. I saw a pair of headlights follow in my rearview mirror. What if Bud's attacker was inside the vehicle, or maybe Carter King? They could be one and the same.

I had to act, but I didn't want to do it alone. For the second time that night, I took Merle Haggard Drive to Rosedale. I drove my news van all the way behind the strip mall and parked next to the van.

Bouncer and his mother were still there doing their illicit work. He heard me and came out the back door. "Why are you back?"

"I don't want to cause you or your mom problems." I glanced down the alley, but didn't see the pickup.

Just in case, I pushed past Bouncer and entered the back room. "Let's talk about this inside. I could use a pair of strong hands to help me with something."

His mom still sat at the table slicing pages out of Bibles. "Don't you have friends to help you?"

"They wouldn't be good for this kind of thing. I need someone strong."

Bouncer puffed up. "What exactly is the problem?"

"I'm being followed. The guy might be dangerous."

I explained what I wanted to do and why I'd need help. Bouncer agreed partly because he liked using his main asset, his muscles, and partly because he would have done anything to ensure I didn't hurt his mom. I also wondered if I was the recipient of a little bit of that chivalry the dancer had mentioned.

Before we left, Bouncer went to get his coat. As soon as we were alone, I asked his mom, "Were you and Carter a couple?"

"For a few months. We covered El Centro, the Salton Sea—all those towns down there at California's butt hole—pretending to be father and daughter."

"Why father and daughter?"

"Partly the age difference, and partly because you sell more Bibles that way. Folks like families when they're buying religious stuff."

Bouncer walked in wearing a leather jacket. "I'm ready if you are."

I stood, but asked her, "Is Carter dangerous?"

"Nah. There was never any meanness in him. Just couldn't stand to be weighed down by anything." She looked at Bouncer, then quickly away. "He thought love meant being stuck to someone with Krazy Glue or something. He didn't want that."

TWENTY-THREE

I drove out west of the city toward Interstate 5. Bouncer rode shotgun with me in the news van. My first instinct was for an immediate and even violent confrontation with the driver of the pickup that had been following me. Fortunately, I'm aware that my first instincts aren't always good. Anxiety over Rod's safety urged me to quick action, but I needed to pick the terrain with care.

The sun would soon be up, but with all the fog, you wouldn't have known it. Consequently, the pickup stayed close. It followed us through a series of house farms where stucco ranchers blossomed in rows like heads of lettuce.

I wondered if Carter King lived in a similar neighborhood. A thief and small-time grifter hidden among the happy families. Would a man like that ever settle down to respectability, even late in life? Bud hadn't. Maybe Erabelle had been the closest he'd ever come to becoming Allan Hawkins instead of good old Bud.

The modern buildings ended and actual farms and orchards began.

I took my eyes off the asphalt in my headlights to glance at Bouncer. "I didn't want to say this in front of your mom, but there's a chance that Carter King is the one following us."

"So?"

"You won't have any hesitation taking him down, will you? I mean, he was a friend of your mom's."

"I get it. You think maybe he's my dad."

I didn't, but maybe I should have.

"The math works out," he continued. "But, you know, either way, he ran out on her. I have no loyalty to the man."

"Hasn't Laurie ever told you who your father is?"

"She said he died in the war and stuff, but I looked it up. There was no war in 1984."

I felt bad, so I said, "Maybe he was in Granada."

"Operation Urgent Fury was in 1983 and only nineteen men died."

I hesitated. "Lebanon?"

"It doesn't matter." His voice lost its indifference. "I figure either he's dead or he's gone, and they both amount to the same thing."

After a moment's silence I said, "My dad's dead."

"Then you know I'm right."

We rode in silence for a few minutes until we reached a suitable orchard. I stopped at a narrow access road cutting into the almond trees. The pickup, now just a pair of tiny headlights in the rearview mirror, slowed too. "You good to go?"

He lifted the roll of duct tape. "Ready whenever you are."

"Why would you even bring that?" I grabbed for it, but his hand jerked it away. "What is it with you and duct tape?"

"It's convenient for tying people up."

"Like you tied me up? By the way, how's your eyebrow? How did that work out for you?"

He struggled, not wanting to admit I was right. Finally he said, "There are two of us. You can rip the tape while I hold him down."

"Whatever."

I turned into the orchard. After driving a short distance I stopped. I jerked the van into park and slammed on the parking brake. My hand wrapped around the bat. The Mace was already in my pocket.

I left the van idling and ran into the trees on my side of the van. Bouncer went the other direction with the duct tape.

The orchard would have been a nightmare of fog and darkness except for a streetlight on the road. I went toward the hazy glow, but froze when I heard an engine. The pickup approached, idled, and backed up. The engine shut off, followed by the headlights. I wanted to go, but forced myself to wait. Then I heard it—the door opening, a long pause, then closing.

I moved. I came through the final trees and hit asphalt. The back end of the pickup peeked at me through the fog. I removed the pepper spray and held it in the air defensively. I still had the bat in my left hand, but I reasoned hitting the wrong person with pepper spray would be better than hitting the person with a bat.

I crept forward, passed the truck, and continued toward the entrance to the dirt access road. The sound of my own van idling reverberated off the trees and the fog, the rumble magnified and distorted.

I reached the break in the trees and stopped. This was where I expected my stalker to be. Why else would he or she have got out of the truck other than to sneak to the access road and spy on my van? But no one was there.

I heard a noise and saw movement directly in front of me. At the last moment I managed to take my finger off the pepper spray's trigger. I had to drop the bat.

"It's me, you idiot." I tried to whisper, but it's hard when someone is holding you off the ground. "Put me down, Bouncer."

"'Bouncer'?" He dropped me. "You don't know my name, do you?"

"Keep your voice down." I tried to get up from where I'd landed. "We can talk about this later."

"I don't believe it." He dropped his voice, if not the subject. "I'm out here risking my neck to help you, and you don't even have the decency to remember my name."

"I never knew it, okay?" I know I should have tried to end the conversation, but a girl's got to defend herself. "You never introduced yourself, so stop acting all judgmental."

"Fine." Bouncer pointed behind me. "I heard somebody get out of the truck. How did we both miss him?"

"I don't know. Maybe he went into the orchard."

I had an idea and looked toward the truck. "Or else he opened the door, saw the fog, and decided not to get out."

Headlights flashed on at the same time as the engine roared to life. Seconds later the pickup barreled forward.

Bouncer tossed me into the trees like a rag doll. He wasn't far behind, but I appreciated my flying head start. We both ended in the dirt on the side of the road just as the truck sped by.

I thought the pickup was long gone, but out of the fog came screeching tires and the sound of an impact.

Bouncer ran straight toward the crash. I found the bat and duct tape in the road, then hurried to catch up.

"I got him," Bouncer yelled. "Hurry, bring the tape."

The pickup driver must have lost control and swerved off the road. The vehicle had plowed through several yards of grapevines only to hit a wood storage shed. In the light from the one still intact headlight, I could see Bouncer holding someone. The man wasn't especially short, but Bouncer was so tall that he easily held him by the back collar.

"Let go of me," the man yelled.

Instead, Bouncer turned him around so I could see his face.

Not Carter King, as I'd hoped. The light was poor, but the red tint of the man's hair was still visible. It was Kincaid, the friendly neighborhood drug-dealing pharmacist.

"Let him go," I said to Bouncer.

He did and Kincaid immediately went to the front of the truck where he'd hit the shed. "The bumper is loose. You know what this is going to cost me?"

"I don't care about your truck," I shouted. "Where's Rod?"

He looked up from tenderly checking the hood for dents. "Who?"

"My boyfriend, Rod. Where is he?"

"How would I know?"

Bouncer practically growled. "Answer the lady's question."

Kincaid flinched and gestured toward Bakersfield. "Isn't he back at that house? The Prius was still parked in the driveway."

"You know he's not there." I raised the bat. Kincaid shrank back. Even Bouncer looked surprised as I brought the wood down on the truck's hood. "Tell me where he is."

Kincaid screamed at the sight of the dent. "How would I know where your boyfriend is? I spent all night following you."

I raised the bat again. "You're lying."

"No." Kincaid jumped between me and the truck. "I swear, I've been following you all night, even up to those crummy mobile homes in the mountains."

I lowered the bat slightly. "Why were you following me?"

He glanced at Bouncer. "Can we talk about this somewhere private?"

"No way," Bouncer answered for me. "You get alone with her, first thing you do is run."

"Please," Kincaid pleaded with me. "Certain aspects of my business require discretion, and we should talk about it privately."

I turned to Bouncer. "He owns a drugstore, but he's selling meth on the side." I looked back at Kincaid. "Now all three of us know, so let's talk. Why were you following me?"

Kincaid looked unhappy, but resigned himself. "I saw you last night out at the King place. I was getting gas and you pulled into the station by the freeway."

I remembered pulling off to check Sally's missing dog flyer. I hadn't seen Kincaid, but since he'd left the farmhouse well before me, the timing worked.

"I got scared," he continued. "You'd been in my store earlier, then I see you near the farm. I figure you're doing some kind of meth exposé or maybe the Kings' sold me out or something." He put his palms together. "Please, I'm begging you to leave me out of your story. I won't survive in prison."

"If you're so scared of getting caught," Bouncer said, "maybe you shouldn't have gotten into this business in the first place."

"I didn't have much choice." Despite the indifferent audience, Kincaid made a valiant play for our sympathy. "You wouldn't believe how tight my margins are at the drugstore. Between paying for a security guard and all the business we've lost to the chains, I'm in the hole every month. It's this or bankruptcy."

I rolled my eyes. "Bankruptcy would be a lot better than dealing drugs."

"I'm not a drug dealer. I've been selling off Sudafed to this guy from one of the biker gangs." Kincaid's gaze shifted to the ground. He seemed reluctant to say the next part. "It's only for a couple people, like Sally, that I've also been acting as a middleman, of sorts."

"You're a drug dealer."

His head shot up. "It's not a regular thing. Just for a couple people. That's why I took such a hit when Sally suddenly couldn't pay."

"Let me guess. She got desperate and offered you a gold brooch in exchange for meth."

He nodded. "I didn't even know it was gold until I got it cleaned up. The entire thing was black and covered in dirt. I only did the trade because I felt sorry for her."

"You're a regular humanitarian," I said. "I'm sure Brandon was thrilled you'd ripped his mother off."

"I didn't rip her off." His indignation rose, crested, then fell. "But, yeah, the kid came to see me. He said the brooch was worth a lot more than what I gave Sally. He wanted it back."

"But you'd already sold it to Pawn Max."

"That's right, but I gave Brandon half of the three thousand I got for it, that's how hard I tried to be decent about it."

I pulled back the bat. "You got five thousand for it, not three."

Kincaid leapt back as the wood hit the already damaged headlight. "Stop hitting my car!" he yelled. "Most people wouldn't have given the kid anything."

"Most people wouldn't have sold drugs." I stepped toward him with the bat raised. "Not to mention how you're making the kid manufacture your meth."

"That was his mom's idea. We agreed I'd stake him some of the ingredients, and he'd make the meth for me. I won't have to deal with the bikers, and he and Sally get some cash."

I wasn't surprised Sally had used her son. Drug addicts use everyone around them until there's no one left. "I'm guessing Sally also gets free meth out of the deal?"

He nodded. "At least this way she won't have to trade her mom's jewelry."

I straightened. "Sally told you the brooch belonged to her mother?"

He nodded. "She said the old lady came through when she asked for help."

I actually believed Kincaid. Maybe that was stupid, but in a weird way it made sense. It also meant I needed to talk with Mida again. Either Carter had given her the jewelry recently because she needed money, or he'd given it to her long ago.

"Okay." I started back toward the road.

"Wait. You can't just leave me out here." Kincaid ran after me. "What about my bumper?"

I stopped.

Bouncer stepped to the front of the truck and evaluated the damage. "I think I can fix it temporarily. Just so you can get home."

"How's that?" he said.

Bouncer pointed to the roll of duct tape still in my hand. "I told you we'd need it."

After dropping Bouncer at his mom's store, I got on the freeway. For the third time in a day I drove north to the Kings' property.

The sun had risen and I could see Warner's electric fence along his side of the road. Still, the haze was coming on fast, and an honest-to-goodness tule fog was almost a certainty now. Children in Bakersfield would wake up to stockings on the mantel, toys under the tree, and severely reduced visibility.

I continued on the public road and found the paved driveway leading to the mobile homes. After a quick U-turn I doubled back and parked behind the same transformer I'd used to hide the news van when Leanore had been with me.

Just as before, I set off on foot. I was lucky. The mist was thinner here and the Christmas lights Sally had strung so obsessively guided me like a beacon. I reached the back side of Mida's mobile home and gazed reluctantly up at the still open bathroom window. The room looked dark, but a soft sound could be heard from the interior.

I pulled myself up—not fun—and climbed in headfirst again. That's when I recognized the sound: moaning.

"Mida?" I jumped up and hurried into the hallway. "Mida, can you hear me? Are you hurt?"

Her fragile voice called from the bedroom, "Help me."

TWENTY-FOUR

I hurried into the dark bedroom. The smell drew a gag from deep in my throat. I held my breath while groping for a light switch, but knew I'd have to breathe eventually. I shouldn't have worried about it. What I saw when the light came on made me forget the smell.

Mida was on the floor next to the bed. Her housecoat, the same one she'd been wearing earlier, had torn, and the fabric now rode up in a tangle over her head and arms. Her body was exposed. She'd soiled the bed, the floor, and herself. Muted sobs came from under the confusion of fabric covering her face.

I should have felt more for Mida, but the shock of seeing my first naked, elderly body momentarily diverted all other thought. Popular culture hadn't prepared me for the reality of breasts sagging to a woman's waist or skin covered in spots, gouges, scars, and plain old weird discolorations.

I snapped out of it and knelt at her side. "Are you hurt? Is anything broken?"

"Help me," she cried.

"I can't until I know if anything might be broken." I tried to gently lower the fabric and free her head.

She saw me and recoiled. "Who are you? Where's my mother?"

"I need to know where you're hurt."

She turned her head back to the floor and wept. "I'm so cold."

With the bathroom window left open, the entire trailer was freezing. I shut the window, turned up the heat, and found a clean blanket, which provided both warmth and modesty.

Mida had been lucky when she fell and hadn't broken anything.

Of course she'd need to follow up with a doctor, but there were no obvious problems other than a cut on her leg.

I found a fully stocked first-aid kit in the bathroom—probably left over from better times when Mida still had an aide. I cleaned the cut and taped a bandage over it. Her legs were thick and swollen. I didn't know what that meant, but it probably wasn't healthy.

I found a pair of heavy rubber gloves, sanitary wipes, and other cleaning items in a hall closet. Mida's bedding was filthy, not just from her recent accident, but from other accidents on other nights. I left it all in a pile in the living room. While I put on fresh sheets, Mida went into the bathroom. She'd wanted to do the more intimate cleaning herself, which I was grateful for.

I heard her coming and called out, "Mida, I'm in your bedroom. I'm the lady who's helping you after your fall."

I'd feared that she'd forget I was there and start screaming when she saw me, but I needn't have worried. Mida accepted me without question.

"Thank you so much, dear. I don't know what I'd do without you."

I finished tucking the sheet in. "I need to ask you a couple questions, if that's okay?"

"I'm sorry, dear." Her hand went to her head. "I'm so sleepy."

I remembered overhearing Sally and Brandon's argument. "You took some cough medicine."

"Why would I do that?"

"I think your daughter gave it to you."

"But Sally's a little girl." She stared at me, waiting for an explanation.

I swallowed. "No, she's not."

Mida hesitated. This indicated that at least some part of her knew it was true. "I don't . . . How old is Sally?"

"Fifty, maybe."

Terror sprung to Mida's face. "How old am I?"

"I don't know." I pulled the clean sheet and blanket back. "Why don't you get into bed?"

She did and I covered her with the blanket. It only took moments for her to forget our conversation about Sally's age, but judging from her agitation, the pain and upset remained.

I reasoned that if someone had punched me, and I immediately forgot it had happened, I'd still have the ache and bruising where the blow had made contact, I just wouldn't know why.

After I'd got her a requested glass of water, I sat down on the bed. "I know you want to get some sleep, but I need to ask you a few questions."

"What about?"

"Did you give Sally some jewelry?"

"Maybe." Her eyes wandered around the room looking for a clue that would fill in the blanks of her memory. "I don't think I have very much. Just some pearls and things."

I shook my head. "I'm talking about two brooches. They were Russian military medals. One of them had diamonds."

She turned quickly to me and her eyes thinned. "I don't know anything about that."

"I'm describing the jewelry your brother stole."

"I don't know about that," she said with more passion.

Was she lying or unable to remember, and how would I know the difference?

I decided to try more recent history. "Sally fired your aide because there was no more money. Did you give her the jewelry so you could have an aide again?"

"You're lying." She started to sit up. "There's plenty of money. Cousin Leland always takes care of me."

"It's okay." I tried to get her to lie back down. "You can trust me. I'm Bud Hawkins's niece."

"If that were true, then you'd already know." She lay back in bed and covered her head with the blanket. "Go away. You're the reason I'm having so much trouble."

"Mida, please," I said, but she refused to answer or come out from under the blanket.

I retrieved the rest of the cleaning supplies and went to work on the floor where she'd fallen. Soon she dropped into a rhythm of deeper breaths and even a few snores.

There was no way around it. I would have to call social services when they opened on Monday. I felt bad for Brandon. I hated the way Sally and Kincaid had forced him into making the meth. If those activities were discovered because I'd called the authorities about Mida, he'd get a long prison sentence.

Ironically, Sally as a user instead of a manufacturer would get a much lighter sentence. But the word *user* seemed a good description of her. She'd fed off her mother's money and indulgences her entire life. Now she was feeding off her son. If she'd been forced to stand on her own and get a job, would she still have fallen into addiction?

The floor was close to being finished when I heard a car. I almost jumped out the bathroom window and ran for it, but without Mida's screaming for help like before, I reasoned I was safe.

The car stopped between the two mobile homes. I peeked out the living-room blinds and saw a black SUV like the one Erabelle had been driving earlier. A man got out and removed something from the backseat.

The door to the other mobile home burst open. Sally, in pajamas and a robe, ran to the man. I didn't hear words, but her joyful squeals and giggles sounded as innocent as a little girl's on Christmas morning.

The man said something and turned to hand her a bulky object. It was Frank, Warner's head of security. I recognized the object as a turkey—fresh not frozen, judging by how giddy it made Sally. After a few more words between them, Sally pointed to where the paved driveway ended and the dirt road began. Frank got back in the SUV and drove into the interior of the property.

Only one thing was at the end of that road: the farmhouse.

What would Frank need to see Brandon about? A bribe? Were they buying the Kings off the way they'd tried to buy me? More important, did this have something to do with Rod's absence?

"Crud." I doubled back through the house. I grabbed the cleaning supplies and threw them in the closet. I left the dirty linens in the pile in the living room and climbed back out the bathroom window. I tried to run to my van, but the fog had got worse. I had to head for the highway and then follow that to the transformer.

Once inside, I started the news van and drove as fast as I dared. I knew the relative distance and tracked it on my odometer. The first time by, I missed the Mountain Dew bottle I'd left by the side of the road. I pulled a U-turn—dangerous in the fog—and found it on my second pass.

I zeroed the odometer and entered the property. The trail of flattened weeds again led my way, but visibility was down to several feet. I crept along at a snail's pace. When I'd gone a quarter mile, I stopped.

If my calculations were correct, the trees on the ridge above the farmhouse were just ahead. I couldn't risk driving any closer and plummeting over the edge. I reached into the back to grab Bouncer's duct tape.

There was movement under the tarp again. "Thing!" I couldn't even remember when he might have stowed away, but there was no denying the dog liked me.

"I don't have time for you right now," I called into the back. "You should have gone with Freddy to the TV station." The dog's playful movements continued under the tarp. He was almost as stubborn as I was.

I got out and secured the tape to the front of the van. I took one last moment to orient myself before following the crushed weeds on foot. With each step I let out more tape. I reached the end of the roll, but still hadn't found the ridge.

I glanced back into the fog. If I let go of the tape, I might not be able to find my way back. Visibility was nonexistent. I could be inches from the van and not know it.

Even more discouraging, I couldn't hear Brandon's heavy-metal music. What if I was nowhere near the farmhouse? What if I'd made a wrong turn and was lost somewhere on the Kings' barren land? And how long had it taken just to reach this spot? Frank had probably completed his business and was already gone.

I tightened my grip on the cardboard circle. It had previously been the duct tape's hidden core, but now the last of that flat, silver material ran off the end and disappeared into thin air. This was my lifeline. I had come far for Bud and for myself, but it was time to go back.

Instead, I let go. What if Rod was in trouble? I'd never forgive myself if something happened to him.

Three steps. Four. Ten. Twenty. Then I heard it—an engine running. I tried to identify where it came from, but the fog bounced the sound as if it were a rubber ball let loose in a box.

Nothing to do but go forward. Five more steps. Ten. Then I saw it. A tree trunk to my right. I rushed to it like an oasis in a desert.

Unlike the last time I'd looked down the ridge, a car was parked in front of the house. I could hear the engine and make out the dark outline of the vehicle as the fog shifted.

Other sounds emerged from under the engine's mechanical rumbling. Sharp, quick stabs followed by shuffling clumps. Digging? Why would anyone be digging in this remote spot?

A grave? Fear gripped me. Was it possible that they'd actually killed Rod? Had Frank been dispatched to hide the body?

I felt my way down the hill as quietly as possible. At least twice I slipped. The second time I made noise grasping for weeds to steady myself.

The sound of digging stopped. "Hello?" It was Frank's voice.

I froze. My chest heaved from exertion, but I tried to quiet my breathing.

"Hello?" he said louder. "Who's there?"

I heard a door open. "Are you calling me?" Brandon must have come out the farmhouse's front door. "Is everything okay?"

"I heard something," Frank said. "But it was probably just an animal."

"There are a lot of those out here." Steps on the porch. "I'd come out and take a look with you, but I'm in the middle of some delicate work."

The digging sounds resumed. "The less I know about what you're doing in there, the better, kid."

Frank actually had the gall to sound judgmental. Frank! The man who'd kidnapped me last year and who'd made an entire career out of breaking laws for Leland Warner.

If Frank's hypocrisy had tweaked Brandon's pride, he didn't let on. "How much longer?"

"I'm almost done. The digging was much easier than I thought."

"My mom dug that entire area up a couple weeks ago to get the jewelry. The dirt was probably still soft."

Kincaid had said that the gold brooch was black and filthy when Sally traded it for meth. Mida must have told her it was buried out at the farmhouse. Had the diamond star been buried with it?

"Whatever the reason, I'm thankful." Frank paused to grunt as he exerted himself. "I'm not as young as I used to be."

Brandon laughed. "Neither am I, and I'm only twenty-two."

If Carter King had buried the jewelry before fleeing town, and Mida had known about it, why hadn't either of them dug it up and sold the brooches before now?

I heard footsteps back across the porch and then the door closed.

Frank continued to dig. The breeze shifted blocks of fog, revealing short glimpses of Frank's black SUV with its headlights on. I guessed Frank had parked so he could work in the headlights, hoping they might help with the fog.

After waiting in silence for a few moments, I finished coming down the slope. I paused, but Frank gave no indication that he'd heard me.

I crept toward what I hoped was the vehicle. If Rod was inside, I had to know. It might not be the worst. I might still be able to help him.

All at once the digging stopped. Some muffled, smoothing sounds were followed by footsteps. "Hey, kid?" Frank called.

I froze in place as Frank crossed in front of me.

"Hey, kid?" he repeated louder.

The farmhouse's front door opened and Brandon said, "I'm here."

"All done." I heard Frank opening the hatch at the rear of the SUV and the shovel falling inside with a thud. "I've got the first half of your money. You want to count it inside where you can see better?"

Brandon's voice sounded unsure. "I don't . . . Do I need to count it?"

"You don't need to, but you should." Frank moved toward the house. "You should always count money."

"Careful not to trip," Brandon said. "There are steps up to the porch."

I reached out and continued forward. My hand touched metal. I followed Frank's black SUV to the rear. The hatch was open.

I heard footsteps on the porch's old wood planks. "Here it is. Mr. Warner says you get the second half when you produce the diamond brooch."

"I'd give it to you now," Brandon said, "but it's not here at the farmhouse and I can't go get it until I finish this work I'm doing."

The two men went in the house, but the door stayed open.

I stood and looked into the rear of the SUV. Black plastic sheeting covered the cargo area. I slowly lifted an end.

Frank hadn't been burying a body, he'd been digging one up.

TWENTY-FIVE

Pieces of rotted black cloth covered the decayed figure, which had become little more than bones. Without a degree in forensic science I couldn't say how long it had been underground, but it would have to have been decades.

I looked up and out the windshield. Through the fog I saw that the rope of the swing had been severed and the tire tossed to the side.

Someone had been buried here for all these years with the brooches. There's no statute of limitations on murder. If this person had been killed, it was still prosecutable today.

Did Bud know about the body's and jewelry's being here? Is that why he was so upset when he saw the gold brooch in the pawnshop—because it meant someone had found the body too? And what about Rod?

I climbed inside, careful not to disturb the gruesome cargo, and looked into the backseat. It was empty except for the shovel and a few folded blankets.

"I'll be back later today to exchange the rest of the money for the diamond brooch." Frank had exited the house and crossed the porch.

I made a split-second decision and climbed into the backseat. I grabbed a blanket from the seat and covered myself on the floor of the car.

"Thank you," Brandon said. "But make sure you call my cell before coming over."

"I have no desire to overlap with your other business." Frank slammed the rear hatch shut, then got in and backed the SUV up.

Frank drove slowly because of the fog, but after a time the feel of the road changed. The ride abruptly smoothed out and I guessed we'd switched from dirt road to asphalt. Frank didn't stop this time to speak with Sally at the mobile homes.

I expected him to drive down the public road to the freeway, but after only a few minutes he slowed and turned left. We were driving into the refinery. The car stopped at what had to be the gate. I heard a window roll down.

"Sir, just let me call ahead to Mr. Warner." This was a young voice, probably a guard at the entrance. "He specifically said he was expecting you in twenty minutes."

"I don't want to wait here. Just call and warn him I'm coming."

"Yes, sir."

I heard smooth-running and well-maintained machinery doing what it was designed to do—unlike the gate at KJAY, which creaked and groaned as it opened.

Frank started the car moving again. We drove for a long time. Even with the fog forcing Frank to go slowly, we covered quite a distance. I was surprised. I knew the property stretched for miles and miles—all the way up to the mansion on the bluffs—but I didn't think Warner or his people would use the oil field as a cut-through.

I used the time to think about who might have been buried at the farmhouse. If the body and jewelry had been buried together, then the John/Jane Doe had probably died around the time of the theft. In this entire sorry tale, I'd only heard of one disappearance: Mrs. Paik's first husband. Bud's army buddy and fellow smoke jumper had returned from Alaska only to abandon his wife. Maybe he hadn't done it voluntarily.

Finally Frank slowed the car even more and then stopped. He cut the engine and got out.

"You're twenty minutes early," a man yelled. "I wasn't ready for you."

"I'm sorry, sir." Frank used the submissive tone reserved for male members of the Warner family. "The digging went much faster than I thought."

"Do you know how I had to scramble after the gate called and said you were on your way?" It was Warner's son. I hadn't recognized Junior at first because his angry voice was so much sharper. "I almost didn't get the security cameras off-line in time."

"I'm sorry, sir. I didn't want to linger at the gate where someone might have seen into the back of my SUV."

"If you'd concealed your cargo properly, then that wouldn't have been a problem." I heard footsteps and then the rear hatch opening. "You idiot, it's barely covered."

"I'm sorry, sir. I thought I'd done a better job. It must have gotten jostled on the ride over."

"Don't make excuses." Junior began walking away. "And don't stand there. Let's look at the well so we can get this over with."

"This one should suit our needs, sir." Frank's voice began to recede. "The crew was pulled off because of an emergency H_2S release. Whatever we drop down the casing will land two thousand feet down and eventually be covered in fracking fluid."

I withdrew the iPhone from my jacket pocket, but saw no bars. I opened the camera app and slowly sat up. We were parked next to a huge pipe running slightly off the ground. The fog blocked everything else, but judging from the sound, we were close to several working oil wells.

I leaned over the backseat with the phone. I removed the tarp and took several still photos. When that had been documented, I removed what I could of the rotting fabric to expose the actual body. It looked to my untrained eye as if the skull had been smashed in. I panned down and stopped. That's when I saw it. The bottom right leg was bent back in a deformed arc. This hadn't happened postmortem.

The realization hit me the way most of mine do: fast, hard, and later than it should have. Carter King had polio as a child and walked with a limp. He'd also been dead for over fifty years.

But how was it even possible? Carter King had sent letters to his sister. He'd engaged in a multitude of shady and illegal schemes. He'd gotten arrested in 1984 and been seen later in Bakersfield by Bouncer's mother.

He could have sold sunscreen to a crocodile with that smile.

That was the perfect description of Bud. Could the man Kelvin Hoyt had pursued for the Bakersfield PD and the man who'd been Laurie Bogdanich's lover been my uncle?

Everyone had lied. Mida, Warner, and Bud had all conspired together. How many times did Bud leave Bakersfield to work a shady scheme using Carter King's name? All to maintain the myth that Carter was alive, when in reality he was dead and buried a few yards from the house he'd grown up in.

I heard voices and returned to my hiding place.

I didn't catch the entire conversation, but clearly Junior was still berating Frank. ". . . satisfactory, but there's more to your job than simple discretion. For what you're getting paid, I expect greater attention to detail."

"Yes, sir." I heard the plastic sheeting jostle. "Ready, sir?"

"Yes." Junior managed to make even that simple affirmation sound like an insult. "Try not to be clumsy, if that's even possible for you."

I heard the plastic crinkle as it and the body were lifted and removed from the cargo area. Their awkward, shuffly footsteps receded around the SUV. I crept out of the back and stepped down into the dirt. I opened the phone's video-camera app and stalked them in the fog. I wanted video of Frank and Junior with the body, but with limited memory I had to be careful when I began recording.

They passed a small pumpjack sucking black gold from the gritty earth. My father, who'd worked for most of his adult life in Kern County's oil fields, called these "thirsty birds" after the toy with the bobbing head. This pumpjack was slightly larger than an SUV. Its constant rhythm of ticking, thumps, and spinning belts was filled out by the faint noise of other pumps somewhere in the fog.

The dark outlines of machinery emerged in the white haze. I caught up with Frank and Junior as they navigated around the massive equipment to where a new well had been drilled.

"Keep your end level." Junior was actually the one holding his end askew, but either egotism or delusion prevented him from realizing it. "Do you know what happens if you drop it here?"

"I clean it up, sir."

Had Frank just mouthed off? I started recording.

"What did you just say?"

"The literal truth, sir. I will clean up the mess because that is what I have always done for your father." Frank didn't raise his voice. He spoke with affability and even friendliness, but I knew from experience to be wary.

Junior didn't. "Your posturing doesn't impress me. We both know you're a glorified guard dog."

I was dangerously close to them, but had to be for the phone to pick up their audio. I stayed low and close to the machinery, hoping they wouldn't notice me in the fog.

"It's not posturing, sir." Frank stopped and they both set the body down on the ground near the well opening. "Over the years Mr. Warner has trusted me with quite a few delicate tasks."

Joy flooded my soul. He'd named Warner on video! But it was about to get even better.

Junior gestured to the plastic sheeting. "Like getting rid of bodies?"

"This is the first one, sir. And you asked me to do it, not him."

That's when the phone ran out of memory. As the app closed, the screen flashed. The light must have reflected off the water particles in the air because it was as if a camera flash had gone off.

Frank saw me.

Junior quickly turned. "Who's there?"

"It's Lilly Hawkins." Frank stayed still. "I think she was recording us."

"What?" Junior paused, and when he next spoke, it was in a very different tone of voice. "Lilly, aren't we friends? Why would you trespass and make illegal recordings?"

I didn't say anything. I was checking in vain for a cell signal.

"I would have thought ten million dollars would buy a little more loyalty from you." When I still didn't reply, Junior took a step forward and extended his hand. "Bring the camera here or else you don't get the money."

"It's not a camera, it's a cell phone," I said. "And it's too late. I already e-mailed the video to the station."

"Are you out of your mind?" Junior turned to Frank. "Make her get it back. We're both implicated."

The desperation in Junior's voice erased all his previous criticisms and carping. He was counting on Frank to make the problem go away, just as his father had for so many years.

"Don't worry, sir." Frank returned to his deferential tone. "She didn't e-mail anything. There's no reception here."

I turned and ran.

Frank called after me, "Good luck getting out the electric fence."

He was right. There was nowhere to go, but I ran anyway. I figured best-case scenario if they caught me, I'd lose the video. Worst-case scenario? Considering that I had Leland Phillip Warner II on video disposing of a body and talking about his father's involvement . . . Let's just say I didn't want to end up down that well with Carter King.

I ran the opposite direction from Frank's SUV. I glanced behind me to see if I was being followed. When I turned back, a wall jumped out of the fog. I hit the side of the storage tank and fell. I heard footsteps coming and jumped up. I hurried around the side of the massive structure, but the footsteps continued.

"Lilly, you're behaving very badly." It was Junior. Had Frank stayed to finish with the body or was he circling around from the other side? "Give me that video or, so help me, I will not be responsible for what happens to you."

I cut away toward a light on an electric pole, but stopped short at a set of aboveground pipes. I had no choice but to turn and follow them. The pumping and wheezing got louder. Soon I'd reached a working pumpjack and the noise eclipsed all other sound.

I stopped to try to guess my location. Frank had driven a long time. Despite the fog, I would have expected to see something of the refinery if it was nearby. That meant we'd come over the hill, which was bad since the refinery was probably my only chance at finding another human being out here.

No cell reception, an electric fence that ran for miles, and no people to appeal to for help. I had a crazy thought and wondered what Bud would do.

Without warning, hands grabbed me. The deafening noise of the pumpjack masked the intimate sounds of our struggle. Instinct told me I was in serious trouble. These hands weren't strong and sure of themselves like Bouncer's. They gripped me in desperation. They scratched, pulled hair, and ripped.

I got a good hit in with my elbow and tried to stumble away into the fog. He followed and tackled me. I managed to roll over onto my back, but wasn't fast enough to get up.

It was Junior, not Frank. I saw him now as he loomed over me and grabbed the front of my shirt. Behind him the thirsty bird bobbed up and down as Junior raised his hand in a wide arc. I tried to kick, but he straddled me. The back of his hand came down with all the power in his shoulder. I heard the internal sounds of flesh tearing as his ring cut a line across my face.

Tears flowed involuntarily from my eyes. Junior dropped my collar and my head lolled back into the dirt. He began searching my overstuffed jacket pockets, pulling out mic cables, antacids, and random batteries. The phone was in the back pocket of my jeans, but he didn't know that.

Through my blurred vision I saw him toss the van keys into the dirt. Despite the pain, I raised a hand to my face. I had no idea how much of the liquid there was blood and how much tears, but I managed to wipe my eyes clear.

My hand darted to the keys. Before Junior even realized what was happening, my fist sailed at him. The metal tip of the news-van key penetrated his designer leather jacket and stabbed his abs.

Junior's scream rose above the din of the pumpjack. He clutched his stomach and fell off me into the dirt.

I ran.

TWENTY-SIX

The oil field was a maze. There were no paved roads to follow. I'd find what seemed to be a path only to run into a giant storage tank or a working oil well. Aboveground pipes connected everything and turned in unexpected directions at unexpected times. Some of these conduits reached as tall as me and others I could easily leap over.

I had one thought: keep following the downward slope of the land. It would lead me to the river, then the bluffs, and finally—if I could climb in the fog—to Warner's mansion, where there was cell reception. An observer might have called this running to trouble, but anything was better than turning around and facing Junior again. Also, if I could e-mail the video back to KJAY, there'd be no reason to hurt me.

After what felt like forever, but was probably twenty minutes, the electric poles ended and an increase in vegetation began. Judging by the lack of machinery noise, the pumpjacks had ended too. When I reached an actual tree, I knew I was close to the river.

I remembered looking down from Warner's mansion and seeing a bridge just below. The Kern River is largely diverted for the irrigation of crops, but at times it flows with treacherous volume. I had no desire to wade across when I was already hurt and exhausted. I followed the river and found the bridge a few minutes later.

I tried one last time for a cell signal before attempting to cross. As I held the phone in the air, I recognized Warner's mansion above. The fog was clearing, but enough remained to blur the structure's edges, as though the house had a bad aura.

I lowered the phone. No cell signal. I had no choice but to go across and climb.

The old wooden planks jostled as I put my weight on them, but were far more secure than the railing. That construction of decaying wood looked as if it would collapse if I even touched it. I wondered if the bridge dated back to when all this had been orange groves. Maybe Erabelle had crossed it as a girl when she herself had climbed the bluffs to look out at her father's land.

A pair of headlights erupted in the fog ahead of me. I heard a car door open. "Okay, Lilly." It was Frank's voice. "You've made a good effort, but fun's over. Give us the camera."

"Are you tired, old man?" I had no reason to think Frank was touchy about being in the twilight of middle age, but when everything is said and done, who isn't? "Because I can do this all day."

He slammed the car door and his form emerged from the fog. "I want that video. I'd prefer things stayed polite, but if I have to hurt you, I will."

I held up the phone. "Come and get it."

He marched forward with brisk steps, as I hoped he would. Once on the bridge, he slowed—wary of the loose planks and suspicious of my not running from him.

He stopped two yards from me and pointed down at a gaping hole. "Did you really think I wouldn't see?" He cautiously stepped to the side and around the missing planks. "If that's your idea of a trap, then you'll never get that boyfriend of yours to marry you."

I charged at him with both palms out. He crashed into the decayed-wood railing and tumbled over the side. Half a second later I heard a splash followed by obscenities.

I ran forward toward the car. Just as I hit dirt, the passenger's-side door opened. I sprinted for the bluff. I glanced over my shoulder and got a glimpse of Junior charging.

I scrambled up the hillside. A quarter of the way to the top, the rise became too steep and I had to move laterally. I found a trench where two sections of earth came together in a V and resumed my upward climb. I grabbed handfuls of scrub brush to propel myself forward.

Near the top I glanced back. The fog had thinned as I climbed, so I had no trouble seeing Junior right behind me. A red stain marred his shirt where I'd stabbed him with the key, but that hardly slowed his progress.

I reached the top and kept moving just to stay ahead. I plowed forward despite that the brush reached nearly to my waist. I wasn't far from the house and instinctively ran in that direction. I hoped there'd be safety in other people, even if they all worked for the man chasing me.

As I ran, I held the phone up waiting for a signal. I must have slowed to look at the screen. I heard Junior at the last moment. He jumped on me like a junior-varsity high school football player—graceless, hard, and desperate to prove himself. We both fell into the brush, but he had the advantage of being on top.

Junior drew his fist back, deciding this time to hit me with a punch instead of a slap. At the last moment I kicked up with my knee and knocked him off course. His fist hit the ground next to my head. A rock must have been there because Junior howled in pain.

I kicked him hard in the gut to free myself, then rushed to find the phone in the weeds. Already his cries were drawing people. I heard a noise alerting me to a text message and leapt toward the sound. I found the phone and accessed the two video files.

"Wait," Junior yelled. He slouched, clutching his wrist in agony. "What do you want? Money? A job? Just say what you want."

In my peripheral vision, guards approached with their Tasers out. "What I want is to send the video."

"If you do that, your uncle will be exposed as a murderer."

I paused and looked up.

The morning sun cast Junior in a beautiful golden light. Surrounded as he was by fallow winter grasses, the entire scene might have looked pastoral, except for what lay behind him. The fog below us was still thick enough to obscure the uglier aspects of the view, but I knew the oil field was there.

I prepared to send the e-mail. "You're lying."

"No, he's not."

For a moment I was so shocked that I didn't move. Then I spun around to find the source of the voice.

Rod sucked in quick breaths from running. "I don't know exactly what video you have, but don't send it until we've had a chance to talk." All at once he drew back in alarm. "What happened to you?"

"What happened to me?" I ran to him, the video momentarily forgotten. "What happened to you? I thought someone kidnapped you or worse."

I threw my arms around him, but he pulled back to look at my face. "How did you get this horrible cut? It's bleeding. You're going to need stitches."

I pointed at Junior. "Leland Phillip Warner, the second."

Rod stiffened, then rushed toward him.

"No. No, it's okay." I ran after Rod and grabbed his arm. "You can't beat him up. His hand is broken. It's not a fair fight."

This was probably the only argument that could have stopped Rod. Fortunately it succeeded. I say fortunately not because I cared if Junior was further injured, but because the security guards looked ready to use those Tasers if Rod had continued.

"Why don't we go inside and discuss this." Erabelle's petite form climbed through the field toward us. She wore the same clothes as at Zingo's, but the morning's soft light made her look both younger and fresher than at the truck stop.

I gestured to the guards. "If I decline the invitation, am I going to get tased?"

She waved them off. "Go back to your posts. This lady is our guest."

They looked at Junior for confirmation. Apparently Frank's male bias had been passed down through the ranks.

After a moment Junior nodded. "Go back to your posts."

One of the guards hesitated. "Sir, are you injured?"

Instead of being grateful to the only individual who cared about his well-being, Junior got angry at the guard. "I said get back to your post."

Once they'd retreated out of earshot, Erabelle walked to Rod's side. "Frank called. Lilly has video of the body. You're going to have to tell her the truth."

"That's right," Junior sneered. "Tell her that her uncle is a murderer."

There was a long pause. Rod and Erabelle exchanged a glance, but neither looked at me.

"Rod?" I said quietly.

"Gone mute, have you?" Junior wiped some of the sweat from his forehead with his good arm. "Where's all that macho courage now?"

Rod stepped toward him. "I'm starting not to care if it's a fair fight."

Erabelle intercepted him. "This is stupid and it's getting us nowhere."

While this went on, I took a deep breath and slowly exhaled. I'd been saying all night that I could learn the worst about Bud and it wouldn't change how I felt. Now the moment was really here. I turned it over and looked inside the ugly truth.

Bud had committed a murder. Bud was responsible for taking another human's life. Bud hadn't meant it to happen. Bud would be sorry. Bud would have a good reason. Bud loved me.

I looked at Erabelle. She probably expected me to ask about Bud, but instead I said, "Is Frank okay?"

"Just a little wet." Erabelle tried to smile, but couldn't pull it off. "I told him to find your car and bring it here." She turned and started toward the house. "Come inside. We're probably all going to get Lyme disease from the ticks out here."

Rod put his arm around me and we followed.

"What are you doing here with them?" I said.

"I'm keeping a promise to Bud."

"A promise you couldn't tell me about?"

He didn't say anything, so I called ahead to Erabelle, "I want to see Warner."

She glanced back. "I don't think the nurses will allow it."

Junior tried to assert himself, despite trailing behind as the wounded gazelle of our pack. "Never mind the nurses. *I* won't allow it."

"It wasn't a request. I'm hearing the truth from Leland Warner or I'm sending the video to KJAY." I looked at Rod. "I want you there too. It's time I heard the truth from both of you."

Junior continued to argue with me, but it was only for show. With Rod and Erabelle there, he couldn't use physical force to take the phone. Without that threat he had no leverage.

Once inside the house we had to do battle with the nurses. We were losing until I heard Warner himself bellowing that he'd see us even if it meant getting out of bed. They relented, but demanded some time to prepare him.

We all retreated to what someone called the upstairs sitting room to drink coffee—yes, I felt that lousy—and hold ice packs to our injuries. Soon there was a knock on the door, but it wasn't a nurse.

Frank entered looking damp and annoyed. Given his talent for hiding menace behind an affable façade, I assumed his looking annoyed was akin to another person's being in a blind rage.

"Sorry I pushed you." I was a little afraid of him and hoped apologizing might prevent a future retaliation.

He smiled. "Was it something I said?"

Erabelle poured Frank a mug of coffee, but didn't invite him to sit. "Why don't you change into a fresh uniform? Then I believe you'll be needed to drive my nephew to get an X-ray of his hand."

All eyes turned to Junior. "Perhaps after we've spoken with Dad."

Frank took the coffee and started to exit.

On his way out, Erabelle stopped him. "Did you take care of everything at the King farm?"

Frank glanced at me, debating how much to say.

Junior cut in, "We can speak freely in front of Lilly now. She's in this as much as we are. More, since her uncle is the one who killed that man."

Even though I'd accepted this as probably true, I still felt defensive. "Then why exactly were you the one disposing of the body?"

"I was protecting my father. He helped cover up the murder and could still be charged as an accessory after the fact."

Junior's candor clearly went against Frank's instincts, but he was used to following orders. "The body is gone for good. Even if the Kings change their minds and decide to make trouble, there won't be any proof."

Erabelle nodded. "And the jewelry?"

Junior spoke for Frank. "The gold brooch was sold to a pawnshop and is already lost, but we can still get the diamond star back. I made a deal with the grandson. We'll have it later today."

As soon as Frank left, I said, "Things would have been much easier if you'd been honest with me yesterday."

This prompted sneers from Junior and declarations of ignorance from Erabelle. The way they told it, neither had known anything when I'd first come to the house. Not until I'd called and mentioned Mida and Carter King had Junior got worried.

He'd assumed the monthly payout, which he'd stopped, was an act of charity to an old family friend. Once I told him about the robbery, he wondered if it was blackmail. He and Erabelle confronted Warner. Leland, to no one's surprise, had refused to discuss it.

Then Rod had called on instructions from Bud and changed everything. The news that Erabelle's brooch had been pawned frightened Warner into being honest. Everyone, including Rod, had agreed that swift action was needed to destroy the body and pay off the Kings. Otherwise the murder might be exposed.

We were interrupted at this point by another knock on the door. Warner was ready to see us. I started to follow Rod and Junior out into the hallway.

Erabelle stayed sitting.

"Aren't you coming?" I said.

"No." She began picking up mugs and placing them on a silver tray. "I'm never going to see my brother again."

"You made it clear yesterday that you didn't like him. Why take a stand now?"

"Certain facts came to light last night." She gestured in the direction of Leland's room. "You'll hear for yourself."

I caught up with Rod and Junior in the hallway.

The nurse stood holding the doorknob. "He's weak and shouldn't have too much stimulation. Don't discuss anything controversial or alarming."

I smiled. "Wouldn't dream of it."

TWENTY-SEVEN

Christmas Day, 10:31 a.m.

The nurse shut the door behind us. Unfortunately the second nurse remained in the bedroom.

Leland Warner ran his eyes over our bruised and bloody trio. "I take it things did not go well."

I walked to the edge of the bed. "We need to speak privately."

"What on earth happened to your face? You need stitches." He pointed to the nurse. "Get an ice pack for her immediately."

Rod stepped to the other side of the bed. "Your son and that henchman tried to kill her. Considering she's the main reason Bud wanted this mess kept secret, I don't think he would have approved."

Warner turned to the nurse. "Never mind about the ice pack. Just get out."

"But, sir, the doctor—"

"Get out," he roared.

She obeyed. Warner took a moment to calm his breathing.

Junior took advantage to try to tell his side of the story. "She recorded video of me with the body. What was I supposed to do? Let her put it on TV?"

Rod looked ready to fight again. "There were other ways to handle it."

"The thing is, I got a good look at his expression just before he did this to my face. Your son enjoyed it." I stayed looking at Warner, but hooked my thumb back toward Junior. "How many of his ex-girlfriends have you had to pay off to keep them from pressing charges?"

I could tell by Warner's expression and Junior's sudden silence that I'd guessed correctly about his history of violence.

Warner looked past me to his son. "You're bleeding. Go get some medical attention. I'll handle this."

"She still has the video. I'm not leaving until I know it's been erased."

Warner didn't raise his voice, but maybe real power means you don't have to. "Don't talk back to me. I'll handle it."

Junior walked toward the door. "Remember, I was out there cleaning up your mess."

Warner waited until his son was gone and the door had closed. "Do you still have this video you shot of my son?"

I nodded.

"Is it very incriminating?"

"Yes."

"Destroy it."

"I want the truth first." I looked from him to Rod. "Was that Carter King's body and did Bud kill him?"

Warner paused to suck some oxygen through the tube in his nose. "Yes to both."

I waited for Rod's answer.

"Yes."

Maybe I don't have the best judgment when it comes to reading people, but they both looked genuine to me. "Then who shot Bud yesterday?"

Warner shook his head. "I have no idea."

Rod also shook his head. "He was conscious when I found him, but he didn't say anything about his attacker."

My voice rose. "How exactly did he forget to mention *that*?"

"He was hurt. Bud drifted in and out of consciousness and didn't always make sense." Rod paused to rein in the emotion that threatened to overtake him. "But he knew someone had dug up the jewelry and was terrified Carter King's body would be discovered. He made me promise you wouldn't find out what he'd done."

"I'm sorry, but you're going to have to break that promise and tell me."

Warner got testy. "We already told you the truth what—"

I cut him off. "You told me Bud killed him. I want to know the how and the why."

Warner looked at Rod.

Rod steeled himself. "They were both drinking. They argued. Bud went too far."

A piece of my heart broke. Not because Bud had got drunk and killed a man, but because Rod was lying. Under different circumstances I might have celebrated my being able to tell, but at this moment when I'd been able to truly know him, we'd never been further apart.

I suddenly felt too tired to keep standing and sat in one of the wingback chairs by the bed. "Then why the secrecy?"

"He killed a man with his bare hands." The disgust was evident in Warner's voice, despite his labored delivery. "There are no extenuating circumstances for that. At least not in the eyes of the law."

His tone made me feel defensive, even if what he said was true. "What did Bud and Carter argue about?"

Warner shrugged. "Something trivial, I'm sure."

"You weren't there?"

"Mida King called us for help after it happened. She was sympathetic to Bud and didn't want him going to jail. He was a veteran and a firefighter. Not to mention that your father, whom she cared for very much, would have lost his only living relative."

I didn't buy it. "Was she setting you up for blackmail? How much money have you given her over the years?"

Warner's heart-rate monitor rose. "It wasn't like that. Our mothers were close and Mida was almost family."

"Just not the kind of family you invite to Thanksgiving or tell anyone about."

"Her parents and brother were dead. She was all alone and I promised I'd take care of her."

This actually gelled with Mida's calling him Cousin Leland. I wondered if they'd each cloaked what was basically a quid pro quo—in exchange for a check every month, Mida let them bury Carter's body at the farmhouse and lied to the police—in the veils of family and friendship. Maybe they each needed to do that for his or her own self-respect.

But even with those self-deluding veils, I was surprised Mida had been so mercenary as to sell out her brother's memory. Carter had been branded a thief for stealing the jewelry.

Which brought me to my next question. "Why is Erabelle not speaking to you?"

"That's between the two of us."

"Did you stand over Carter King's body and tell Bud you'd help for a price? Did you make Bud promise never to see her again?"

"If you mean, did I protect my sister, then yes." The heart-rate monitor rose again. "Would you want your sister married to someone who'd just killed a man—and that's leaving out how unsuitable he was to begin with?"

"No, I wouldn't, and I can actually excuse you for that. Maybe Erabelle could too, but I don't think she can excuse the jewelry."

Warner didn't flinch or take his eyes away, but all the same, something in his expression looked guilty. "We needed a credible way to explain Carter's disappearance. The theft of the jewelry did the job perfectly."

Rod eyed the medical equipment. "Let's try to take everything down a few notches. Remember what the nurses said."

I ignored him. "You could have pretended Carter stole something that belonged to you. Instead you stole from Erabelle."

"She would have gladly given Bud the brooches if she'd known he was in trouble."

"Yes, but it would've been her choice, and even if she'd given up the jewelry, she would've still had Bud. You made sure she lost both. You wanted her completely dependent on you."

"You think I like being responsible for everyone? You think I like having to save them from their own idiocy and poor judgment?" His hand went to his chest and he had to struggle to keep talking. "But you protect the people you love. You fight for your family and do your duty."

An alarm sounded on the medical equipment. The nurses rushed in.

"Both of you, out," one said as she cranked up the oxygen. "I told you not to upset him."

As we walked out, the other nurse was putting a nitroglycerin tablet under Warner's tongue.

I stopped at the open door to the sitting room with the intention of talking with Erabelle. She sat listening to the medical drama unfolding in the next room, but showed no sign of going in.

I raised the phone. "I'm erasing the video."

Erabelle nodded. "You didn't believe me earlier, when I said I'd never see my brother again."

"That's the kind of thing people say in the heat of the moment, but don't mean." I glanced back at Warner's bedroom. It sounded as if his attack was receding. "But I understand now."

"I thought you were someone who might." A small flutter of emotion passed through her body, but she quickly suppressed it. "I'm sorry about Bud. Is there any hope?"

"People say there's always hope, but . . . usually there isn't, really."

Rod and I left. I paused at the landing to look out at the oil field one last time. Through will and intelligence Warner had obliterated his father's orchards and created this new landscape. He'd gained power and money, as well as provided people like me with gas for our cars. All the same, it didn't look like a happy trade.

Junior intercepted us at the front door. "I want proof the video is destroyed."

We kept walking. "There is no proof. You just have to take my word for it."

"That's not good enough."

Rod pushed open the copper door and held it for me. "I saw her erase it. The video is gone."

Frank stood outside with my news van.

"How did you find it?" I said.

"I called Brandon King and asked him to check up on the ridge." Frank smiled. "Once I knew it was there, I sent two of my men to get it."

I laughed. "How did Brandon react to finding a news van parked near his meth lab?"

Frank flinched. "I have no idea what he's doing there, but, as you say, he was very unhappy. I promised him you'd be minding your own business from now on."

Rod looked confused. "How did they even get it started?"

Junior indicated the bloodstain on his shirt. "Your girlfriend scratched me with her keys."

"I think you mean *stabbed*," I said, although truthfully it was probably little more than a flesh wound.

Junior, inflamed by my minor dig, pointed to the van. "I want all her video equipment confiscated. Any tapes or cameras in the vehicle are not to leave this property."

Frank looked confused. "Sir, she didn't have access to this equipment in the oil field. There's no way she recorded you on anything in the van."

"I don't care. I want it all."

"He's just trying to be a jerk," I said. "Which is sad and a little pathetic."

Frank appeared to agree, but took the keys around to the rear of the van.

"Hold on." Rod followed. "This van and everything inside is the property of KJAY."

"I couldn't care less," Junior said. "It's not leaving here."

Frank stepped back from the open rear hatch. "Lilly, do you have some kind of animal in the back here?"

That's when I remembered Thing.

I turned to Rod. "It's that dog again. It keeps sneaking into my stuff. I saw it playing around under the tarp just before I left the van. There wasn't time to do anything about it."

"Your dog? How domestic of you." Junior pushed Frank out of the way. "Unfortunately, I may need to inform animal control that it's vicious and needs to be put down."

I felt an unexpected surge of maternal instinct. "You hurt my dog and I will break more than that hand."

Rod looked at me in surprise, but then added, "That dog is our personal property. We'll sue if anything happens to it."

Junior smacked the tarp where it moved. "I think it's getting riled up. If it attacks me, Frank may have to fire his Taser at it."

Junior hit the tarp again.

"Stop doing that," I yelled. "He's just a little dog. He never did anything to you."

Erabelle had come out. "What's going on? Why is there shouting?"

Junior reached for the edge of the tarp. "Get ready, Frank."

I grabbed Frank's arm before he could remove the Taser from his belt. "That many volts could kill a small dog."

Junior whipped back the tarp. I had visions of Thing's leaping out and defending me, which was exactly the excuse Junior needed to kill it.

But I needn't have worried. Thing didn't leap at Junior. Thing didn't bite him. Thing didn't even pee on him. Because Thing wasn't under the tarp.

A thirty-foot python was. I sooooo owed Freddy an apology.

The snake bowed up. Its mouth opened and a loud hiss sped past its huge fangs. Junior screamed. I don't mean he cried out or yelled for help. I'm talking primal-scream time. Everyone jumped back as the snake lunged. Junior, being the closest, couldn't get away. The fangs shot straight into his thigh. He fell to the ground with the animal still biting him.

That's when the rest of it began slithering out of the van—and there was a lot of snake to slither out.

Frank raised the Taser, but Junior kept moving and screaming so Frank couldn't get a clean shot.

Rod was the first to come to his senses. "Hold still." He jumped in and tried to grab the snake at its head where it was still lodged in Junior's thigh.

I shook Erabelle's arm. "Go get help."

"Are you kidding?" she said. "This may be the greatest thing I've ever seen. Two snakes in a death match."

"Exactly. A death match," I yelled. "It could be poisonous."

She shook her head. "Sorry, no. That's a python. I've seen plenty of them abroad, although never one this big. There's no venom. They squeeze their victims to death." She pointed at her nephew's leg. "See, like that."

The snake was indeed coiling itself around Junior's leg. Rod still tried to get control of the reptile's head, so Frank pulled on the midsection in an attempt to remove it from the leg. The only result was that more of its lower end fell out of the van.

"Kill it," Junior screamed. "It's squeezing me. Just kill it."

Security arrived. I would have hoped that someone screaming his head off would have elicited a faster response, but since one of the guards quit on the spot after seeing the snake, I don't think they were Frank's best men.

Their arrival freed me, on a moral level, to do what I'd been longing to do from the start—shoot video!

My iPhone easily captured the moment when all seven guards

pulled on the snake and, instead of freeing Junior, only raised him leg-first off the ground. The audio quality wasn't great, so his screams sounded like a high-pitched girl's.

That recording of Junior I didn't erase.

They finally got the monster snake uncoiled and subdued. While everyone was busy tending to Junior, Rod and I got in the news van and drove away. I was a little worried they might stop us at the front gate, but they had bigger problems.

Even though Rod was driving, I still put my call to KJAY on the speaker.

Freddy answered on the second ring. "KJAY, we're on your side."

"That little dog is still with you, right?"

"Little dude is finally in his crate. I scrounged some wire and locked him in."

I didn't really think the snake had eaten Thing, but it was a relief nonetheless. "I know what they're looking for at the crash site."

"The city sent out a press release saying they're making an announcement at noon. Is it toxic waste?"

"No. A giant python was in one of the crashed vehicles and escaped."

"Dude!"

"That's probably why the animal control officer never came back to the station yesterday. I think they were trying to find the snake before they had to announce it to the public."

"But I totally said there was a snake in the crash."

"I know. I'm sorry. But in my defense, you also said there was toxic waste."

I e-mailed Freddy the video of Junior, then held the phone up so Rod could give Freddy instructions on how to handle the story. We also called the city and told them that the snake, probably attracted by the heat in my van, had crawled inside the open door when I'd chased the officers, Freddy, and Thing into the alley near the crash site. We tried to explain that it was now at Leland Warner's mansion, but I'm not sure they believed us.

We reached Rod's house and again parked the news van next to the Prius. I went inside with him, mostly because I feared that if I said my piece in the van, I wouldn't be able to get him out of the vehicle.

He shut the door and headed to the kitchen. "We should only stay long enough to get something to eat. You need to see a doctor about your face."

I followed him. I watched as he checked the pizza, hoping it was still good. "We're not going to eat or do anything until we talk."

He looked up. My tone obviously alarmed him, as it should have.

"I may not be smart about understanding people or even knowing them." I made sure we were looking each other square in the eyes. "But I know you lied to me about the murder."

TWENTY-EIGHT

R od shook his head. "Warner and I told you the truth."
"Mostly, but not all of it."

He struggled for a moment, then yielded to a burst of uncharacteristic anger. "You weren't supposed to know any of it. I promised Bud. He begged me. He was dying right in front of me, and all he cared about was you never knowing what he'd done."

"Your promise to Bud is just an excuse."

He pulled back. "What's that supposed to mean?"

"It means trust me or give me up. If you don't like me the way I am, there's no point in being in a relationship. I'm not a salad bar."

His expression changed and he leaned in and looked at my pupils. "Do you have a concussion? Maybe we should've gone straight to the hospital?"

"I'm not delirious. I'm trying to explain that you can't pick and choose the parts of me that you want." I pointed to myself. "This is it. The good and the bad are a package deal. If you can't even trust me to handle the truth about my own uncle, then why would you want to be with me?"

"This is about trust, but you've got it backward." His voice rose. "All I've ever done is twist myself into knots trying to prove I love you, but nothing is ever good enough. We could be together for a hundred years and you'd still expect me to hurt you."

Even in my angry, defensive state, this had a ring of truth to it, but I wasn't ready to give in. "You're treating me like a child who needs to be managed and controlled."

"I'm trying to protect you."

"That's what Warner said about Erabelle." I turned and walked out.

My KJAY ID card was one of the things Junior had taken from my pocket and tossed into the oil field when he'd been looking for the phone. I had to call the newsroom and ask Ted to come open the side door for me.

A Yule log had run in place of our local morning show. Ted was preparing for the noon while the demon was out covering the snake story. Other than a skeleton crew of control room staff and Freddy on the assignment desk, nobody else was in the building. Even Callum was home in bed.

Ted opened the door. "Did you find Rod?" His eyes focused on my face and he did a double take. "What happened?"

"Rod's fine. I'm sorry. I should have texted you."

"That's great, but what happened to your face?"

"Don't worry, you should see the other guy." I entered and we walked together through the empty building. "He needed X-rays."

"Maybe you should see a doctor. You might need stitches."

He clucked over me like a mother hen, which would have been nice except I was still upset about Rod's being so overprotective. Just to make Ted stop I got the first-aid kit and went into the anchors' dressing room.

What I saw in the extremely well-lit mirror surprised me. I knew it was bad, but not your-face-looks-like-ratatouille bad. An alarming cut ran across my cheek and ended at my split lip. Blood had dried on my neck and shirt. Despite the ice I'd applied earlier, my cheek had swelled to resemble a tomato. My lips, normally a pleasant rose color I rarely covered with lipstick, looked like an eggplant.

After cleaning up, applying Neosporin, and changing into a clean KJAY polo, I texted everyone that Rod was safe. I debated calling Lucero, but finally decided I didn't want to talk to him and sent a text instead.

I thought about calling the hospital and checking on Bud, but I was afraid of what they'd tell me.

I applied more ice and killed some time helping Ted feed the animals. His mood had improved considerably from last night. He'd agreed to re-air the pet segment on the noon show, and viewers had immediately begun tweeting the news. Several had even suggested Ted and the demon would make a great morning-show team.

Ted also planned to use the video of Junior and the snake. My only regret was that Junior was probably in the hospital and wouldn't be able to see it live.

I avoided sleep, despite my body's fatigue. Experience pulling overnighters for work has taught me to power through the next day and go to bed at my usual time. Otherwise my sleep cycle goes haywire and I'm miserable for weeks.

At quarter to twelve, I gathered my things.

I drove through the empty streets and past the closed businesses. Festive decorations were everywhere. They'd been mounted by business owners and the city government in celebration of Christmas morning, but no one was around to see them.

December is a month of anticipation. A month of parties. A month of planning and shopping. A month of food. A month of television specials and holiday movies and packages in the mail. A month of dreaming what gifts might still be given and received. A month of baking. A month of Christmas cards from forgotten friends and tree-lighting ceremonies at malls.

It all leads to this. All that money, time, and energy spent in service of Christmas, which I've always found to be a sad and monotonous day.

Maybe that's just a sign of how broken my family and childhood were. Maybe normal people wake up on Christmas morning and gather with loved ones in a way that fulfills all that anticipation.

In my house, my mother vanished into the kitchen. Instead of the holiday meal being an excuse to bring us together, it became a physical manifestation of her worth as a human being. She allowed no assistance or interruption and attacked her task with the precise execution of a general going to war.

My father, home for the holiday from the oil fields, vanished into himself while sitting in plain sight on the living-room couch. If I attempted to show him what Santa had brought, he'd nod and listen, but nothing was there. He was like a robot programmed with appropriate responses.

My sister, two years older than me, might as well have been from another planet. We shared no real touchstones. We spoke different languages. Other than our DNA, we had nothing in common.

Bud had been the only one I felt a genuine connection with. I consoled myself with the knowledge that even if he died, I'd still have that connection and everything he'd meant to me.

I reached the airport and parked. The number of cars in the lot surprised me, but then I guess this was not a day when people told their relatives to take the airport shuttle home. I debated waiting outside because of my face, but decided I couldn't risk missing her.

Inside the airport's only terminal, a small crowd waited for the passengers on the plane from Phoenix to disembark. I spotted Mrs. Paik's granddaughter with her parents. The mother and daughter shared a physical resemblance, but their body languages and attitudes couldn't have been more different.

I tried to stay out of sight near the rental-car counter. I avoided people by pretending to look at the posters advertising the amenities available in Bakersfield. Our motto had once been "Sun, Fun, Stay, Play," but even the Vacation and Visitors' Bureau had realized how silly that sounded in the context of farmland and oil fields. Now they wisely pushed our country-music heritage, which at least had the advantage of being real.

The first trickle of passengers appeared, followed by a gush. Family members reunited, then quickly left for the parking lot or baggage claim. Mrs. Paik emerged toward the end.

Her dowdy clothes looked meticulously maintained. No

wrinkles or stains marred the simple blazer—a Herculean task considering she'd just got off a flight. The gray hair I'd last seen under a hairnet now rested close to her scalp in the tightly spun curls of a permanent. The only flaw in her orderly appearance was a slight curve of her aging spine.

Mrs. Paik's granddaughter, all sloppy and loose, hugged her with a childish enthusiasm that surprised me. I felt bad for the girl's mother, left out as she was. If my sister and I spoke a different language, then Mrs. Paik and her granddaughter spoke the same one, despite their age and cultural differences.

I intercepted the family at the door. "Mrs. Paik?"

They each stopped abruptly. Confusion and a little fear were evident in their startled expressions.

"I'm sorry," I hurried to say. "You probably don't recognize me because of my face. I had an accident. We met last summer when my uncle Bud was working at Double Down Donuts. I'm Lilly Hawkins."

"Yes, I remember." Recognizing me didn't relieve her tension. She stayed as tightly wound as the curls on her head. "You need stitches."

"It looks bad because it just happened, but once the swelling goes down, it should be fine." I tried to laugh. "You should see the other guy."

The joke did not go over. It actually made the daughter more uncomfortable, not less. "What are you doing here? I made it clear on the phone last night that you'd made a mistake."

"I only have a couple questions for your mom." I turned to Mrs. Paik. "Bud was shot yesterday and I'm trying to untangle some of his affairs. I know it's Christmas, but could you spare a few minutes?"

For a moment no one knew what to say. Being intercepted at the airport by an acquaintance with a messed-up face is bizarre. There's no real protocol for handling a situation like that.

"But I don't understand," Mrs. Paik's daughter finally said. "How did you even know we'd be here?"

I had no answer, which was stupid because it was bound to come up.

Fortunately the granddaughter had thought ahead. "I texted her this morning and asked how Bud was. I said Grandma would want to know when she arrived." The granddaughter rolled her eyes. "Suspicious much, Mom?"

Despite being in the country for over fifty years, Mrs. Paik still spoke in accented English. "How bad are Bud's injuries?"

I debated before saying simply, "There's no brain activity."

Mrs. Paik's shoulders slumped even more than age had already lowered them. "That is terrible. I'm sorry for you and your family."

"Do you mind speaking with me for a few minutes? I promise not to keep you too long."

The daughter looked at her husband. "We have a long drive back to Elizabeth and we have people coming for Christmas dinner."

"Dad said he wanted to stop at Starbucks." The granddaughter looked at Mrs. Paik. "You could talk to her there. It wouldn't take long." She paused to wait for an answer. When none came, she spread her arms and said, "It's for Bud."

We drove in separate cars to a nearby Starbucks just off the freeway. I wanted to suggest that I drive Mrs. Paik so we'd have more time to talk, but feared it would spook the daughter. She clearly viewed me with suspicion. She was right, secrets were being kept from her, they just weren't mine.

Mrs. Paik and I took a small table in the corner to talk while the rest of the family ordered drinks.

"If you're handling Bud's finances, he and I finished our business last summer." Mrs. Paik rubbed her hands together as if cold, but it looked more like a nervous gesture. "He was very generous to take such a low percentage of our profits. I understand if you want that money for his care, but I can't help you. It's already been spent on my condominium in Phoenix."

"That's not why I'm here."

She appeared to relax a little. Her hands still rubbed together, but she lowered them to her lap. "He would only take fifteen percent. I felt it wasn't fair, but he knew I needed money to retire. Seventy-seven is too old to be working."

Bud had told me they were splitting the profits. I wondered how many other good deeds he'd done that I'd never know about. It made me feel better about the bad deeds I'd also never know about.

"I have some questions about your first husband. I believe he was friends with Bud."

She looked over at her family.

"I haven't told your daughter or her husband anything. I want to respect your privacy."

"Why do you need to know this?"

"I think Bud's shooting is related to something that happened back in the 1950s. Were your husband and Bud close friends back then?"

She nodded. "We moved here after the war because of Bud. My husband couldn't hold a job. He was drinking. Bud said to come here and there would be new jobs and a new start."

"What happened?"

"New place, old problems."

"What about Bud? I heard he had trouble adjusting after the war as well."

"He had trouble, but not from the war." She laughed. Her rigid face came to life and I even thought her curls loosened a little. "Bud had girl trouble. There was one in particular who wanted to marry him. Men like Bud are not made for that life. Her brother made trouble too."

"Is that why Bud went to Alaska?"

"He and my husband both ran away from their problems. The

pay fighting wildfires was astonishing, much better than the jobs my husband kept losing here, but they did not do it for the money. They wanted to be free. Free of the people who loved them."

She looked down at her hands. They'd gone still. "Bud ran from the girl, my husband ran from me."

The girl had to be Erabelle. Mida had said he'd had trouble after the war, which I took to mean post-traumatic stress disorder. Now it sounded as if Bud left because he'd seduced his friend's sister and didn't want to face the consequences.

That was dishonorable enough, but he'd also been my father's only living relative. With Bud's own father and stepmother recently dead, he'd had a responsibility to care for his orphaned half brother. Instead, he'd left for Alaska and abandoned my father to the care of strangers.

An instinctive rejection of that idea swelled inside me. Bud loved my father just as he loved me. He would never abandon him. Out of that denial, an idea began to take shape. What if Bud hadn't left my father with strangers? Mida had said Warner recommended her and Carter because they needed the extra money Bud would pay. What if Mida had lied to me? What if Bud had already known and trusted Mida?

I had to stifle the urge to reach across the table and grab Mrs. Paik. "Do you remember a night when Warner's jewelry was stolen?" She looked uncertain, so I continued. "Bud was a witness. It would have been right after he and your husband returned from Alaska. The theft was a big deal and was probably in the papers."

She nodded slowly. "I remember because my husband did not come home that night."

I glanced at her family as they doctored their drinks at the condiment bar. "Your granddaughter told me that your husband disappeared, but is there any chance he's still alive?"

"Why?"

"I have to talk to him about Bud. He's the only one who might know the truth."

She pulled back and managed to straighten her curved spine a little. "I lied to my granddaughter. I wanted her to believe I had no choice about the divorce, but that was not the case."

It was difficult for her to say these things, so I managed to stay silent and not push her.

After a pause she continued, "Alaska was good for my husband. He stopped drinking. The rigid lifestyle of the firefighters was similar to the army. When he returned, he said he would do well if he could find more work like that, but we both agreed the marriage was over. We divorced as soon as my citizenship was finalized."

"Do you know if he's still alive or where he's living?"

She nodded. "Kelvin got a job working for the Bakersfield Police. He still lives in town."

I felt my skin flush. I didn't know if it was excitement or embarrassment at being made a fool of. "Kelvin Hoyt?"

She looked up with startled eyes. "Do you know him?"

"Yes. I met him last night at the hospital. Kelvin has cancer."

TWENTY-NINE

K elvin Hoyt, retired sergeant of the Bakersfield PD, lived in an upscale senior-living community. He'd given me the name when I'd taken his phone number the night before.

I waved a poinsettia I'd taken from the community's own driveway at the kid behind the sign-in counter. "I'm visiting Kelvin Hoyt. Which apartment is he in?"

I had a detailed backstory ready to explain who I was and how my face had been cut. I even had a response in case he told me I needed stitches, but the young man gave me the number without question. The smarter and more attentive employees probably had the holiday off.

I took the stairs to the second floor instead of using the elevator. I felt stifled enough by the heat and potpourri of the place without getting in a small box. This was probably just a symptom of both my eagerness and apprehension.

The tastefully carpeted hallway, with its framed prints of horses and flowers, was just as empty as the streets downtown. Maybe the residents had all gone out to spend the holiday with loved ones. I knew this would not be the case with Kelvin.

I rang the doorbell. His neighbors had each decorated their doors with Christmas cards and tinsel. The only thing on Kelvin's was a simple sign reading K. HOYT.

There was no answer to the bell so I knocked. After several tries I heard a frail voice inside. I waited. After another minute the door opened.

I'd only seen him reclining in the chemo chair. Now, face-to-face,

I was surprised by how tall he was. His thin frame loomed over me.

"Hi, Kelvin. It's Lilly Hawkins." I held up the plant. "I stole a poinsettia for you."

"Dear girl, what happened to your face?"

"Can I come in?" Instead of waiting for an answer I pushed past him. "How are you feeling after your chemo?"

"But your face. Have you seen a doctor?" He shut the door behind me. "You need stitches."

I laughed. "You should see the other guy."

Kelvin didn't laugh. "Who is the other guy? It wasn't that boyfriend of yours, was it?"

"Not at all. I'm offended on Rod's behalf."

I smelled vomit. Other than that bitter odor and about a dozen pill bottles sitting on the counter in the kitchenette, the apartment could have been the model they showed potential renters. The small living/dining room was clean, the immaculate carpet vacuumed, and the bed I glimpsed through a doorway was even made.

Was this more of the militaristic structure Kelvin had told his wife he needed to survive? Maybe forcing himself to get dressed and make his bed was the only thing getting him through the chemo.

Kelvin stayed at the door, but I could tell he was using it to prop up his weight. "Who hit you like that?"

"You might be surprised to hear it was Leland Warner's son." I set the poinsettia down next to unopened mail on the dining-room table. "I shot some incriminating video of him this morning. He wanted it back."

"I see." Kelvin wobbled—that really was how he walked—toward the living room. "Someone should go have a talk with him."

He said it as though that someone would be Kelvin, in a week or so when he'd got some of his strength back. It also didn't sound as if there'd be much talking done.

"Don't get any ideas about beating up Leland Phillip Warner the second. Although I appreciate the sentiment."

He stopped and made the effort to turn toward me. He was

smiling and warmth twinkled from his eye. "Don't worry. I wouldn't fight fair."

I spread my arms. "Why then, by all means, have at him. But you should know I left Junior with a broken hand, a stab wound in the gut, and a nasty snakebite on the thigh."

This warmed him even more. "Good for you."

"I only stabbed him with a key, so it wasn't very deep, but, you know, I felt good about it."

He continued wobbling toward a recliner. "I feel good just hearing about it."

The conversation petered out and so did the warmth. He collapsed into the recliner. A bucket was on the floor next to it, probably for throw-up emergencies. The end table next to the chair overflowed with cans of 7UP, a digital thermometer, and one of those plastic organizers to sort pills by day and time.

I sat on an ottoman since it was closer to the recliner than the chair it went with. I scooted to the edge and leaned toward him with my elbows on my knees. "Why didn't you tell me the truth last night?"

"I did."

"You left a lot out. Like how you and Bud were friends. How Carter King, the man you hunted for all those years, had been dead and buried all along. How Bud had impersonated him and you diligently added those fake leads to the police file."

Kelvin must have guessed when I arrived that I knew at least part of the truth—why else would I be there?—but he still looked upset. "Bud doesn't want you to know this, Lilly. You should stop. It's bad for everyone."

"I'm guessing he called you at the same time as he called Warner, right after he found the brooch in the pawnshop. It was good of you to drop everything and help him, especially since he couldn't get Warner on the phone."

Kelvin's face tightened as he debated what to say. "All I did was put my treatment off for a day."

"Driving backhoes into pawnshops is hard enough when you're at full strength. I wouldn't want to do it with chemotherapy drugs in my system."

He reached for the soda and took a small sip—probably stalling for time. "How'd you find out about that?"

"The police have surveillance video of you and Bud from the store. They ID'd Bud from one of his tattoos, but they have no idea who you are."

"That's good. The only thing worse than being old is being old with cancer. The only thing worse than being old with cancer is doing it in prison. The only thing worse than being old, with cancer, in prison, is doing it as a former cop."

I had to laugh. "It really was good of you to help him. I think you're the only real friend he ever had, except for Warner when they were young."

"He would have done more than that for me." Kelvin looked away to hide his emotion. "He saved my life up in Alaska. A bunch of us got on the wrong side of the wind and had to run for it. I tripped and sprained my ankle. Everyone ran. Bud ran too, but first he threw me over his shoulder."

"Do you know who shot him?"

Kelvin shook his head. "No. We busted into the pawnshop, like you said. All we wanted were the records to know who'd pawned the brooch. We got back here and I just about collapsed."

He hooked his thumb back toward the bedroom. "I went in to get some sleep. Bud stayed up going through the paperwork trying to find a name. When I woke up, Bud was gone."

Hoyt reached under the side table and withdrew a thick, black binder. "Here's the paperwork from the pawnshop. I went through it myself yesterday afternoon. The fella who pawned the brooch is named Kincaid, but I can't figure how he got ahold of it in the first place."

I took the binder from him. "He's Sally King's drug dealer. She traded it for meth."

Kelvin took this in, but it seemed to frustrate him. "Why would Bud go tackle that fella without me? Why take off by himself while I was sleeping?"

I didn't think that was any great mystery. If Kelvin had been exhausted after the robbery, and he had chemo scheduled for later that day, Bud probably decided he'd imposed on his friend enough.

Instead of saying that, which might have made Kelvin feel weak and useless, I said, "What happened to the gold brooch?"

"Last I saw, Bud had it."

I shook my head. "It's missing now."

"Whoever shot him probably took it. I know he had fifteen grand stashed at your place too."

If Bud was planning to pay someone off, or even to buy back the more valuable diamond brooch, it would explain why he'd needed to use the house so suddenly that morning.

"Kincaid, the drug dealer, is the best-looking suspect." I pointed at the binder in my lap. "You could spin an easy scenario where Bud gets his name from the paperwork, arranges a meeting, and Kincaid shoots him."

Kelvin nodded. "He'd keep the jewelry and Bud's money that way. And drug dealers tend to react bad when questions get asked about their business."

It made sense, but somehow I didn't read Kincaid that way. As morally reprehensible as his actions were, he wasn't a violent street dealer.

I took a deep breath. "Tell me about how Carter King died."

"No."

"Why not?"

"Because I made a promise to Bud. Mida knows what happened because she was there, and Warner and I know because she called us for help after, but it's going to die with us."

"There's someone else who knows. Bud told my boyfriend, Rod, at least some of the truth while they were waiting for the ambulance."

Kelvin's eyes widened, but he didn't say anything.

"Bud was frightened that Carter King's body had been discovered," I continued. "He asked Rod to warn Leland Warner so he could throw money around and make sure the truth didn't come out."

Kelvin hesitated. "Did your boyfriend tell you how King died?"

I nodded. "He and Warner both did."

"Warner did what?" Kelvin looked like a man who wanted a fight but couldn't get out of his chair, which was exactly what he was. "One promise to keep in his entire life and that SOB tells you—the last person in the world Bud would want to know."

"Don't be so hard on Warner. He made sure the body got destroyed and is giving the Kings a bagful of money to forget it was ever on their property." I paused. "Also, I'm pretty sure he lied to me. My boyfriend definitely lied."

Kelvin went still. "What did they say?"

"That Bud killed Carter King during some kind of drunken fight over something that nobody really knows or cares about."

Kelvin leaned back in his chair and closed his eyes. After waiting for too long, I finally realized he wasn't going to say anything.

"I believe Bud did kill Carter, but it's the why and how that nobody's being honest about."

Kelvin's eyes stayed closed.

"What was Bud's relationship with Mida King?"

His head tilted down and he looked at me. "What do you mean?"

"You want to explain why instead of calling the police, Mida called Bud's friends to come and help cover up her own brother's death?"

More silence from Kelvin, so I continued, "I think Bud and Mida were having an affair. He was doubling up—Mida and Erabelle at the same time—but he'd decided to marry Erabelle. He'd written to her from Alaska promising."

Excitement moved me to stand. "Carter got angry. Bud had

used his sister. Back then, premarital sex was a big deal. Maybe Carter thought she was ruined or something."

My mind raced through the ugly scenarios I'd devised on the way over. I grasped for one horrible enough that everyone, even Rod, would be determined to keep it from me. "Maybe she had an abortion. Some kind of horrible back-alley thing. Maybe Bud even forced her do it so he'd be free to marry Erabelle. Carter would have been furious. They fought. Carter died."

Kelvin stared at me. He only broke eye contact to blink. Then he said, "That's it. I'm sorry, it's terrible, but that's the truth. Mida and Bud admitted everything when Warner and I arrived."

With great difficulty, Kelvin forced himself to stand. He patted me on the back before wobbling into the kitchenette. "Try not to hold it against him. Bud made a mistake. He would've taken it back if he could."

Kelvin's feet slipped across the carpet. I heard him fiddling with the pills in the kitchenette.

How did I feel? I'd fought to discover the truth. I'd even risked danger and injury. Bud was flawed. He'd made terrible mistakes out of self-interest and greed, but I loved him. Why had everyone doubted me? Even Bud himself didn't believe I could handle this. I couldn't wait to find Rod and tell him how wrong he'd been, how seriously he'd underestimated me.

But in the background of my pride, a part of me knew something wasn't right.

I followed Kelvin into the kitchenette. "How did Carter King die? Warner said Bud beat him to death."

"Don't mind that," he said after too long of a pause. "Warner exaggerated, is all."

I watched as Kelvin picked up one of the pill bottles, looked at the label, then set it down.

"I don't think so," I said. "Warner looked genuinely disgusted. I think it fundamentally changed the way Warner thought of Bud, to know he was capable of something so violent."

"Nah. Erabelle is what ended that friendship." Kelvin picked up another pill bottle. "One bad punch killed Carter. Bud didn't mean it to happen."

"I saw the body. The entire skull was smashed in."

Kelvin tried to open one of the pill bottles. "I told them not to give me the childproof ones. Do I look like I got kids?"

I reached out and stopped Kelvin's hand on the bottle. "You already have your pills set up in that plastic container in the living room."

He tried to laugh. "You're right. I plain forgot. I guess that's what you call a senior moment."

He was lying, of course. Kelvin hadn't needed or wanted pills. He came into the kitchen to avoid me. He left now for the same reason.

"I'm sure you've got more questions about Bud and Mida," he said on his way back to the recliner. "But I'm real tired. Let me get some of my strength back and we'll talk again in a few days."

Kelvin's voice rang hollow in my ears, and not because of his fatigue or illness. The tone was that of a parent telling an anxious child that nothing bad would ever happen. It was an obvious lie, but so much better than admitting that cancer, housing bubbles, and terrorist attacks probably waited in the future.

I followed and stood in front of Kelvin as he sat down. "Was I wrong about Bud and Mida?"

"No. You got it." He pulled a blanket over his legs. "But maybe we can talk about it in a few days. I'm running a temperature."

"Bud wouldn't beat someone to death." But even as I said it, I knew it wasn't true. "He'd have to be so incredibly angry. There's nothing that could make him that angry."

Except there was something.

The idea tore its way through me. Even then, I couldn't summon the strength to say it out loud.

THIRTY

Kelvin took a sip of 7UP. "Let this rest. You figured it out. Time to let it go."

I tried to ask the question, but gravity increased tenfold. My legs gave out and I sat straight down on the ottoman.

Kelvin's eyes widened in alarm.

I struggled and finally said it. "Did Carter King hurt my father?"

Kelvin flinched.

Tears came to my eyes. I tried to speak, but it was so hard. "How bad?"

After a long pause Kelvin looked up. "Bad."

"Was it just physical or . . ." My throat closed and I couldn't get the words out. I let a sob escape to clear the way, then said, "Was it sexual abuse too?"

"Folks didn't talk about it back then. Nobody knew what *pedophile* meant, but we had them around, all the same."

"How did Bud know?"

"Mida told him. She caught her brother at it, but didn't know what to do. She felt responsible. That's why she helped us hide the body, not cause there was anything romantic between her and Bud."

"My dad didn't . . ." The rest of the sentence got lost in my tears.

Kelvin ripped two tissues from the end table and forced them into my hand. "I'm sorry, dear. I couldn't make that out."

"My dad didn't talk until he was nine. Bud had to tell the school he was mute."

Kelvin sat back. "Abuse at that age, it's hard to overcome, but your dad did better than a lot I've seen. He never hurt nobody else. Didn't get into drugs like a lot of survivors do. He worked hard and had a family of his own."

"He killed himself, didn't he?"

Kelvin didn't answer.

"Didn't he?" I yelled.

He recoiled, startled by my suddenly raised voice, but then said, "Bud always figured he did. I guess he tried once before when you were real little. Bud blamed himself, of course."

Rage gushed inside me. It was like a previously untapped deposit that had always been there. It flowed now because I was forced to admit that my father's pain—his depression, sorrow, and own rage—had all been stronger than his love for me. He'd left me without his protection. He'd made a choice to leave.

And my father had, in his turn, been abandoned by Bud. Dumped, after the recent trauma of losing his mother and father, to live with a pedophile because Bud couldn't be bothered with his own brother. Bud had chased excitement and adventure. He'd run from Erabelle, responsibility, and obligation.

I raised my hand to my face and jabbed at the open wound. It didn't work. The real hurt did almost nothing to dull the one inside me.

Kelvin jerked to attention. "What are you doing? Your face is bleeding." He ripped more tissues from the end table. "Here, put pressure on that."

I ignored the offered tissues. "I hate him."

He struggled to stand. "I know. I hate Carter King too." He held my chin and pressed the tissues to my face himself. "But there's nothing to do now. He's been buried for fifty years."

"No." I paused to sob. "I hate Bud."

Kelvin lowered his hand. His eyes glassed over, but he managed to hold in the tears. "That's what Bud was afraid of."

I had to move. I couldn't bear to be trapped in the little

apartment. At the door, I stopped and turned around. I still held the pawnshop binder to my chest as though it were a shield. "Thank you for your help. You've been very good."

I left the building and got in the news van. I drove, but not to any place in particular. At one point I had to pull over. Rage swelled in my limbs. I pounded the steering wheel and kicked blindly. I didn't even know why. I just did it.

I passed Westside Hospital—a different facility from the one Bud was in—and stopped. Because, apparently, there was no limit to what I could be wrong about, I decided to see if I needed stitches. My pride was salved only slightly by their use of glue instead of needle and thread.

The physician's assistant said I'd have a scar, but a relatively minor cosmetic procedure might remove it in the future. I walked back to the car with a prescription for a light painkiller and an antibiotic. It reminded me of Kincaid.

I drove to Rosedale. It wasn't rational, but when I saw Bouncer through the window of his mother's store, I felt better.

I parked and he opened the front door for me. "What happened to your face?"

"Can I come in?"

He stepped back so I could enter, then locked the door behind me. He'd been alone in the store, unpacking boxes and restocking the shelves, but said he had coffee made in the back.

We sat at the same table his mother had been using to cut pages from the Bibles the night before. I wrapped my cold hands around the warm ceramic mug, but didn't drink its contents.

I told him about Bud—how he'd killed Carter King and why, how he'd assumed Carter's name, and how Bud had been the one selling Bibles with Bouncer's mother in '84.

When I finished, he crossed his arms. "Why are you here telling me this?"

"I thought you'd want to know about Bud, I guess."

"You guess?"

"I don't know." I pushed the coffee away. My rising annoyance absolved me of having to pretend I liked it. "Maybe I didn't want to be alone."

"You've got people. You've got a guy who obviously loves you and friends."

I stood. "I wish I could push a button and make them all go away."

"Why?"

"Because I hate being tangled up in their lives. I don't want to feel hurt or angry when they let me down, and I don't want to be terrified that something bad might happen to them."

Instead of being judgmental, as I expected, Bouncer nodded. "I feel that way about my mom sometimes. She won't go straight. I don't think it's even about the money. When I tell her how hard it is for me to know she could get that third strike, she tells me not to worry, like it's a choice or a switch I can flip."

He stood up and started back out to the storefront. "There's no way for me to stop worrying about her. That's part of being in a family, even if it's a family of two."

I followed him to where he'd been unpacking boxes. "I don't want to be in a family."

"But you don't want to be alone either."

"Why do you say that?"

"Because being alone is an easy dream to realize." He grinned. "And instead of doing it, you came here to tell me that we might, in fact, be family."

He reached down and picked up several Bibles, then placed the stolen merchandise on an empty shelf.

"If I'm so desperate to connect with you, then why don't I know your name?"

"Because until this moment you haven't cared enough to learn that my name is Jake."

"Exactly. Because caring is the worst."

"You'll get no argument from me." He shelved more Bibles.

"And short of the person you love dying or magically ceasing to exist, there's no way out. You're trapped."

A fantasy of running away dazzled me for a moment. Erabelle had escaped the ties that bind by moving to Indonesia. It felt so seductive—severing every claim on me, every relationship that required something I wasn't able to give. No more feeling guilty because I'd hurt someone. No more feeling angry because people had hurt me.

It came just as suddenly as the truth about my father and Carter King. I sucked in a breath and rocked back.

"Are you okay?" Bouncer said. "Is something wrong?"

"I know who shot Bud." My mind whipped through scenarios. I reached a particularly awful one and jumped up. "And I think they're going to do it again."

I raced back to the van. I flipped through the pawnshop binder trying to see what Bud must have seen. I didn't look for the brooch, but rather I focused on the transactions from the previous weeks. I saw enough to confirm I was right and called Lucero.

I also started driving. After several failed attempts to reach him, I left a long message on his voice mail. I even called Handsome, who also didn't pick up, and left a similar message. As a last resort, I called 911.

Despite all that effort, I was alone when I reached the Kings' land. I followed the road along the refinery's electric fence. The van shook as the speedometer climbed to ninety. After what felt like an eternity, I slowed at the asphalt driveway and turned in. I approached the mobile homes with dread. When I didn't see the Escalade, my dread turned to fear.

I stopped and got out without turning the engine off. The overcast day cast a depressing tint over the unkempt flower beds and crooked shutters. Even the Christmas lights looked cheap and sad.

No one answered at Sally and Brandon's house. I ran across the drive and pounded on Mida's door. If she'd been there, I would have thrown her in the van. Saving at least her would have been enough of an excuse to run away and let the police handle the rest.

But she wasn't there.

I listened for sirens in the distance, but no cavalry was charging in. The only sound on the lonely property came from the wind beating through the dead grasses. I had no choice. I was going to have to drive to the farmhouse.

I returned to the van and drove forward past the mobile homes. The asphalt ended and spit me out onto the dirt road. A trail of dust and earth blossomed behind me as I sped farther and farther into the property.

I honestly didn't know what I'd do when I did eventually reach the farmhouse. Should I park some distance away and try to sneak up on it? Should I charge in? I might be wrong. I didn't have proof, just some circumstantial evidence and an understanding of what might be driving Bud's shooter.

A formation of odd black streaks and sharp angles appeared on the horizon. I'd never visited from this direction, and it took me a few moments to identify the collapsed barn.

Time to decide. The farmhouse appeared and I decided on a direct approach. If it turned out the worst was true, I'd stall until the police arrived. It might not be too late.

I slowed. Four vehicles were parked in the dirt clearing at the rear of the house: three pickups and Sally's Escalade. I parked a short distance back and shut off my engine. Through the windshield I eyed the trucks.

The duct tape on the front bumper identified one of them as belonging to Kincaid. The second was much older and looked like the one Brandon had been driving the previous day. The third was easily the biggest and most expensive. I recognized it as part of Warner's fleet of vehicles. Erabelle had given me a ride in a similar one the previous day.

Not all of the trucks were empty. Someone's head cast a shadow on the back window of his or her vehicle. The head didn't turn at the sound of my van. It didn't glance down to read or examine something. The shadow didn't move at all.

I had a bad feeling, but took the bat and got out of the van. Outside, the air reeked of diesel fuel from the rumbling generator.

I walked slowly, partly from caution and partly from dread. I stopped one last time at the rear of the pickup. I tapped the CHEVY lettering with the baseball bat. The wood hit the metal with a loud thud, but the figure didn't move.

This dead stillness implied that the individual was past being a danger to me or anyone else, but I still approached with care. The driver's-side window was rolled down. I didn't want to look, but forced myself.

My stomach lurched and I had to fight my gag reflex.

Frank had been shot. There wasn't much blood where the bullet had entered just above his ear. His skin was still warm and I didn't think he'd been dead for long. The money, the second half of Warner's lump-sum payment to the Kings, wasn't in the truck with him. Neither was the diamond brooch he was supposed to obtain in the trade.

I pictured Frank arriving in the souped-up pickup. Doing yet another dirty errand for the family he'd spent decades serving. He probably hadn't even got out of the truck. The killer could have stood in the same spot as me, smiling and making conversation. Frank probably hadn't known what hit him.

I'd got here too late to save Frank's life, but I might not be too late to save the others.

I stepped up and crept through the kitchen. The plastic sheeting had been lowered over the doorway into Brandon's lab. I cautiously looked inside. With all the windows boarded, the work light on the stand still provided the only illumination. The leftover tools of meth production were still in place, but the room was empty.

My relief proved short-lived. A faint noise beckoned from farther inside the house. The long, low sounds reminded me of water sloshing in a bucket.

I stepped softly on the plastic covering the floor. I reached a large archway on the opposite side of the room and pulled back the sheeting.

A chemical odor filled the dark room. Faint light, as well as the sloshing sounds, came from a hallway. As I crossed what used to be the living room, I recognized the dim outlines of the front door. It was good to know I could get out without running all the way back through the house.

That's when I tripped. I found the Mini Maglite in my coat pocket and shone it down.

This time my stomach didn't lurch. It was as though my over-whelmed brain had shut off certain reflexes.

Kincaid lay splayed on the floor. His open eyes stared straight up at the ceiling. He'd been dead longer than Frank, and it appeared his death had been much more painful.

THIRTY-ONE

Kincaid had been shot in the stomach and bled out. The swell of dark liquid had reached a particularly wide space between the wood planks and fallen straight down under the house.

I swallowed, despite my mouth's feeling like a dry sponge, and reached down to check for a pulse. I didn't doubt that Kincaid was dead, but it seemed the proper thing to do. Touching him, I realized that he'd been covered in some kind of liquid. The wood floor glistened with it too, without actually feeling wet.

Judging from the smell, some kind of flammable chemical or accelerant had been poured on the body and around the room. I stifled my panic by reasoning that the killer was unlikely to ignite the house while still inside.

A lot of people would have walked back to their car and waited for the police. Even more people wouldn't have ventured past the public road in the first place. That I'd driven all the way here, continued past Frank's body, and now found myself inside a firebox standing over yet another body placed me in a select group.

Despite the danger, I continued toward the hallway and the odd sloshing sounds. If I ran away now and more people died, I'd always have that weight on me. I'd know I'd been selfish and left others in danger with disastrous consequences. Isn't that the weight Bud had lived with for fifty years? I had no desire to emulate him.

I killed the flashlight and entered the dark hallway. The chemical smell increased the closer I got to the sounds. Its sharp odor burned my nostrils and I had to cover my face. My foot slipped, which was unusual in my boots, and I guessed the accelerant had been poured here only moments earlier.

I had an odd realization that this was the place where my father had been hurt. Within these walls he'd been unable to defend himself against a predator. I wanted it to burn. I wanted the match to be struck. That the wood still stood and that I could stand inside this place all these years later was an abomination.

I stopped at an open bedroom doorway. A flashlight sat on the floor pointing straight up. The light it blasted on the ceiling reflected downward and cast the room in a soft glow. Two figures lay on the floor. A down comforter spread under them protected them from the dirt and coarse wood planks. Pillows had even been placed under their heads.

At first I feared I was too late to save them, but then I saw the rise and fall of their chests and guessed they'd been drugged.

The third person in the room was not drugged. Brandon turned from pouring turpentine on one of the walls. He saw me and froze.

"You don't have to do this," I said. "You've got all the money, the jewelry, and the meth. Take it and run. I won't stop you."

He looked more annoyed than surprised to see me. "You're the lady from KJAY, right? Warner's security guy promised you wouldn't come back. He said you were taken care of."

"It's a good thing I did come because maybe I can stop you from doing something that you'll regret."

He shook his head. "The only regret I have is that I didn't do this sooner."

The window to try to talk Brandon out of harming anyone else was closing. Instead of lying to him or tricking him, I decided to speak honestly. "I understand you can't do this anymore. Your mother is a drug addict and your grandmother needs round-the-clock care, and each is getting worse. Anyone would think about leaving, and a lot of people would actually do it."

I stepped into the room. "I understand that you're desperate, and I know one way or the other you're going, but you don't have to kill your mother and grandmother. You can walk out of here right now without hurting anyone else."

He still hadn't moved. "How did you even know I was leaving?"

"Someone got Mida to sign papers mortgaging the land, but the money's not in her account." He looked surprised I knew, but didn't interrupt me. "There was also your mother's dog. It didn't run away. The animal shelter has it because the owner turned it in. I thought it was Sally until I saw the pawnshop records. You've been selling things for weeks, probably at other pawnshops too. Appliances, Hummel figurines—anything that's not tied down. You've built a nest egg to take with you."

"Why do you even care? Didn't Warner give you money to go away?"

I made a split-second decision not to tell him about Bud. I hoped I might still be able to avoid more violence. "I understand why you need to leave. You're under so much pressure here and it's not fair, but you don't need to kill anyone else. You can walk right out of here and drive away."

"You say you understand, but you're clueless." He looked down at his mother and grandmother. "When I was a kid, I found a stray cat. Every night I brought her inside to my bedroom so the wild animals couldn't hurt her. One day Mom and Grandma say how we're going to Disneyland for three days. I begged them to let me leave the cat inside, but they thought she'd wreck the house."

I had a feeling this story wasn't going to end well for the cat.

"When we got back, I looked everywhere. Finally I found her out in the brush. She'd been torn open. Parts of her were even missing." He looked up at me. "It happened because I wasn't there to protect her."

"That was a cat. Your mother and grandmother are human beings. They'll survive without you."

"No, they won't." He threw the metal can of paint thinner. It crashed into the wall with a bang that sent me jumping back to the doorway. "When the money stopped last month, I saw how it was. My mother is gone. She doesn't exist anymore. Before she dug up the jewelry, she actually traded sex for meth, that's how desperate she was." He pointed toward the living room where Kincaid's body still leaked blood. "I'm glad I killed that monster. I did the world a service."

"But you don't have to kill your mom too. She could still get better."

"She's been to rehab twice and each time she's gotten worse. This is the only way. If I leave her here, she'll OD in an alley or worse."

"Then what about Mida? Even with the Alzheimer's, your grandmother still has the capacity to love you. She can experience joy and happiness. You may think this is some kind of euthanasia, that you're being good to her, but trust me, it's not what she'd want."

"In another year, maybe two, Grandma won't be able to talk or walk. She can't even go to the bathroom now without help. You can't argue that a quick, painless death isn't better than what's coming."

Despite the weird love in his words, something in his tone sounded a warning. I watched as his hand whipped behind his back and withdrew the gun. I wondered if it was the same one he'd used to shoot Bud.

"In a way," I said, "maybe it's better that you won't walk out of here peacefully and ride off into the sunset with all that money."

"Why's that?"

"I'd always feel guilty for letting my uncle's murderer get away."

He jerked in surprise. "Your uncle?"

"Bud Hawkins. You shot him yesterday in my living room in Oildale."

"That's your uncle?" Brandon said it as though we'd just

discovered a friend in common, not a murder. "I'm sorry about the old guy, but I couldn't risk him making trouble."

"And the money you stole?" He frowned and I said, "I know he had fifteen thousand at the house. Isn't that why he wanted to meet you there?"

He nodded. "I told him I'd pawned those things and sold the brooch to Kincaid in order to pay our bills. He offered to give us the money to help until we got things straightened out with War-ner again."

"And you decided you'd kill him and keep the money and both brooches?"

"Mostly, I wanted to shut him up so I could get away clean today. I've been planning this ever since Warner's money stopped coming last month. I couldn't risk your uncle ruining it the day before I was scheduled to go." Brandon lifted the gun. He actually looked sorry. "I wish you hadn't come here."

I held up the bat. "You're right to wish that."

He laughed. "What, are you going to swing at the bullet?"

I'd thought Brandon was pretty smart, but then again I'd thought he was nice too.

I took a step closer. "When a gun fires, there's a small explo-sion. That's what propels the bullet. If you pull the trigger, the spark could ignite all this accelerant you've spread everywhere. You'll blow all of us up, even yourself."

I withdrew my hand from my pocket. "Fortunately for me, that's not how Mace works."

I sprayed it right at him. His hands shot to his face as he cried out. It wasn't military or law-enforcement grade, so it didn't take him down. Blind and desperate, he lunged at me. I jumped out of the way, but he still clipped me and we both fell.

He landed on top of Sally and I hit the floor.

I'd dropped the bat in my fall and now saw it rolling away. I heard Sally's confused voice as she woke from her drugged sleep.

Brandon rose from where he'd fallen on her and started to move toward me.

Still on my hands and knees, I dove for the bat. I took hold of the fat end and jammed the wood shaft straight back under my arm. It hit him in the gut just as he leapt at me again.

I heard something and turned my ear toward the front of the house—sirens. Brandon was already making painful noises because of his eyes and the blow from the bat, but I heard a louder, clearer cry when he recognized the sirens too. He had to know there was no way out now. Even if he did get by me and to his truck, he couldn't see to drive.

I feared he might try to retaliate in his last minutes of freedom. Despite Brandon's injuries, a man with nothing left to lose and a grievance can do a lot of damage. But instead of lunging at me again or trying to stand, he went still. He wiped fluid from his face, but it did nothing to stop the flow coming from his eyes and nose. I was even tearing up and having trouble breathing from all the chemicals in the air.

That's probably why I didn't see him reach into his pocket. Brandon had the lighter out before I knew the danger. He was too far for me to get to him so I threw the bat. It stunned him, but he still held the lighter. One motion from his thumb and we'd all go up in flames.

I leapt across the women and dove for his hand. Outside, the sirens reached a crescendo and stopped. We struggled, falling over Mida and Sally.

"Help!" I screamed. "Help! We're inside. He's going to blow the building up."

In retrospect that was not something likely to make people run into a structure, but to his credit I heard Lucero calling back, "I'm coming, where are you?"

"One of the bedrooms," I yelled. "Hurry."

Sally tried to push us off her as she came more fully awake, but we continued to struggle.

When footsteps pounded in the hallway, Brandon played his last card. His mouth opened and bit down on my arm. I had to let go.

He rocked back on his haunches and held the lighter up. He smiled as his thumb moved. He really was getting out today, one way or the other.

That's when I saw Sally. She rose up on her knees and swung the bat at her son. In her case, self-preservation trumped mother love.

THIRTY-TWO

T he officers responding to my 911 call had been the first to arrive, but they hadn't proceeded beyond the mobile homes. Lucero had led the charge to the farmhouse.

Mida and Sally were taken to the emergency room in an ambulance. I gave a statement and promised to come in for a longer Q&A later. Brandon was arrested for Frank's and Kincaid's murders and also taken to the hospital. Nobody said it, but I knew they'd up the count to three homicides when Bud died.

Brandon's pickup contained the meth, Warner's $500,000 bribe, another $340,000 in cash, and both brooches.

I called Leanore and asked her to come get me since the police didn't want my van moved until they'd finished the investigation. We briefly returned to the station, where everyone was celebrating Ted and the demon's triumphant noon show. Predictions were that a record number of viewers had tuned in to see the pet segment. That wouldn't matter to KJAY since it wasn't a ratings period, but Ted and the demon were sure to become household names. The morning-show idea seemed to be getting real traction.

Ted had also presented the video I'd shot of Junior and the snake. It was already garnering massive hits on the KJAY website, and the *Huffington Post* was going to link to it.

I stayed at the station long enough to sit for a quick interview about my confrontation with Brandon. Callum said it was the best Christmas present I ever gave him.

Before leaving for the hospital, I called Erabelle and explained what had happened. She agreed to make sure Mida was placed in a dementia-care facility, and I promised to try to keep the Warners out of my official story to the police.

"How's Bud?" she said before hanging up.

"Last time I called, there was still no brain activity."

"I keep thinking . . ."

"What do you keep thinking?"

"What would all our lives be like if Bud and I had gotten married? You'd be my niece."

I had a flash of how I might feel in fifty years if Rod and I broke up now. Somehow I knew that I'd never be happy with someone else. "Do you want to come see Bud? I can tell them you're family."

"No." My offer seemed to depress her more, but maybe she felt like a coward for not coming. "I'm flying back to Indonesia tomorrow. I'll make arrangements for Mida before I go."

I hung up and got the keys for van #3. It felt strange not to be in my usual #4, but I figured a lot more was going to change at KJAY than which van I drove, so I should try to adapt.

As I prepared to back out, I heard a yipping sound outside. I put the van back in park and opened the driver's-side door. Thing had got out of his crate again and sat looking up at me with its irregularly shaped eyes.

"What do you want from me?" I said. "What am I supposed to do with you?"

Leanore passed on the way to her own car. "You're supposed to take him home and love him."

"I don't think so."

"If nobody adopts him," she called back, "the shelter will kill him."

"Leanore, you are diabolical." I reached down and picked Thing up.

I couldn't imagine being responsible for a dog for the rest of its life, but then again, I couldn't imagine allowing anyone to hurt it. "No peeing in the van or in the house." Its stumpy, little tail wagged as I set it down on the passenger seat and shut the door.

At the hospital, I left Thing in the news van with a cup of water and some pee pads I'd bought at the grocery store.

When I entered the ICU waiting room, I thought it was empty. Then I saw Rod sitting alone in a dark corner. He'd shaved, showered, and changed clothes, but it didn't look as if he'd got any sleep.

"I'm sorry," he said, "but there's still no brain activity. They'd like to take him off the respirator."

"Where's Annette?"

He paused and took an awkward look around the room. "She's not coming. I talked to her on the phone and she's exhausted. Just can't face being here if there's no hope."

"I guess it's you and me, then." I took a deep breath. The words were hard to say, but I knew that I had to say them. "I'm sorry that I make things hard for you sometimes. I'm sorry that you keep having to prove that you love me. I hate that about myself—"

"Lilly, no." He looked surprised. "I never should have said those things."

"Yes, you should have. I'm glad you were honest. I'm going to try harder."

"I should have been honest about a lot more than that. I've been sitting here beating myself up. What you said about Warner and Erabelle . . . I'll tell you the truth about Bud, if that's what you want."

"I already know."

We sat down and I told him about visiting Kelvin Hoyt, whom Rod hadn't known about, and how I'd finally guessed the truth. I also told him about Brandon and what had happened at the farmhouse. I glossed over the more dangerous parts. Rod would hear about it eventually, but for now I wanted to focus on Bud and my father.

"There's a part of me that wishes you'd succeeded and I never found out the truth." I didn't like admitting it, but I thought I owed it to Rod. "But that's the weak part of me. It's not the part that you should be encouraging."

"I went way too far and lost my bearings, but it wasn't just you I was trying to protect." Rod paused. "You don't understand what it was like when I found Bud. He was raving and terrified. I asked who shot him and he wouldn't tell me. He didn't even want his shooting investigated because he was afraid you'd learn the truth and hate him."

I'd assumed that yesterday, when Rod had invoked his grandfather's recent death, it had been a ruse designed to explain why he wanted me to stay at the hospital. Seeing his emotion now, I realized that grief from his own loss had probably heightened his reaction to finding Bud. Maybe that's why he'd gone to such lengths to honor Bud's wishes.

When I suggested it, he quickly agreed.

"I'm sorry you didn't get to say good-bye to your grandfather," I said. "But I'm almost glad that I never said good-bye to Bud."

"Don't say that."

I looked down where our hands rested together. "I wouldn't know what to say to him."

"You'd speak from your heart."

"What if my heart is full of anger and bad stuff?"

"You have a giant heart, Lilly. If it were full of anger, you wouldn't try so hard to protect it."

The doctors came and spoke with us. They said that Bud was essentially gone already. Once they took him off the respirator, his body would stop breathing and die.

I believed them, but somehow couldn't sign the papers yet.

I finally went in to see Bud. The hollow and sunken appearance of his face surprised me the most. Even though he wore tape and padding around the ventilator tube, I could see that his skin looked as thin as Saran Wrap as it clung to his cheekbones.

After Rod and I had been there a short time, a nurse came and told us someone wanted to see Bud, but since he wasn't family, they couldn't let him into the ICU. I went out to the waiting room expecting to see Kelvin Hoyt, but it was Bouncer.

"I thought I'd try to see him, at least."

"Did you ask Laurie if he's your father?"

Bouncer shrugged. "She wouldn't talk about it. I know that sounds weird, but if you knew her, you'd understand."

I told the nurse that Jake was my cousin and they let him in. Rod took the news of Bud's possible paternity the way he took everything, with kindness. We offered to leave, but Bouncer said not to. He stayed long enough to hear a few of the better and crazier Bud stories. In a way it felt like a wake, except Bud was in the room with us.

When Bouncer was ready to go, I walked him to the door of the ICU. "If I ever need some duct tape, can I call you?"

It was a corny, stupid joke, but he laughed anyway. "I always have an extra roll handy."

I think we each wanted to know the other better, but were wary of both pushing too hard and being pushed ourselves.

When I returned to Bud's room, Rod got up to go find coffee and Mountain Dew. We were each emotionally and physically exhausted and needed some artificial stimulation.

After he'd gone, the only sound in the room came from the ventilator pumping air in and out of Bud's lungs. The quiet intensified the pressure I felt. Finally I scooted my chair close to the bed and took Bud's hand.

I was going to tell him that I knew the truth and didn't blame him, but in the end I didn't think he'd want to hear it. For all his folksy wisdom, Bud was a practical man. Forgiveness for breaking something wouldn't concern him so much as fixing the damage.

I instinctively knew that's what lay at the heart of Bud's wish to protect me—the knowledge that the damage to my father had rolled down through the generations and hurt me as well. He must have looked at every self-destructive mistake I'd ever made as a direct result of his own failure to protect my father.

"Bud, it's Lilly. I'm here with you in the hospital. I'd like to talk for a minute or two, if that's okay. There are some things I want you to know."

I paused just in case there might be a miracle and he'd squeeze my hand, but nothing happened. The tattooed arm, its skin now thin and brittle like old paper, remained still. I knew in that moment that he was really gone. I'd said it before to Rod, but now I truly believed it. Whatever had made Bud who he was, no longer existed in that body.

"I love you, Bud. I will always love you. I'm so grateful that I got to have you in my life. I always knew that you loved me and I could go to you for help."

I had to pause because I'd started crying.

"I also know that you worry about me. I know that you're frightened of not being here to help me. I've made bad choices sometimes. I've hurt myself and rejected people who care about me.

"I understand why you're frightened, but you don't need to worry anymore. I'm going to be okay. I'm going to marry Rod and we're going to make a life together. We're going to love each other, and even when bad things happen, I'll handle it. I promise. You don't need to worry about me anymore, Bud."

I looked up and saw Rod standing in the doorway. Our eyes met and I knew he'd heard what I'd said.

Without saying a word, Rod stepped into the room and set down the drinks. He withdrew the engagement ring from his coat pocket. My hand shook as I held it out so he could slip the ring on my finger.

As I kissed him, I couldn't help but think how unchanged I felt. I'd worried so much about taking this step. Now that it had happened, I felt as though it had always been this way.

A few hours later I signed the papers. They removed the ventilator tube and Bud's body died quickly.

I've heard people say that their loved ones are with them in their hearts. I thought it was hokey, self-delusion. My father had died and I never felt him with me.

Now I understand. Bud was in that hospital room when I said good-bye, and he was there when Rod put the ring on my finger.

I know because he's always with me.

Acknowledgments

As always I'd like to start by expressing my sincerest thanks to everyone at the Friedrich Agency. Molly Friedrich, Lucy Carson, Molly Schulman, and Becky Ferreira are the best in the industry. This book, and pretty much my entire writing career, wouldn't exist without them.

The character and tone of a place is created by the people who inhabit it. Touchstone has been a supportive and enthusiastic publisher of all three Lilly Hawkins books because the people who work there are so supportive and enthusiastic. My editor Lauren Spiegel's outstanding guidance shaping this manuscript, as well as her attention to detail while shepherding it through publication, has been more than any author could dream of. I'm also deeply indebted to Kiele Raymond for her generosity and invaluable notes.

My publicist, Shida Carr, has been in the foxhole with me for all three books. I don't have words to properly thank her or Ashley Hewlett. Also with me through thick or thin have been my copy editors, Steve Boldt and Jessica Chin. How do they manage to make me sound literate? We've never met, but I picture them as superheroes in some kind of grammatical Bat Cave.

Special thanks to Jo Imhoff, Ceasonne Reiter, and Kim Zachman for reading drafts and giving invaluable feedback. Thank you to James Lincoln Warren for the many e-mails and conversations allowing me to hash out plot ideas.

I couldn't have written this book without the technical expertise of Walter Reiter and Tracey Imley, MD. Any mistakes are mine and not theirs.

I'm a devoted mystery fan myself, so when Spencer Quinn

and April Smith both offered their endorsement of my second book, it meant more to me than I can say. Chet the Jet and Ana Grey are very different protagonists, but they share equal space in my heart.

Finally, I thank my dear husband, Jeff, for always believing in me.

TOUCHSTONE

READING GROUP GUIDE

INTRODUCTION

TV news photographer Lilly Hawkins is back, and this time the story she's chasing is her own. It's Christmas Eve, but Chief Photographer ("Shooter") Lilly Hawkins and her comrades at KJAY-TV are experiencing anything but a silent night. From the moment the police scanner announces Lilly's home address as a crime scene, life as she knows it is over. Murder has struck closer to home than she ever imagined, and the investigation leads Lilly to discover long-buried family secrets.

FOR DISCUSSION

1. At the beginning of *Going to the Bad*, Lilly is torn over how to respond to Rod's marriage proposal after accidentally finding an engagement ring in his pocket. What does Lilly's conversation with Leanore about her hesitation to marry Rod reveal about Lilly? If you have read other installments in the Lilly Hawkins series, how does this characterization compare with what you already know about Lilly?

2. How does Lilly react to the potential loss of someone she holds so dear? How does her reaction differ from Rod's? How do you personally cope with grief? In what ways are you similar to or different from Lilly?

3. Nora McFarland provides brief glimpses into each character's personal history, shedding light on their actions and motivations. Which character in *Going to the Bad* did you find yourself feeling the most sympathetic toward? What is it about the character's story that elicits your compassion? Which character in the story did you find yourself struggling with the most?

4. Describe the relationship between Leland Warner and Lilly's uncle Bud. What secret bound them together? What impact did it have on them individually, and how did this secret propel the narrative?

5. Throughout *Going to the Bad*, "Thing" consistently shows up in unexpected places and at unexpected moments. How do Lilly's feelings toward Thing change over the course of the novel? What significance does this seemingly small character play in Lilly's emotional development?

6. Were you surprised by what Lilly learned about her father? Have you ever had a similar experience of learning something about a friend's or family member's personal history?

7. Throughout the story, Lilly repeatedly states that there's nothing she can learn about her uncle Bud that will change the way she feels about him. Did you find her conviction admirable or arrogant? How is that conviction tested when Lilly learns the truth about Carter King? Did your own opinion of Bud change?

8. What surprising role does Bouncer play in Lilly's personal evolution and the ultimate solving of the murder investigation? In what ways are Lilly and Bouncer similar?

9. Lilly's work on the murder investigation is interspersed with humorous exchanges with various characters from KJAY and the police department. How did the use of humor throughout the narrative influence your reading? Which character's sense of humor did you enjoy the most?

10. There are several families in *Going to the Bad*, each with multiple generations. What are the dynamics of each family? In what ways do the members both love and harm one another? How have Lilly, Bouncer, Junior, and Brandon all been shaped by their families?

11. Were you surprised to learn the identity of the murderer? Why or why not? What was your impression of this character up until the final revelation? Which character did you guess was the murderer? If you guessed incorrectly, describe what made you suspicious.

12. Describe the most surprising twist in the plot from your perspective. What did you enjoy the most about the story line?

13. If you've read any of the previous installments in the series, how has Lilly's world changed? What effect have advances in technology had on the KJAY news department? How have Lilly's friends and coworkers changed from the start of the series to the end?

14. At the end of *Going to the Bad*, Lilly says good-bye to her uncle Bud. Have you ever had to say good-bye to a loved one with a terminal illness? Do you think Lilly handled the situation well? What does it say about how she's changed?

How did it feel to complete the final installment in the Lilly Hawkins trilogy?

It's very satisfying, but also a little sad. I'm emotionally invested in Lilly and she's been a big part of my life for the last five years.

What was your inspiration for creating the fictional newsroom at KJAY and its cast of characters?

I've worked in several newsrooms, and they each had more than their share of eccentrics. I don't know if journalism attracts people with distinct personalities or if the job sharpens their character traits. There's an enormous amount of pressure and tense situations, so it may be the latter. They say pressure makes diamonds, but I think in the news business they're slightly irregular diamonds, which is a lot more fun.

How did Lilly's growth and transformation by the end of *Going to the Bad* compare with what you initially imagined for her character?

I've always wanted to end with Lilly and Rod getting engaged. For someone who's protective of herself and used to holding back, that's such a huge step. I had difficulty getting to that moment in an organic way because of everything Lilly was going through in this book. The trauma of losing Bud and the tension in her relationship with Rod made it all the more difficult to take that step. I even wrote a draft that ended with Lilly telling Rod she wasn't ready for marriage. Fortunately I was able to find a moment that felt right in a later draft.

What was the most enjoyable or memorable moment in the process of writing *Going to the Bad*?

Writing Bud's death was very emotional for me. I was actually crying. I know he's fictional, but I really loved the old guy.

Going to the Bad weaves an intricate web of secrets and relationships. How challenging was it to architect all of the connections and deceptions?

I wrote a twenty-five-page outline and got feedback on that. It helped enormously because I was able to eliminate characters and plot points that were easily confused. Then I made more changes as I was writing.

The characters in Going to the Bad react to and handle loss in many different ways. Why was it important to you to portray these different reactions?

I like to pick a theme and have it reflected in different ways by the supporting characters' stories. Lilly's main character flaw is a fear of abandonment, which is really just a fear of loss. For the final book I knew she needed to overcome that and made it the focus of the book.

What have been some of your favorite or most memorable interactions with readers of this series?

When I'm working, I'm in a bubble and forget that other people are eventually going to be reading my work. Sometimes a stranger will e-mail to let me know how much they enjoyed one of the books and the bubble pops. It's a wonderful surprise and means a lot to me.

Has writing this trilogy changed you in ways you didn't anticipate when you first started writing? If so, how?

I'm a very different writer now than when I began the first book, *A Bad Day's Work*. Back then I had the luxury of writing only when I felt inspired. Now I'm much more disciplined and keep to deadlines. It can be difficult with humor. Being funny even when you're depressed or anxious is a challenge.

Where do you think your sense of humor comes from?

Most of it I have no control over. A sense of humor is probably something that we're all born with to various degrees. If anything has influenced me, I'd say it was watching tons of old screwball romantic comedies and even sitcoms like *WKRP in Cincinnati*.

Have you always been a fan of mysteries? What are some of your favorite characters or series?

I've been reading mysteries for as long as I can remember. I'm a huge fan of Ross Macdonald, and his work inspired *Going to the Bad* more than anyone else's. Most of his books involve characters' long-buried secrets coming back to haunt their children. I doubt I was as masterful at constructing my plot, but he was definitely my inspiration.

You used to work as a community relations manager at Barnes & Noble. How did this experience influence your decision to start writing? What are some of your favorite bookstores?

I always wanted to write a mystery, but it wasn't until I began working in the bookstore that I committed myself to making the attempt. Working in the presence of so many books inspired me, but the authors who came to the store also played a big part in my finishing. They were all very supportive and encouraged me in ways I'll always be grateful for.

I love Barnes & Noble for obvious reasons. I'm sad that they carry less stock than when I worked for them, but I understand the business pressures that led them to make those decisions. In Southern California, where I used to live, I love Book 'Em Mysteries in

South Pasadena and Mysteries to Die For in Thousand Oaks. The owners really know their customers and do a fantastic job serving them. In New York, the Mysterious Bookshop is like coming home to the mother ship.

What are you working on now? What can readers expect from you now that the Lilly Hawkins trilogy is complete?

Right now I'm working on a fictional book about a pandemic flu like the one in 1918. I'm also plotting a humorous mystery for children set on an island off the Georgia coast.

Someday there is a fourth Lilly Hawkins book I'd like to write. Since all the books take place in roughly a day, I think it would be fun to write one set on Lilly and Rod's wedding day. It would be a disastrous turn of events, but they'd eventually get to the ceremony and live happily ever after.

1. Nora McFarland was inspired to start writing based on her own experience of being a shooter for a local television station. In the biography section of her website, www.noramcfarland .com, she writes: "I recognized almost immediately that the job was a perfect setup for a mystery. Shooters, as they're called in the industry, work grueling hours at a frantic pace and report on everything from heinous crimes to bizarrely comical feature stories." Devise a character and a setting for a mystery based on your own personal experience. What would be your character's name? What kind of mystery would your character solve?

2. Spencer Quinn, *New York Times* bestselling author of the Chet and Bernie mystery series, called Nora McFarland's second novel, *Hot, Shot, and Bothered*, "fun, funny, tautly suspenseful, and very smart. Lilly Hawkins, the heroine, is irresistible. I couldn't put it down." Write your own blurb for *Going to the Bad* and share it with your book club members!

3. Play a game of "Two Truths and a Lie" at your book club meeting. Have each book club member prepare three statements about themselves—two that are true and one that is a lie. In any order, share your three statements with the group and then vote on which statement is false. This classic icebreaker will test which book club member is the best detective!

DON'T MISS ANY OF THE
Lilly Hawkins
MYSTERIES!

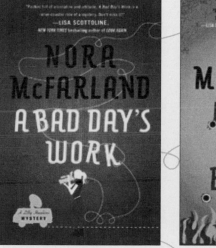

"A breath of fresh air to the world of lighthearted mysteries . . . A charming new series."
—*Suspense Magazine*

Available wherever books are sold
or at www.simonandschuster.com

TOUCHSTONE
A Division of Simon & Schuster
A CBS COMPANY